More **LOVE** for the Florence Love series:

'A funny, sassy, page-turning debut'   Jenny Colgan

'Heaps of fun! ****'   *Heat*

'I am in LOVE with Florence Love – she's flawed, feisty and funny as hell'   Mel Giedroyc

'Plenty of twists, and a fresh, funny new voice that made me laugh out loud'   *Woman & Home*

'Clever page-turner'   *Woman*

'You will laugh, cry and ultimately fall in love with Florence Love'   *Bookliterati*

'One of those books that you hope to grab the odd five-minute break so you can pick it up and dive into it again'   *Whispering Stories*

'With a smart, feisty heroine like Florence Love this is sure to be a great series'   *Book Magnet*

'Hugely entertaining'   *Linda's Book Bag*

'A fascinating insight into the world of detection'   *Prima*

'A sassy, feisty heroine to die for . . . She's smart, she's sexy, and she's very, very funny'   *Reader's Digest*

'Delightfully witty'   *Writing Round the Block*

'Refreshi'   *The g She Reads*

'Florenc   e enjoyed by many   *ook Lovers*

A Whole LOTTA LOVE

LOUISE LEE

HEADLINE

First published in Great Britain in 2018 by
HEADLINE PUBLISHING GROUP

1

Cataloguing in Publication Data is available from the British Library

ISBN 978 1 4722 2461 3

Typeset in Garamond MT Std 12.25/13.5 pt by
Palimpsest Book Production Limited, Falkirk, Stirlingshire

Printed in Great Britain by Clays Ltd, St Ives plc

Headline's policy is to use papers that are natural, renewable and recyclable
products and made from wood grown in well-managed forests and other controlled
sources. The logging and manufacturing processes are expected to conform to the
environmental regulations of the country of origin.

HEADLINE PUBLISHING GROUP
An Hachette UK Company
Carmelite House
50 Victoria Embankment
London EC4Y 0DZ

www.headline.co.uk
www.hachette.co.uk

For my grandad, Tom; and my dad, Tom;
and him indoors, Tom

Putting Old Ghosts to Rest 101 – Tip #1:
Offload

Unlike the other emergency services, private investigators do not get on-the-job counselling. Nor off-the-job. You're too here, there and everywhere to have friends, never mind regular therapy; too legally bound by confidentiality agreements; too much of a one-man-band. Sometimes you crave an encouraging slap on the back.

Utilise your best resource – the client. They're sitting ducks and, boy, do they want to know all about you. See how long it takes them to ask, 'What's your most memorable case?', which they 100% will. Use it as your cue to hop on the psychologist's couch. Metaphorically.

- Never mention identities or the specifics of a case, mind you.

- Err towards broad brushstrokes and a few juicy titbits.

- Feel free to wax lyrical about the marvel of you.

- Make the case a cracker. Get your heart involved. Tell your client the one that's closest to it.

The result: you are a rock star. No amount of psychotherapy can buy that level of validation. Neither will you see your client more emotionally transparent. While massaging your own ego, study their truth portals and micro-expressions – dishonesty going forward will be as flagrant as a fart.

Part I

Dorset Daily,
Saturday, 13 February 1988

A local man has been found dead in a remote corner of Twisted Acres Farm, Christchurch. Eric Steensen, 39, from Sandbanks, was discovered in the passenger seat of a fume-filled car, in the early hours of this morning. The owner of the Nissan Sunny coupé, Bambi Love, 37, from Laurelbridge, is thought to have driven Mr Steensen to the clearing, her intention also to kill herself. Mrs Love is currently missing.

Detective Inspector Tim Rice, Dorset Police, said: 'Paramedics and firefighters were called to the farm shortly after midnight. A chemical response team ensured the area was safe before the car doors were opened. A male, deceased, was found in the passenger seat. We believe he had been accompanied by a local woman. Her whereabouts is currently unknown and of great concern to her family. We would urge the public to report any suspected sightings of Bambi Love.'

Emma James, parishioner of Our Lady of the Saints Church, Laurelbridge, said Mrs Love was 'a lovely

Catholic, but fragile as a sparrow. The baby blues got a hold of her.'

It is believed the couple had been strangers until four days ago, meeting only once to plan their deaths. Each left a suicide note, explaining their intentions.

Jackie Collier, counsellor for Mind, explained. 'Less than 1 per cent of suicide pacts occur between strangers. But when they do, it has nothing to do with needing support or empathy. The primary aim is always efficacy.'

Total Rebound

The woman on my bed is sensational. Huge, intelligent eyes – predominantly iris, onyx black, framed by ice-white slivers of sclera. A good-sized symmetrical nose with pretty, pinched nostrils. Full, moist lips, off which I want to bounce a gentle fingertip. She's also Punjabi, so looks nothing at all like my ex-boyfriend.

Still, she reminds me of him.

The mole on her neck, for example – it's as risen as a velvet button. She rides a Vespa. There's the fact she's an alpha – the domineering type, chockful of poise and incapable of taking me to heart. And just as Tommaso shortens his name to Tom, she opts for something equally punchy; something like Fi, or Bea, or Tee.

Oh, the tenuousness with which we cling to lost love. Indignity, however, is part and parcel of the grieving process – I cut myself some slack.

Fi or Bea or Tee and I met in Bournemouth. Bar So. Queuing for entry to the Ladies, we chatted about the role of the toilet attendant – specifically, how they and their accoutrements bring a tense claustrophobia to the peeing process.

'Remove her and her stool, and there'd be room for three more,' she'd complained, posh as the Queen.

I'd shown her my pound. 'I only want to put some lipstick on.'

That was that. She'd pulled a compact from her bag,

pointed its mirror towards my face and taken my coin. 'I'll put it towards your next drink.'

We've not stopped talking since.

My brother, Michael, binned us off. He hates being super-fluous. Later, I'd explain everything to him – that she's a Capricorn and I'm Cancer. When those signs meet, it's to resolve a story our ancestors failed to, which sounds fantas-tical, but it's actually not. Ask Albert Einstein, Carl Sagan, Ptolemy, T. S. Eliot and Pythagoras.

After Bar So, we shared a Zinger Twister. She told me about her name, which definitely translated as a plucked stringed instrument used in Hindustani classical music. Then it was back to mine.

Laurelbridge. A village north of Christchurch. Here are some of the landmarks I pointed out to her. The duck pond to which ducks don't come. The cemetery behind Our Lady of the Saints; it was where I lost my kissing-virginity. The village post office that belongs to my dad.

I told her, 'When I say "my dad", I mean, me. But only when he's dead.' Then I performed a sign of the cross. So that he doesn't die, *ever*. Post-office fact: I don't want one.

'So, what do you do for work?' she asked.

The downside of being a private investigator is an inability to boast. Your existence is akin to Bruce Wayne's. Revealing your job title is professional suicide.

'Oh, loads of interesting stuff. Next year I'm starting a forensic psychology course.' I winked. 'The dream is to cure psychopathy.'

'Tall order. How do you plan on altering the genetics?'

'There are environmental factors.' Then I came clean: 'Bottom line, I'm medically nosey, especially when it comes to people who lack a moral compass. Serial killers, especially. I'm so interested in them I thought I was one for a while.' She laughed. I shook my head. 'I stuck magazine articles about psychopaths to my wall. I had a poster of Patrick Bateman. I got myself tested in the end.'

'How did that go?'

I smiled. 'Better than I thought.'

The taxi dropped us off two kilometres north of the duck pond, at the top of a black and winding road, just shy of the cattle grate. Giggling, we stumbled along a short, dark track, our arrival at the driveway tripping the security light.

Cowslip Cottage – the family seat. At night, it's ever so cosy – more rustic than tired. The Purbeck stone, its jaunty demeanour – the place could have sprung from the ground, like a tor. The wooden sashes date back to the post-hobbit era. Clamped to its exterior is an asymmetrical flue that resembles a very pretty landslide – its crannies provided excellent footholds for a child who needed to climb to the roof.

Which is where I reside – in the loft room.

It boasts the only window with a view beyond the woods. On a bright day, you'll see in the distance sheets of rapeseed, a belfry's finial; the English Channel – a pigeon-grey infinity pool that crashes too abruptly into the horizon. As a child, I longed to look over that edge – my mother was somewhere beyond it, I was sure.

Inside the cottage, I turned only the side lamps on. To provide ambience. And to hide the cracks. The place is always tidy, but in need of a makeover. Paint peels around the skirting boards. The shabby-chic sofa errs towards dilapidated. The rug recedes in six places, each bald patch the work of a foot, because we always sit in the same order – Dad on the left, Michael in the middle, then me.

On the upside, the room boasts a two-hundred-year-old hearth on which you could roast a pig; there's a wall of wine in the lean-to; and a fifty-inch television, acquired by my brother, specifically to take his mind off the dated decor.

Remote control in hand, I said, 'Netflix is our oyster. What do you fancy watching?'

Fi, Bea or Tee stopped me there. 'Are we *actually* going to watch Netflix and chill?'

'You suggested it,' I argued.

'Florence, you do know that it's a euphemism for rudies?'

'I did not know that.'

'Sweetheart. You've been living under a stone.'

She was wrong. 'I've been in Italy, falling in love, then getting dumped, mainly.'

'You've said.'

When on the rebound, never go on and on about your ex. It's tedious and rude. All forms of cold turkey (be they the result of addiction to a substance or a person) involve living in the moment. But Capricorns are infuriatingly good listeners.

This one shuffled along the couch until our hips touched. Her endgame, putting nimble Asian fingers through my hair, scratching with her nails as she went. I dropped my head towards her, so she could pet all sides.

'I do get it,' she rued. 'I split with my ex in the summer. You'd think I'd have stopped feeling empty by now – but I do, usually in a room full of people.'

'Like now?' I nodded at my lap.

That made her snort. 'You do know what they say, Florence? To get over somebody, you gotta get under someone.'

I looked up into her face, tried to live in the moment. Admired her skin – Type IV on the Fitzpatrick Skin-typing Test – she produces collagen naturally and in abundance, giving her a natural plumpness and deep satin finish. Her Cupid's bow is voluptuous enough to nestle a peanut in. Thick, mid-length hair, raven black and shiny as a snooker ball.

If I was a lesbian, she'd be exactly my type.

I told her, 'Rebound sex never fills the void in you.'

She wasn't talking marriage. 'But it does fill a void in space-time.'

'I hardly know you.'

Shuffling away from me, she put her hands on her knees to remind me of a few things. 'Veena. Thirty-five. I love Janis Joplin and am allergic to prawns . . .'

Veena. Vee for short.

Relieved, I missed most of what she told me. Especially when she mentioned the prawns. It got me thinking about Fra Diavolo, my favourite seafood dish; Tommaso had insisted I have it in Rome, on our first date.

'. . . so I threw her out. Leaving me with a mortgage made for two.' Veena slapped her own cheek, playfully; then remembered an earlier conversation. 'But that's not a problem, because I'm a Capricorn. Making me dogged at digging myself out of a shitstorm. Good job I do everything with – what did you call it?'

'Delicate horns.' I kept her off the subject of rudies. 'How do you pay for your mortgage for two?'

'Usual way. I work my arse off. Bournemouth County Court. I'm an assistant coroner. And currently my medical opinion is: you need a massage.'

I paused.

There. *Right there.*

Kismet.

Serendipity.

Fate.

One and all came a-knocking.

'Vee, you are a bloody star.' I pointed at my scapula. 'My shoulders are shot to pieces.'

Access to my bedroom is via a svelte staircase designed for only the healthiest BMIs. Shutting the door behind us, Vee insisted I sit on a stool and slip off my top.

Massage is something I know a lot about, though I didn't tell her this. Entrapment specialists use it as foreplay – manipulating the acupressure points oversteps a mark without being overtly sexual.

Very important aside: entrapment is not a classy form of prostitution. We *never* sleep with the client. That demeans all involved. My aim is one kiss, five seconds, with tongues, case closed.

Vee's massage was too steamy. I groaned. Expertly, she elbowed my shoulder well, celestial window and heaven's pillar. While I said things like, 'Oh my god, this is the best massage I've ever had.' And, 'You actually have magic elbows.' And, 'I'd have *loved* to be a coroner.'

'Every day, a new riddle,' she agreed.

'What qualifications do you need?'

She said this especially close to my ear. 'A medical licence. A big dollop of curiosity. And the legal authority to determine a cause of death.'

It tickled. I shivered. Then asked about data protection, which is a private investigator's favourite topic. 'To get a copy of a pathologist's report, you have to be the next of kin, right?'

'Or the law. And even they have to have a cracking reason. There are hoops and a lot of paperwork. It costs money, too.'

'And what if you're not a relative or the law but, say, a student of forensic psychology – how much would it cost you then?'

Vee knelt in front me and placed her thumbs on my temples, rotating them counter-clockwise. 'Well, that depends on the efficacy of the coronary officer.'

For a while I let her press my cranial nooks, massage the inside edges of my eyebrows, manipulate the bridge of my nose. When she stopped, I opened my eyes to find her admiring my clavicles, and I let her, because *never* have I had an asset at the coronary office before.

'Everybody has a price,' I said.

'What's all this interest?' She stood up, took my hand, indicated that we were to sit on the bed.

'I'm going to be a student of forensic psychology,' I reminded her. 'It's for research.'

The truth. There's a case I have in mind. One I've been working on for twenty-five years. And although you should never become emotionally embroiled with a contact, the sexual meeting of minds is permitted; especially when your contact is as valuable as Veena – she has access to every Dorsetian post-mortem, ever.

And so, here we are now. Vee pushing my fringe behind an ear, attentive to every strand. Before kissing me, she pauses to showcase her eyes. They are unequivocally massive. What they're not is every shade of green known to Crayola – no hues of olive, pistachio or lime. Neither does she smell like him. Tommaso wore Tom Ford Neroli Portofino. She wears Bulgari Omnia Crystalline – I can smell the lotus flower, white sandalwood and musk. By the time our lips touch, my heart has vacuumed itself shut – her tongue is too small.

I go with it for five seconds. Then gently pull away. 'I forgot the internet booster.'

'I'm using it,' says Michael.

Rocket fast, Vee and I stand up. My brother has his back to us. Busily, he roots through my make-up bag.

'Where the fuck did you come from?' I shout.

'My room,' he tells a pair of tweezers.

'I didn't know you were in.'

Michael turns, hatefully. 'I arrived home at nine-oh-six. It was after you abandoned me.' He doesn't move or comment beyond this, just stares.

'Hello, again,' says Vee.

'Dad's back,' he tells her.

'No?' I say.

Michael tells Vee, 'I'm not lying. He is.'

I tell her, too. 'He's not. Look.' I point at the arc of yellow that sweeps across the room. 'Vee, you have to go.'

'Are you not allowed friends?' she asks.

Michael's confused, too. Puts his hands on his hips, awaiting my response.

'He'll guess, Vee. You're gorgeous. He knows what I'm like.' But I don't know what I'm saying. Dad and me fact: I remain an absolute enigma to him. I gather her jacket, bag, shoes. Hand them to her. 'He's very Catholic.'

She empathises: 'Hindu.'

Michael puts a hand to his heart. 'I love Hindus.'

We hear the front door slam. Michael's presence and now Dad's has made me feel icky – I want Vee gone. So I flick my brother a very secret gesture. The one we had in the olden days, when I entrapped men.

Back then, my brother was my sidekick; his job, to burst in and behave like the aggrieved husband. Michael was superb at bringing a case to a close, largely because he's built like a rower. Sometimes, however, he needed prompting. And, being a slave to the Method, he always needed time to prepare. He was also insistent that we used a particular gesture to prompt his entrance. I gave in. He adores *Star Trek* and can say 'Live long and prosper' in actual Vulcan.

FYI: *Dif-tor heh smusma.*

I do a Vulcan salute behind Vee's head. The signal is as powerful as a hypnotist's finger click. Michael's switch into professional mode is alarming. How to murder an ant with a shotgun . . .

He glowers at Vee. 'Sorry, who are you exactly?'

'Veena,' she replies slowly. 'Florence's friend. You were there when we met. Bar So, tonight?'

Michael points the tweezers squarely at me. 'You do know she's married.'

Vee smiles. 'She's not.'

I bob my head weakly. 'I was.' Then throw my brother to the wolves, because I'm looking like a fool. 'Michael, are you on drugs?'

'Yes,' he answers, like I'm stupid.

Vee takes a concerned step towards him. 'What have you taken?'

'Vitamin D, glucosamine and half an aspirin.'

'I see.' She nods thoughtfully. 'Has this become a habit?'

'Yes.'

Veena pats his arm, unfazed. 'Good. But remember, glucosamine is useless unless administered in very high doses.'

'I do know,' he says.

She smiles, then slips her shoes back on. 'Let's get the introductions over with.'

And so we follow her out of my bedroom, down the skinny stairs, into the kitchen. Me kicking Michael's calf, because Asperger's is a pain in the arse in all situations that require spontaneity.

Vee, it turns out, is just the tonic Dad needs.

Flirting as effectively with him as she did me, I find I'm pleased they met. The last few weeks, Dad has taken to staring blindly at inanimate objects, his shoulders bowed by the weight of his grief, because his 'companion' chucked him.

Vee is also the type of friend that makes me look good. 'Crikey, this is fantastic.' She sips, delighted. 'It's a Rioja, right?'

Dad reads the label. 'Finca Allende, Aurus, Rioja 2010. To new friends.'

We clink glasses. I let him have his first sip before I say, 'That wine's a hundred smackers a bottle.'

Alarmed, Dad holds the glass away from him. 'Jesus Christ! I'd no idea.'

'It was a gift for his sixty-fifth.' I wink at Vee.

She reassures him. 'You can taste every last penny. It's a total treat. Thank you, George, for sharing. Next time we meet, I'll reciprocate. I have a Terrazas de Los Andes Malbec, 2012. Not quite as pricey as yours, but my absolute favourite.'

Immediately appeased, Dad takes an over-enthusiastic gulp. 'That sounds grand.'

'It has very silky tannins.'

'Aye.' Why my dad employs a Newcastle accent is anyone's guess. Mine is that the woman is mesmeric enough to discombobulate linguistic function – there's no denying she sounds exactly how cashmere feels.

When she excuses herself, it's with the grace of a Bollywood superstar. I walk her to the cattle grate, where we wait for her cab. The taxi's lights wind up the track towards us, while we swap numbers, then kiss again, which – now we're familiar with one another's mouths – is much nicer than the first time. It's also comfortingly final, because she's definitely going home.

When I return, Michael is buffing the kettle with a tea towel.

'Where's the old man?' I ask, picking up Dad's half-full glass.

'Deadheading.'

'It's midnight.' I peer out of the window. 'He never wastes wine.'

Dad wears a head torch and kneels on a gardening cushion, his posture burdened once more. The pity I feel for him is debilitating. To make myself feel better, I try to sneak my arms around Michael's waist, then clamp on to his back, but he flaps me off like I'm a wasp.

So I tell him off instead. 'You didn't have to go the whole entrapment hog. I just wanted to bring the evening to a gentle close.'

Now he turns around. 'I didn't have *any* time to plan my character or motivation.'

'Neither do you have to tell everyone I was married.'

'Twice.' He says earnestly, 'You're irresistible.'

'That's not the point.'

'Well, I liked her.'

'Me, too, Michael. Just not like that. Unfortunately, I'm not a lesbian.'

Appalled, he whispers, 'That's homophobic.'

I don't have the energy to argue. Just finish Dad's drink.

The hydrangea Dad fails to prune has brown, crispy heads the size of hedgehogs. Despite his lack of movement, his mouth and nose spit tepid steam.

'You all right?' I ask, approaching him.

When he turns to me, I'm blinded by his head torch. I use a palm to block its glare. There's a wet streak on one cheek; I pretend not to have noticed. 'Dad, it's Baltic out here.'

'I'm warm enough.' A brisk wipe of his face, then he reaches for his secateurs.

'I drank your wine. There was a tenner's worth left in the glass.'

'I hadn't finished,' he half smiles. 'I liked your friend.'

'Told you I had one.'

'She's quite the siren. Where's she from?'

'The Punjab.' I laugh. '*Siren?*'

He zips up his body-warmer to clarify he is not a sexual being. Then says, 'So she's a coroner.'

'Just an assistant one.' I play it down, so he doesn't get suspicious.

Dad won't talk about what happened to Mum. The gazillion questions I had were batted for six. Not a day has passed where I haven't felt wounded by that. Of course, I've carried out my own enquiries. Things have become a little clearer. Though I am not allowed to tell him the things I've discovered. He made me swear never to involve him, and especially not Michael.

He's not thinking about Mum now, so isn't suspicious. Placing dead petal heads in his punnet, as though each is frail as a soap bubble, he mourns another woman.

'How's things with your squeeze?' I say. 'Are you still estranged?'

It's a pointless question. Of course they're over – that's why he spends his nights poring over dead wood. 'It's more of a sabbatical,' he says.

'From what?' Dad won't tell me why Darcie broke it off. The guilty truth is I know more than him. 'Do people have sabbaticals from retirement?'

'From me, Florence. She's having a sabbatical from me.'

The side of his face is translucent in the glare of his head torch. All cheekbone and arteries and capillaries and eye socket. He's tired. And almost seventy. But mostly, he's gutted about being dumped. Then again, for my whole life, he's looked like that. Apart from when he and Darcie became an item – her presence was like a rejuvenation serum; and, of course, when my mother was around, back in the days when he was my real father.

'I'm sorry.' I join him on the grass. Put a hand on his shoulder. 'That sucks.'

'Yep.'

'What happened?'

He stares at me for a while. Ruffles my hair, then stands

up. '*The Loves* happened. Our family is a bit alternative for Darcie.'

'Alternative?' I follow him across the lawn. 'That's a new one. Well, I didn't like her, anyway. Her daughter was the Antichrist.'

He turns. 'The *Antichrist* won't be working at the post office any more. So, all in all, a good outcome for you.'

'No, it is not.' I catch him up. With the post office unmanaged and Dad looking so mentally doomed, I'm ethically obliged to take the helm. It's where I end up during life's ebbs. Duct tape, envelope glue, the ancient stamp-moistener – they're all synonymous with making me want to score diazepam.

My sudden urge is to fly back to Italy for just one more conversation with Tommaso. 'Actually, I'm grieving, too,' I sulk. 'I met a man.'

'In Italy?'

'Tommaso.' Saying 'Tommaso' out loud makes him dangerously real.

'The one who nursed your brother when he took a tumble?'

I nod. Dad had been interested in that part of my trip to Italy. The part where Michael bumped his face and lost a tooth. Concerning anything else: zip-all interest.

'Michael and I stayed in Trieste.' I make this fact especially clear. 'That's in the *north*. Literally, a hike from the Slovenian border.'

This reassures him. His shoulders relax. North Italy is definitely not the south of Italy, which is where my mother is. I know it, and he knows it.

He pretends to be jealous. 'Did you fall in love?'

'Up to my neck.'

He smiles. Because Italy may have been a genuine holiday, after all. Had I been investigating my past, I'd not have had time to be falling up to my neck in love. I certainly wouldn't have visited the Mezzogiorno, specifically Bagnara Calabra, a town so far south it sits on Italy's big toe.

'Is there any hope for you and this Italian?'

My smile is thin. 'I'm too alternative.'

'Then he's a muttonhead.'

'He is, isn't he?'

'A *tom*fool.'

'You're on fire. High five.' We pat hands. 'Do you know what we need?' I lead him towards the back door. 'Family therapy.'

My dad loves family therapy. It involves no talking whatsoever. See how he takes my arm. How we tangle fingers. How he pushes our clenched hands into his Barbour jacket, keeping me warm, like when I was little.

Once inside, he's proactive. Dishes out glasses the size of goldfish bowls. Shares a bottle of Co-op Australian Cabernet Sauvignon equally between the three of us. Pulls the spare duvet from behind the sofa. Assuming our positions on the couch, he tucks us all in, then does something outrageous – puts his feet on the apothecary table.

We follow suit.

He points the remote control at the large flat screen and says. 'Are we all sure?'

'Yes,' Michael says.

'Because family therapy requires commitment.'

'We do know,' my brother nods.

'You'll be in for the long haul?'

'You *always* say that.'

'Dad and I are grieving,' I explain.

'And me,' he tells us both. 'I'm grieving the most.'

'Yes, you are.' He's not. He's forgotten Sebastien Tremblay exists. They were *engaged*. The wedding was booked. He'd bought a Groom and Groom cake topper and my best woman's dress. Sometimes, I envy his condition – how easy it is for him to park pain in favour of his own private Xanadu.

I suggest a pledge. 'We should honour our communal angst. Mourn our individual losses together, as a family. Deal?'

'I'm in,' says Dad.

Michael's sigh is stagey. 'All right, then. But it sounds awful.'

'Not when you enlist family therapy,' smiles Dad.

For one anaesthetised moment, everything feels rather perfect.

Binge-watch (also **binge-view**). *To watch multiple episodes of a television programme in rapid succession.* A contender for the Oxford Dictionaries word of the year in 2013, the word beating it being 'selfie'.

As it's a relatively new craze, psychological analysis of binge-watching is in its infancy. Though the *Daily Mail* has warned that it makes you fat, lonely, carcinogenic and a little bit socialist. Less was made of the fact that, for some, it's a bona fide addiction.

My opinion . . .

The box set, used sparingly and always in groups, is a useful psychological crutch. A means of simultaneous escapism. The normalisation of vicious circles, heartache and adversity is quite the anaesthetic, enabling you to tie up your own existence in a boxset-sized bow. The producers know they're doing it. They use tried-and-tested formats that humans, regardless of race or genre, find entirely comforting. In short, it makes the medium as underutilised as medicinal cannabis.

I have never got over *Lost* ending. *Ever*.

Tonight, Dad gives us a choice of three: *Breaking Bad*, *Game of Thrones* or *House MD*.

We take a vote. Michael uses both hands to vote for *House MD*. Trouble is, Dad and I are more important, right now.

While Michael has processed his grief, we're only at the start of ours – to be precise, the denial phase of DABDA, a universally accepted model charting the five stages of grief (Kübler-Ross, 1969).

Dad and I win, four hands to his overly splayed two – so plump for something visceral.

Game of Thrones.

I love it. So does Dad – though he wanders in and out when the rude bits are on, particularly the incest. He is staunchly present, however, for the gratuitous violence.

When Ser Jaime Lannister starts having sex with his twin sister, an event swiftly followed by the attempted murder of a child, Michael declares it, 'Too disturbing.'

'It's just pretend,' I reassure him.

'It has no respect for screenwriting form.'

'I think it's bloody brilliant,' states Dad.

'Dad,' Michael says, ever so kindly, 'big characters don't get killed when you're not expecting it.'

I frown. 'Is that what they teach you at acting school? To never push the envelope?'

Michael points at me. 'Which envelope?'

'The metaphorical one . . .' My voice peters out, because Michael already fires up the iPad.

'I'm going to watch *House MD* instead,' he states.

The downside of Michael's condition: an unwillingness to push the envelope. 'It isn't family therapy if we're watching different things,' I tell my dad.

He puts a soft hand on mine. 'Next episode?'

We need headspace that only the two of us inhabit. 'Err, yes,' I say, and decide *Game of Thrones* will always be ours.

Given its underlying theme, it's uncannily apt. Beneath the gore and debauchery is the survival of family. Internal feuds, time-honoured mistakes – the whole human condition. Yes, mostly it's about the negative bits of being a blood relative, but you can't help – despite all the deceit – get a raging thirst for loyalty.

We watch three episodes. Then Dad turns in. Fiercely, he kisses my head. He even performs a swish of his imaginary mace before exiting the room.

And for a moment, I feel empowered too, think about calling after him, telling him exactly what happened to me three weeks ago.

Florence Love fact: going to Italy was the most enormous thing to happen in my life.

The moment dissipates too eagerly. My father's happy. Listen to him, humming the theme tune in his deepest church-choir voice. I let him hum his way to bed. Because George Love doesn't want to hear it. Not tonight, or ever. A martyr to her cause, the man still pretends that his wife killed herself. That she was a brittle-minded woman, prone to depression and in receipt of a tricksy Latin temperament.

Bambi Love fact: my mother is neither weak nor dead.

He knows this, because he's been secretly communicating with her for the last twenty-five years. I know this because I found her.

A Mother's Love

Shell-shocked and disorientated, I'm not sure how I got to
the airport. Yes, in the taxi. But alighting, paying the driver,
passing through Security – all are lost memories to me. I
don't recall taking my boots off, nor removing the laptop
from my suitcase. I definitely did, because I have awoken
from my brain freeze as part of a fat queue waiting for
Boarding Gate 5 to open; everyone itches to enter the glass
holding cage, their aim to bag a moulded seat close to the
woman who unhooks the barrier.

I frown at them all. My all-consuming sentiment; having
been failed by everyone and everything. How dare the whole
world plod along perfectly well without my mental participation.

A secret about abandoned children. We pretend we were
born of fair-minded women; their *raison d'être*, us, despite
fate's wickedest twists. A very secret secret about me: I had
a hunch my mum loved me a bit more than anyone else.

And then we met. It was a good half an hour ago now.
A quarter of a century had passed, yet in unexpected ways
it was as though nothing had happened in between, which
is ridiculous and cruel.

Ridiculous, because I haven't seen her since I was eight.
Seven being the age at which prior memories dissipate.
Children lack the sophisticated neural architecture needed to
form and hold dear complex memory. Without mastering

calendars and language and the art of empathy, their auto-biography is destined to be a tiny fraction of the truth.

Yet I found my mother's every micro-movement was ingrained in my psyche.

Cruel, because she then forgot to provide an explanation or apology. Lost mums have a lot to make up for. Even more to live up to. No longer a saintly idea, they're flesh and bone and capable of a lot of reassuring platitudes.

My mother, however, was decidedly oblivious to me.

Our meeting was brief – two minutes, if that. It was also an accident. She'd travelled to Trieste to see Michael and me. When I say 'see', I mean *observe*. Yes, her lover slipped us her address. The one I already knew. Her intention, however, was to remain unseen. Still, two minutes is enough time to touch my cheek, stare hard at my retinas, rub my thirty-five-year-old triceps and tell me how overwhelmingly proud she is of the woman I've become.

But too quickly she'd heard Michael calling for me – our taxi to the airport had arrived. That was a stinger; just the sound of his voice solicited in her a primal response – Bambi was suddenly all over *his* safety and the importance of *his* continued ignorance. Just like our dad.

What about me? I didn't say.

Michael's voice had edged closer, leaving me with a few seconds to warn her of the danger she was in. That her secret past had come back to bite us all on the arse. A past I know nothing about. Just the fact that Italy wants her dead.

Tommaso told me so. Shortly after ordering that I leave the country on pain of death. Whatever it was she'd done, the nation was hell bent on revenge. That puts a biological family in the firing line.

And so, before returning to England, I told my mother to go missing again. Properly, this time. Nobody has ever taken my word so seriously. The bitch forgot to finger-wave me a *ciao*. The most notable event of my earthly existence was over.

The passport official marches through us to his booth as though we're as insubstantial as balloons. Rage makes me breathless, not because of him, because I was less than eight years old for 90 per cent of our relationship – my memories are an unequivocal sham. Otherwise, she'd have asked if I was peckish, pulled my cardigan around my chest, neatened my hair into a centre parting.

This version of her could barely look at me.

A rule of private investigation: impetuousness is forbidden. If you've not thought it through, you're responding to a biochemical surge.

I tell Michael I won't be long – I've left my credit card back at the hotel reception. In the meantime, he is to enter the glass cage and stand by the window. There he will check that the plane's safety procedures are carried out correctly. He's all for it – the task gives him an opportunity to use his detective notebook. Though I'm first to examine his tooth.

'It's still not there,' I say.

'Why did it have to be the front one? Everyone can see it,' he complains.

'It's fine,' I lie. His facial haematoma is as alarming as the Phantom of the Opera's mask. It's been four days since he fell on his face, so it's in full bloom – a tiny measure of the pressure Bambi Love, or whatever her real name is, left on my eight-year-old shoulders and ever since.

I push a fifty in Michael's pocket; it's more than enough for his taxi from Bournemouth airport to Laurelbridge.

'Won't be long then.' I hold out a palm. 'Half an hour tops. I'll meet you on the plane.'

My brother's handshake is heartfelt. 'Can you get me a Twix?'

*

I sprint from Trieste airport, ignoring the taxi rank and bus stop, running left instead against the traffic. Emerging on to the SS14, I jog along its hard shoulder.

Manifestations of impetuousness should be preceded by a bout of intense activity. This works off the bile, leaving you deplete of every self-serving interest, revealing only the bare bones of your mission.

Mine: to ask my mother why she doesn't love me any more.

Barely aware of the lorries that rattle past, I jut through cars and scooters, cross a major roundabout. Twelve minutes later, I arrive in Ronchi dei Legionari.

I should be hiding, ducking in and out of parked vehicles, avoiding the CCTV, especially not striding past Hotel Ronchi – the owner had been watching our every move. But I'm too sweaty to go incognito. And tortured-looking. How can people be so fickle? Tommaso and I were in love. I know we were: I was there.

Then he said, 'You have twelve hours to leave Italy, give or take. We're on opposite sides now, Florence.' Just like that.

I don't know why we're on opposite sides, but if the sins of my mother are to stalk me for ever more, I want to know what they bloody well are.

My mother was hiding just fifty metres from my hotel.

Sacro Cuore Immacolato di Maria. I fling open the church's oak doors, head straight for the confessional booth. Because that, people, is where I found my mother – cowering in the penitent's seat, unable to look me in the eye, failing to confess a fucking thing. Which is very much the deal when you're sitting in a holy cupboard.

The ironies are tragic.

Instead, she looked lost, forgetting to explain in full where she'd been since I was eight. One truth glared. Bambi Love hadn't spent it mourning me. Not since leaving the UK and

27

returning to a homeland that wants her head. Especially Tommaso and his family. For pity's sake, before he knew who my mother was, Tommaso and I had legs.

The confessionary booth's doors are shut. I don't bother to knock, just pull them both open.

Of course, she's not there. So, I sit on her seat – the sinner's seat – touch the wooden grate that had separated us. The one she didn't touch back. I inhale the air, but the cabinet's oak is too dominant, any remnants of Chanel No. 5 lost beneath its fragrance.

This occasion illustrates the downside of impetuousness. No forethought, plan of action, surety of desired outcomes. I sit in a confessional booth with no idea what to do next.

God tells me:

You've left your brother, toothless, and in receipt of mild special needs, at an airport. He's noting safety procedures – you know he will be taking this very seriously. He's also returning to a broken engagement, which you really need to tell him about. And the questions from your father – mainly concerning the location of your moral compass – will leave him lost as a lamb. Do not abandon him at the airport, my child. She might be a piss-poor excuse for a mother, but you are not.

Right there is the problem I have with God. He only arrives to remind me of my responsibilities to everyone else.

I exit the confessional, genuflect, tetchily, at the holy-water bowl, then do as I'm told. Though this time I jump in a taxi, because my run here was neither tempered nor undertaken in appropriate footwear. I have calf-shake. That's a build-up of lactic acid and nerve confusion.

For a second time this morning, I slip off my boots. Use the opportunity to massage my peroneal tendon – it's tight as cheese wire. Then tune into an Italian woman's voice – she argues with the official. I've no idea what she says, but its texture is a drop kick to the heart. Whipping my head up, I gawp at the back of her skull. Listen to her elongated double consonants and the inconsistent outcomes. Her phonetics tinged with something unbearably familiar – a secret hint of Dorsetian.

The missing voice that once made our family's full set.

Yet her behaviour is immediately perplexing.

The customs officer tackles a bottle of water from her. Flustered, she decants her toiletries into a clear bag. She's supposed to be flying under the radar. Basic airport procedure – no liquids, flammables, weapons. The body scanner beeps. She removes her watch, walks through again, briefly stopping to volumise her hair. The woman is a blueprint for artlessness.

I'm not angry, I'm furious. This isn't how she used to be. Yes, she was ditzy, but charmingly so. Yes, she seemed scared a lot of the time, but that was just her mien. Yes, she barely left the house, unless it was a church do, but God was the only thing she loved as much as her family.

Thank the Lord, my mental legacy is the result of her insistence we watch old cop shows together. It was she who bought me my first detective's notebook. And some red plastic binoculars. We were training to be girl PIs. An infamous crime-fighting duo. The certainty of that memory is my number-one safe place.

Yanking my other boot free, I stay out of view.

Follow her swiftly through Security.

The Morning After

House MD: a power precis, according to Michael. 'It's a complete mixture of *Diagnosis Murder*, *LA Law* and *Scooby-Doo*.' He's telling me this now, even though I'm very much a-fucking-sleep.

Last night, I slept in the living room on the window seat. It looks on to the front garden, our gravelled drive, a cattle grate, track and woodland. Mum and I bagsied this seat, because it has an excellent view of the TV.

'The Angels' Seat', she called it. Here we'd lie, entwined, listening to her mesmeric stories about mermaids, Jesus, flying cars, my Italian family – boy, was I looking forward to meeting them.

Piccolina, they will throw such a party. Italians love only one thing more than their own babies – their babies' babies!

Did she even say that?

In hindsight, this window seat gave her the heads-up, should we have visitors. Sometimes, we'd pretend we were hiding out. That was fun. I'd have to do slow counting to stop myself from doing a number two.

After she'd gone, I'd sit here a lot. Watching the trees sway in an array of breezes, the light changing from one minute to the next, the different types of rain: sun showers, snow showers, spiteful hail. The moon, especially; we've had many a conversation. Over the years, however, the view from this window has remained constant in the worst way – it never included her.

Last night, once Dad had gone to bed, I folded myself in half and encased myself in the musty guest duvet. I don't know when I dropped off. Last I saw, the clouds were an inky blue, punctuated by slivers of a new pale sky. Immovably, tomorrow waited behind them.

And even though Michael has shaken me violently, three times now, I decided, after the first shake, not to open my eyes again. Although nothing happened here between Vee and I, the room is tinged with betrayal. A lipstick-stained glass. My graduation photo – returned to the wrong shelf . . .

'*Flo!*' Michael shouts loudly into my ear.

'What the . . .?' I throw myself into a sitting position. The manoeuvre involves sliding my face up and along the freezing window sash.

'I was just wondering . . .' *Now*, he whispers.

Murderously, I open an eye. 'Wondering *what?*'

'What time you'd like waking up?'

'Are you having a laugh?' It's a fruitless question. The answer is no. My brother has an altruistic thought and must carry it out instantly. 'Please fuck off,' I say.

'Point taken.' He shows me an apologetic palm.

Furious, I fall back into the foetal position. The duvet over my head, I squeeze my eyes shut. Feathers belonging to a long-dead goose stab at my face. Then I think about dust mites. And the fact that I have a very morally suspect act planned for this afternoon.

There's no way I'm getting back to sleep now. Especially when I hear the theme tune to *House MD*, again.

I kick the duvet away like it's a giant stingray. Point furiously at the television. 'Why has Huge Laurie got a walking stick?'

My brother's more of a morning person than me. Sitting down beside me, he breaks it gently. 'Because his leg is in pain.'

'You do know the volume control is above thirty? Above thirty is for after midday.'

'It is after midday.'

'Shit. Why didn't you wake me?'

He offers me a bowl of something delicious. A fry-up for a baby. The bacon, tomatoes, scrambled egg, sausage and pancake are cut into small, equally sized chunks. 'Tabasco sauce or syrup?' he asks.

'Both,' I say, with a full mouth. The guy can cook.

'Where are you going?' He sits back down next to me, too close.

I'm squashed, but like it. Say, without thinking, 'I'm meeting Noah.'

'Who's Noah?'

That is a very good question . . .

He's a man I've kept off Michael's radar. The less he knows, the better. Plus, Michael might tell Dad, who very much knows Noah and will be unsettled that we're in touch.

'You remember – the guy I kissed in the nuclear bunker?' His look says, *You disgust me*. 'We were at primary school. And it was just the once. Why are we sitting so close?'

'Oh, you know,' he sighs.

I squint. 'What's happened?'

'Sebastien called again.'

'What do you mean, *again*?'

'I didn't tell you because I wanted to make my own mind up.'

'It's made. What did he say?'

'That he was sorry and embarrassed, and that he'd battle heaven and earth to win me back.'

'What a tool.'

'He's too romantic.'

'Michael, stop it. Remember what he did.'

To facilitate this, we sit in silence.

And I recall Sebastien's appearance. A very small, off-duty vampire. His civvies too tight. A face smoother than cling film. His voice, a precise and eerie Canadian. I shudder and turn to Michael. 'Have you remembered yet?'

He nods, resigned. 'I was going off him in the end.'

'If he phones again, cut him off. In fact, block his number. I'll do it.'

While he digs for his phone, I give him a speedy kiss on the cheek – you have to be fast with Michael, he dodges lips like a boxer dodges jabs. When he's finished scrubbing his face with a wrist, he passes me his phone.

Openly, I snoop through his messages. There are no new ones, so I give him instructions. 'I'm jaded so will be needing another bowl of this. And a coffee. Not the one Dad saves for guests.'

He fakes a retch. 'It's older than me. Flo, you're comfort-eating.'

I pull my T-shirt over my belly. Punch his thigh. 'No, I'm in mourning. Christ, I miss him *so* much, Michael.'

He punches mine back, harder. 'Who?'

'Tommaso!' I snap.

'He was your soulmate.' He nods. 'Flo, in three words, I can sum up everything I've learned about getting through hard times such as these.'

I smile. Only he can put a smile on my face this soon after my regaining consciousness. He points the maple syrup at me. 'Momentum is survival.'

'I told you that.'

'You didn't.'

What's not to love? My protégé. I pass him his phone back. 'All blocked. When are you thirty?'

'You always ask me that.'

In four months. On March 10th. It's a Tuesday, and he won't technically reach the big three-oh until 17.56 p.m. Born here at the cottage, Mum had let me cradle him, blood, mucus and all. 'I don't know him, but I love him,' I'd told her, perplexed.

Apparently. Or maybe I didn't say a word. Maybe I complained about the yucky long sausage that attached him to my mother so he couldn't float off and away. Maybe I wasn't there at all.

What I do know is Michael's a Piscean, which makes us a textbook match, sibling-wise.

Both signs are passionate about truth so err towards jobs that provide access to the human psyche. It gives us tangible clues as to the point of existence. Our job choices, however, vary. Cancerians tend towards becoming teachers or psychiatrists. Pisceans make up the largest proportion of saints and serial killers.

I'd be lying if I said my brother didn't have a smidge of the latter. His ability to move on so fast being one of them. Look how he turns the TV volume up to forty. Points at it and says, with large eyes, 'The camera is actually going into somebody's brain.'

'Any chance of an adult portion this time?' I jiggle my bowl.

After lunch, I whip up to my loft room. Put my dressing-table stool back in its place. Flap the memories free of the single duvet. Open the curtains to welcome a different day. I then clean my teeth over its little pink basin and get dressed. There's no point in washing – I'm about to cycle the equivalent of a half-marathon.

This is what I wear: black jeans, black hoody, black hooded cagoule, black hat. Trainers, black.

Shouting goodbye to Michael, I double check my rucksack.

Its contents: cash, phone, sugar solution and an atomiser.

Warning: I can't pretend that what I'm about to do is legal. For that reason, I'll be keeping it entirely to myself.

Noah declines to give me even a conciliatory shoulder barge when I arrive at the hotel bar. To be fair, I'm perspiring and grubby. He frowns at my get-up, forgets to stand up or offer me a drink.

'Robbing banks again, hen?'

I take my gloves off. 'Stagehand. Voluntary work.' Sitting opposite him, I become conspiratorial. 'If anyone asks, I've been with you since 2 p.m.'

'Because . . .?'

'We're friends.'

'Don't push it.' His face lights up, marginally, which I'm pleased for. Noah looks much nicer when there's a peak of insouciance. At nine, he was very insouciant, his air invincible. It was what drew me to him. Unfortunately, life got to Noah. His melancholy is palpable, not helped by the Scottish accent. Often, he forgets to be sociable, like today.

'I'll get my own drink, shall I?'

He pushes himself slowly into a standing position, makes his way to the bar, while I have a look around the joint.

The Travel Inn, Christchurch West, is identical to every other. Ostensibly moulded from plastic, an antibacterial wipe away from surgical sterility, everything thoroughly attached – the televisions, the beds, the side tables, the body wash. The carpet is generic – a stain-resistant cacophony of purple. The chatter is muted, meals are freshly micro-waved that day and the anonymity it purveys is a welcome reprieve.

'It's quite pop-up, this chain,' I tell Noah when he returns. 'Like it's been assembled at the hotel factory and airlifted in – fixtures, fittings and staff.'

'What are you talking about?' he asks.

'It's very *Westworld*,' I nod.

'Sorry about that.' Noah likes to take everything I say personally.

So I point at the window, a verge of grass and the A35 beyond. 'It's brilliantly convenient, though. If you're passing through, like you.'

Downing the rest of his pint, he starts a new one. 'Let's get to the nitty-gritty.'

'Yes. I'm sorry it's been a couple of weeks since we chatted . . .'

'I always feel like I'm chasing you.'

That's because looking for my mother is nobody else's business but my own, I don't snip.

It frustrates me that Noah's parents were part of Bambi's story, too. That he wants the truth as much as I. Discovering what happened to our families has become his *raison d'être*. In an amateurish way, he's turned out to be an asset. Trouble is, despite his looking like a handsome Scandinavian paladin, his aura sucks the air free of joy, as does the reason for our connection . . .

Noah's father's name was Eric Steensen. When Bambi disappeared, Eric did, too. The coroner might have said that he was the gassed man in Mum's passenger seat, but he wasn't. Eric had fled to Scotland. Later, his young family joined him. Theirs was a cloak-and-dagger existence, with no questions asked, until a year ago, when Eric Steensen passed away, for real.

Noah and I discovered that his father had been a witness protection officer. For twelve years, it was his job to look after my mother. Until Eric and Bambi decided to do a flit – and take out a man, for good measure.

On paper, there's a touch of the Bonnie and Clyde about it.

Neither Noah nor I knew how closely our lives were entwined. Until recently, my recollections of Noah were: we played together as children, and then we didn't. And the cemetery bunker kiss, of course. I get it – Noah's as desperate as me in his need to know everything. Still, I'm possessive of *her* story and, more especially, mine.

'I've done some research,' Noah is telling me. 'Witness protection officers protect victims of crime. But, mostly, society's dregs. There's a big chance she's a bad egg or a snitch.'

'You're so down on her.'

'Aff!' He shows me a finger. 'Let your mum off her pedestal for a moment.'

'No.' I flick the digit away. 'She already dangles from one by a toenail.' It's a fact Noah knows already – he's the only person I've told about meeting Mum.

'Hen, loyalty clouds your vision.'

'I'm trained to be detached.'

'So why are we arguing about facts? Ninety-five per cent of protected people are criminals, one way or another.'

'You keep telling me you remember her. Then you'll know she's not the career hood-type.'

'The mafia are hell bent on revenge. It's obvious she's an informant.'

'Nothing's obvious. Your dad was a bloody policeman, and you didn't have a clue until a month ago.'

Noah lowers his voice. 'He had to live in secrecy – *everybody's* life depends on it. Witness protection is a dangerous world.'

'Lives depended on his *deceit*.' I take a messy gulp of wine. 'Making me right. Things are far from obvious.'

Secret: there's a very high likelihood that my mum grassed on the mafia. But until I've got my head around that, he's not going to, either.

'What about King Arthur?' I hate it when Noah pretends he's forgotten a name. 'The guy you met that time you fell off a hill.'

The horror of that memory puts my heart rate through the roof. 'It was a mountain. And I dangled.'

Thankfully, somebody passed by. His name was Lancelot and it didn't suit him at all. Agile as a mountain goat, he was also, facially, not dissimilar to one. He was up to no good, milling around Castilla de Friuli, hiding in undergrowth. I recall the disconcertingly acrobatic way in which he'd rescued me and the enmity with which he ordered me to tell no one about seeing him, especially not Tommaso.

Which I did not – other things got in the way.

Now I know, of course, the Mountain Goat knew things I didn't at the time. That Tommaso's father, Rocco Bellini, was a gangland boss soon to retire, leaving my lover days from the biggest promotion of his life. Lancelot even left a note on my pillow, advising I get out of Italy fast.

> *Florence,*
>   *Your choice of boyfriend is inadvisable. For your family's safety, I beg you return to England and stay away from everybody Bellini-related.*
>   *You will not see me again. Please destroy this letter.*
>   *Lancelot*

I change the subject. 'How did you meet your wife?'

Noah baulks, doesn't quite know what to say. 'She worked reception at RBS in Inverness, I dropped in letters and parcels. What's this got to do with anything?'

Nothing. I'm disarming you, so you stop talking about Bambi.

'You play your cards too close to your chest,' I say. 'It's very unfriendly.'

'It was how I was brought up.' Placing elbows on the table, he drops his head to the side.

'You get that, too. I know you do.'

I get it with knobs on. Noah and I were living on different

sides of the country, knowing we were implicit in something but having no idea what. A parent's subterfuge rubs off on you.

Noah will not shut up. 'For UK and Italian government agencies to assist one another in relocating a witness to the UK, that witness has to tick some *big* boxes.' He pauses. 'Aren't you interested in what she did?'

'Not any more.'

'You met her, and that was hard, I get that. You feel cheated. Trouble is, I know you. You're not leaving it like that.'

'I am,' I lie.

'Well, I'm not leaving it.'

'She's *my* mother.' There, I said it.

The look he gives me. This is what he silently transmutes . . .

We share too much history. Your quest for truth is inexorably conjoined with mine. Hell's bells, woman, I have unearthed truths that have led you to a reunion with your dead mother.

I do not believe in being inexorably conjoined with anyone. 'You're just so unyielding. Always in my ear, everything on your timescale . . .'

He nods. 'Fair enough. From now on, you're the boss.'

'I was *always* the boss.'

'And everything will happen at your speed. Take time to digest things. When you're ready, I'm here.'

'Here?' I show him his surroundings.

'If necessary.'

'That doesn't make me feel claustrophobic at all.'

'It's not meant to.' He frowns. 'I'm visiting friends. It's allowed.'

'No, you're not. Go home, Noah. You've a wife and kid in Scotland who need you. It's not fair on them, you hanging around me all the time. You do know we're not boyfriend and girlfriend?'

This he says with gravitas: 'The last woman alive and I'd not prod you with a turkey baster.'

'OK, Macbeth.' I stand up, knock my chair backwards. 'But no more stalking me, like you did in London. I'll be in touch when I'm ready.'

'You owe me for the drink.' He nods at the evidence.

'Scottish and tight. You're an actual stereotype.' I slap a fiver on the table. 'Goodbye, Noah.'

I'm at the door when he shouts back at me. 'You're forty-five pence short.'

Bigamist

Openly, I stare at the mother I formerly knew as Bambi Love. Leaning against a pillar, my view is unfettered.

Currently, she is pretending to inspect the ingredients of a night cream. I know she is pretending because her body language says otherwise. Contracted – hunched shoulders, chin tucked in, elbows tight at the waist – my mother's stance is too defensive. She concentrates squarely on external stimuli. Especially for someone to arrive.

I use the opportunity to absorb her sixty-three-year-old face.

Physically, she's as I remember. A Charlie's Angel, specifically Jaclyn Smith. Large, brown curls that bob about her shoulder blades. Aviator Ray-Bans. She even sports a playsuit, which is very cute and shows off a figure enviable for a thirty-year-old. Then there are the little white pumps, ready for action. And a cashmere pashmina that could double up as a headscarf, should she need to disappear in a crowd.

Behaviourally, however, she's an enigma.

My mother would never have stuck out like a sore thumb. Look how she sprays perfume inaccurately at tester strips. She is clueless as to the rubrics of disappearing in a crowd. It's a miracle she's survived the last twenty-five years.

I spot him before she does – the man for whom she waits. His lanky stride makes him appear lazy, but legs that length

41

cover more ground. I've seen him and his pannacotta-coloured hair before.

See the change in her body language as he approaches. Her shoulders pull back, her arms slacken, her neck lifts. External stimuli are no longer of interest; it's all about the square foot of ground on which she stands. They don't hug; she simply touches his cheek.

That makes me mad.

What's his cheek got that mine hasn't?

And what about her husband? The one she's still married to. Sitting at home, bringing up their children, pretending he's widowed to save all our bacon, while she's enjoying her happily ever after in a flower-laden villa just outside Bagnara Calabra. I travelled there and saw it. I also saw her daughter, and a granddaughter called Paola. That was hard viewing. The daughter is older than me. I was supposed to be her firstborn.

I look at the lover, husband, gimp – I've no idea what. Bent and benevolent like the BFG, only more Italian. Does he even know who Bambi is? Was? Properly? During all her incarnations?

The airport tannoy system makes everyone stop and point an ear at the gods.

This is the final call for Boarding Gate 5.

I look at my watch. Glance up. My mother does, too, chivvies her pannacotta lover along.

It's difficult to think straight. Boarding Gate 5 is *my* boarding gate.

No, oh no, no. You cannot come home with us. Not today. Not just like that. Not on an easyJet flight to Bournemouth. I don't care that it might be the only place that's safe for you now; there's a more massive issue concerning me.

Michael.

He was pre-school when she went to live with Jesus. He

42

won't recognise her, not at first. She'll recognise him, though. Bambi was older than seven when she abandoned us. Definitely, she had the sophisticated neural architecture needed to form and hold dear complex memories. Of course, I'm assuming children grow up to look exactly as a mother expects. Puberty can send people off on a facial tangent. One thing's for sure: if she does recognise him, she'll whoop and screech and cry, because he is all she cared about. Michael Love fact: he is not equipped to be reunited with a mother he thinks is dead. He never will be.

'Stop,' I state, loudly.

Obediently, Bambi and her lover swing a left at the last minute – they hurry towards Boarding Gate 2. Glancing at the departure board, I see a flight to Tito Menniti (REG) – it takes off ten minutes before mine. They are heading back home.

I'm madder than before.

Because why aren't you getting on an easyJet flight to Bournemouth, just like that, today? I feel rejected all over again.

'Bambi!' I shout.

Everyone looks at me except her.

'Mum!' It feels audacious saying that word out loud. I flinch, uncertainly, awaiting her response.

But the English for *Mama* alludes her. Or perhaps she's just forgotten me saying it. She's about to disappear around a corner towards her gate; I don't recognise my voice.

'What's wrong with me, Mum?'

Bambi's steps falter and halt. Mine, too.

With a tragic jolt, I recognise her stance, my surety the result of bona fide memories: her dropping me at junior school, at Brownies, my granny's; her goodbyes too heart-felt, delivered with tortured eyes. It was crucial to her that I understood the intensity of her farewell. Quite different to her hellos – they were guilty and demonstrative, like she'd had an epiphany and owed us the world. I didn't understand.

Now I do – Bambi wavers between fight and flight.

I look at Pannacotta Man, who stares back at me, his milky eyes seeping too much kindness. Who the hell is he to look at me so fondly? I don't care that he's now acting as my adversary, using those same milky eyes to implore Bambi to turn around.

My feet are too magnetic. It takes everything to drag them towards her, while the questions pour unwanted into my head like a storm of wasps. I can't shake them free.

Did you even love my dad? Was he an easy catch, as besotted as the BFG, prepared to play whichever game you dictated as long as he's in your life? When you were our mother, Michael's and mine, did you spend it *all* wanting to be somewhere else?

Ten steps away, I communicate with her via telepathy, because we used to practise it in the Angels' Seat. The memory is real all right; lucid as this moment – we did mind-reading and I always guessed right.

Just like today. Bambi will opt for the flight option. See her now, walking slow and unsteady.

Humiliated, I freeze. Tears come erratically, cruel ones, the type that make your hands dangle.

A myth . . .

My lost mother was like David Banner out of *The Incredible Hulk*, the 1970s TV series. I can hear the theme music playing in my head now. It's soul destroying. More soul destroying than Barber's 'Adagio for Strings'. Michael Jackson's 'Ben'. Randy Crawford's 'One Day I'll Fly Away'. Even its title's a corker. 'The Lonely Man'. Arguably the saddest music ever produced; it might as well blast from the speakers now.

Yet as I watch her leave me behind, I find I'm not thinking of her. I'm thinking of my father. She doesn't wander lost from town to town, unable to settle for reasons beyond my understanding. It's George Love, ambling from moment to moment with his loss and his abysmal secrets.

Michael's phone brings me round. 'The Lonely Man' fades out. An insistent sci-fi text tone fades in. I remember the owner of that tone. It's like a bucket of piss in the face.

Darcie's daughter, Annie. The Antichrist.

Clumsily, I fiddle with his phone. Wiping my eyes and nose with a sleeve. Eventually, getting up the text.

The woman's hatred of my family is impressive. It's true Annie has been candid with me regarding her ill intentions, her sole aim being that our parents never marry. It's a goal I'm one hundred per cent behind. Our methods, however, are diametrically opposed, as are our moral compasses.

The text she has sent my brother is menacing.

Hurry home, Micky, love. Daddy needs you.

The bitch has even put a smiley face on the end.

Under-age

I practise Fānziquán in the back garden. Also known as 翻子拳, this Chinese martial art is combative and revolves around having perilous hands.

Two fists are fast like the falling raindrops, and fast like a snapping whip.

My imaginary target: Annie's head.

Imagine Kathy Bates in *Misery*, only less likeable. And her name is Annie, like the actual character Bates plays in the film. Though she's called Annie Wilkes, and this Annie's called Annie Something-else.

She thinks my family has too many skeletons. It's the only thing with which we agree. There are certainly more than I can disinter.

As with all martial arts, acute awareness of your surroundings is essential. This involves enlisting all your senses. Mine are too clouded with hatred. When, finally, I spot Michael loitering at the shed, I do a brief scream.

'You always creep up on me!'

'I know.' He wears his compassionate face – it's very good. 'You've been practising fighting since we got back from Italy.'

I stop him right here. 'I will not have you worrying about me, Michael.'

'I'm not,' he states. 'I'm worried about me. You're messing with my mellow.'

I squint. 'I can see that's inconvenient.'

'Good,' he says. 'Now sit down. We need to have a chat.'

But the grass is wet and cold. So we replot to the kitchen, where Michael makes tea and speaks to me as if I'm a child.

'I know Tommaso chucked you, but you can't mope for ever. Breakfast or Earl Grey?'

'Twenty-four days is not for ever. Breakfast. And it was a mutual decision.'

'You weren't engaged. Dad didn't know him. Did you even copulate the relationship?'

I don't laugh because, no, Tommaso and I failed to make the knocking-boots stage. We did, however, kiss and do the motions a bit against a tree, which was one of the most spiritually complete moments of my life – until we got told to stop by the hotel's proprietor.

'I was getting *married*.' He points a teaspoon at his heart. 'Now move on, already.' This is the cruellest thing he's ever said to me. It's also exactly what I have told him to do. He leans his bottom against the kitchen unit and folds his arms. 'We need a case. A brand-new one. It'll take your mind off being a reject. Something to get us out of the house.'

'I don't have the energy,' I say truthfully.

'That's OK, I've sorted it.' He puts a tea in front of me. Waits for me to compliment it.

'Oh, exactly the right colour. Sorted what?'

'A new case.'

'No, you haven't.'

'I have. I suggest we take it.'

I laugh. 'I'm the trained PI – I'll decide if we take it.'

'OK.' He waits for me to decide.

'Do you have any actual facts I can base my decision on?'

'Yes,' he says proactively.

'Can I have them?'

Taking his detective's notepad from an inside pocket, he hands it to me, then says, 'It's all there. Grandmother engaged to gardener. Antiques have gone missing. The family want a background report on him.' And the bit that most concerns Michael, 'He's Welsh.'

'Very *Lovejoy*. I like it. How did you hear about the case?'

'Dee from the sauna bar. Her friend, James, is the grandson.' He places a palm on his heart. 'We have to help him, Flo – he's ever so worried about his gran.'

'The *sauna bar*?'

He shows me a no-nonsense palm. Because the gaff is a gay sauna with private rooms and alcohol on tap. 'Are you in or not?' he demands.

'I'm not sure this case is therapeutic enough, given my current state of heartbreak.'

'OK, but the deal is, I'm in charge.'

'It doesn't work like that. I'm the boss, but in the shadows. You're also in the shadows, but as an assistant.'

He does serious eyes. 'You can't be in charge for ever.'

'I can. What with it being my company, and me having all the qualifications, contacts, equipment, and me getting all the cases.'

'Apart from this one,' he states, placing fly biscuits in a neat circle on a plate, then wiping the kitchen surface lovingly with an antibacterial wipe. Then all the other surfaces. I'm soothed by the serenity of his movement – it's as restful as whale music. 'Housework's my therapy,' he likes to say. Who am I to deny him that?

'Go on, then,' I sigh. 'You can be in charge, but in the shadows and acting like an assistant, for anonymity purposes.' His smile is huge. 'Now pass me the sugar.'

'You don't take sugar.'

'No,' I agree, taking the bowl from him. A fly biscuit between my teeth, I go into work mode. 'Michael, go and make an introductory appointment. First rule, we need to see if the client is someone we can work with.'

Excited, he disappears with his tea into the living room. And I take a clean jam jar from the dishwasher.

How to make a concentrated-sugar solution: one part water

to four parts sugar. Boil, then simmer, stirring constantly until the sugar has dissolved. Decant to glass container.

I put the jar in my rucksack, then look for my bicycle clips.

Our initial meeting with the client, James Jardine, is to take place at his work. This is not unusual. Visiting a punter's office while posing as a business client or customer is an excellent ruse. I've never, however, been asked to attend the till point of a garden centre before. This garden centre temporarily moonlights as a winter wonderland. The door to Santa's grotto is guarded by real reindeers. Elves on stilts are accomplished at raising a smile; especially Elfish Presley. The grown-ups can swoon over log cabins, hot tubs and fire pits. There's a restaurant, a ball pond, a children's club and a choir, fifty-strong. Currently, they're singing 'All I Want for Christmas is You'.

Michael's first job as boss is his usual one. He's my 'second eye', keeping me safe, watching my back. I cough loudly to centre him – he's become very taken with an insectarium.

'Are you sure that's him?' I mouth.

Michael nods from his aisle, waves me forward. I pick up a bauble and proceed to the client's till.

Never appear bemused when approaching a potential punter. They're unsettled enough. Calling upon the services of someone like me stems from a punishing place – one ranging from appalling worry to clinical neurosis. He'll certainly be having second thoughts at this stage – my job, therefore, is to offer an immediate sense of control, but mostly empathy, and definitely not to pull the face I'm pulling now.

But this situation is a first for me. I double-check his Happy to Help badge.

James. That tallies.

So why is he only fifteen? That makes this encounter extremely illegal.

I put my bauble on the counter. 'This is not no win, no fee. You do understand that?'

James wears an orange T-shirt and an orange cap upon which he's attached an avant-garde tinsel arrangement. His blue eyes are lively and sharp. His demeanour: a very skinny lovey. A teenage Benedict Cumberbatch.

'I'm aware of the protocol,' he tells me, in a cadence fit for a grown-up. 'I finish in ten. I'll meet you by the ice rink.'

Taking my bauble, he plops it in a brown paper bag, then gives it back, without asking for payment. Failing to notice that I am an actual grown-up and he's the child. Nor that I'm a proper PI and deserve a little – I don't know – fascination.

I look at my watch. 'Eighteen hundred hours it is.'

When I look back, James is already serving the next customer, as if a PI hadn't just attended his cashier desk, like his current customer is the centre of his universe. I envy the youth of today. Am intrigued by the audacity of them.

The ice rink.

As expected, it's too small. Swarms of children unable to negotiate fine motor skills, let alone skate on knives in an anarchistic bowl of sheet ice.

'It's so wrong,' states Michael. Not to my face, to his phone. He's positioned on the opposite side of the rink.

'Michael,' I say, 'I have a prevalent issue.'

'Go on.'

'What's with Charlie Bucket in there?'

Michael looks up from his phone and at me from his side of the rink. 'Are you doing irony?'

'I am.'

'Nope.' He still doesn't get it.

'Michael, we can't take this case. Have you seen the client?'

'What's wrong with him?'

'In our profession, representing a minor is all shades of wrong.'

'What's wrong with miners?'

Homophones are not Michael's friend. 'He's at *school*. Did you know that?'

'Yes. Dee said. Do you remember when Bruce Miller got his head sawn off?'

'He did not.'

'He did. Matthew Munday skated over his neck.'

Bruce Miller's neck is fine, though Matthew Munday did have to perform an emergency bunny-hop when his friend face-planted. 'It was a nick to the jowl.'

'Jeeeezus!' screeches Michael.

I know immediately what he's referring to. A single-minded dad skating backwards, insistent that his children watch; yet their little legs flail, like dystrophic ducklings. 'I'm going to phone social services, Flo.'

I hang up. My peripheral vision has kicked in. Someone stands to my right, leaning against the barriers, too. I wait a few seconds before appearing to notice him.

A little taller than me, James has taken his orange uniform off, loiters in his civvies, just one of the kids – the weird ones.

James Jardine wears a suit jacket, over a T-shirt and sensible jeans. He has an actual parting and a document folder. Were he anything to do with me, I'd tell him to lose the Brylcreem, buy some skinny jeans and a Slipknot T-shirt – his look cannot do him any favours in the playground. He's the type of boy who looks like a lesbian.

'You're early,' I tell him.

He quotes Shakespeare. 'Better three hours too soon than a minute too late.'

I do half a smile. 'Shall we get a coffee?' That sounds wrong.

James doesn't help things, does a stagey sigh and beleaguered nod. I feel like I'm about to steal his virginity.

It's an edgy walk to the café. I don't know what to say. It doesn't matter; James does . . .

'I've never used a private investigator before,' he tells me. 'But I've done my research on the best way to go about it. My family's grateful you're taking this case. They've heard all about you.'

This is exactly why Michael's not management material. You should procure a case via enigmatic insinuation. You do not pitch for it with your case history – that puts client confidentiality and our own health at risk. Then again, Dee from the sauna bar probably knows all about me, anyway.

An admission: I was in the newspapers through no fault of mine – the incident put a stop to my career in entrapment. Don't go there. 'I think you'll find you and your family have heard nothing about me.' My wink is not a friendly one.

James does empathy, brilliantly. 'Definitely.'

Our destination is the ideal place in which to interrogate a child – big and fluorescent as a supermarket, not romantic at all; we disappear among the patrons and potted shrubbery. Neither of us pushes the issue of refreshments.

'So, thank you for coming.' He places his hands on top of his document folder, like a bank manager. 'I have the bits and pieces your boss asked for. Photographs of my gran, her gardener . . .'

Boss? 'How old are you?' I ask him straight.

He shows me philosophical palms. This is an acceptable and expected question. 'Seventeen.'

'No you're not.'

'We have good genes.' He taps the folder. 'To prove it, I've included a copy of my passport and my provisional driving licence. My dad said I should give it you.'

'Why aren't I talking to your dad?'

'He's a vicar. It's not really appropriate. You can check. His details are there.'

I remove all blocking objects so there's nothing for him to hide behind. Condiments, menu, a white vase with a flower in it. If you don't trust a client, never take on the case. 'They might have considered a more mature spokesperson. You're still at school?'

He puts his elbows on the table. 'I'm studying for my A-levels. English, drama and ethics.'

'Ethics is religious studies, right?'

'They don't call it that any more.'

'At convent school, it wasn't compulsory to do RE, but it was a test of morality.'

He touches his chest. 'Not so much for me. Church of England. Please believe me. I've got this.'

'What about money?'

'We don't have *huge* amounts . . .'

Wrong answer. I'm not here to do him favours. I'm here to do a sterling job. 'This is an expensive game.'

'We have enough, though.'

'Nobody does.'

James leans forwards, alarmed. 'Then what's the point of you?'

I'm half tempted to punch his arm: that was an excellent response. 'Luckily for my clients, I'm frighteningly efficient.'

There follows the routine spiel . . .

'Now, I need to know everything. Rest assured, anything you tell me will be treated in complete confidence. If we cannot help you, I'll tell you. If you feel this is not the right path, that is fine. We *have* to be on the same page. Should we agree to proceed, I'll need five hundred pounds upfront. That buys you forty-eight hours, excluding expenses. Then we'll talk again to see where we're at. Hopefully, we'll discover

that your gran has bagged herself a corker of a gentleman.'
I nod at his folder. 'So, what you got?'

James has everything in plastic envelopes attached with treasury tags. It's like a GCSE project. First, I study the copy of his passport and provisional licence. It looks kosher; nonetheless, I decide to do an ID check on him when I'm back at the computer.

There are three photographs of the target, Alan Knight, and a filled-in questionnaire. Target questionnaires are essential, prior to a case. They proffer invaluable information, such as height, mobile phone numbers, past addresses, family, school, education. A very intrusive CV compiled by someone who half knows you. It can be hugely enlightening. I read through it twice.

Alan Knight, 76, ex-Welsh Guards, served in the Falklands, where he sustained a back injury. Became a school caretaker, then a gardener. Wife, Margaret, died of cancer ten years ago. His only child, a son, died as a teenager. Owns a cottage in Chartwell in which he's lived for years.

There are two photos of the boy's grandmother – one of her alone, and one where she's being cuddled by James and a woman.

'Your mum?' I ask.

James nods, eager for me to see the next sheet of paper. A letter. Written on behalf of himself, his sister, his father, his mother, his uncle and a few cousins, requesting that I proceed and assuring me that funds, within reason, are not an issue.

Crowdfunded investigations are my favourite type. When a whole family unit has clubbed together, the likelihood is an interesting outcome, because a *whole* family is never wrong.

As I read, he tells me: 'He's not a bad man, on the surface. But there's something not right. Small, expensive things have been going missing. Grandad's watch – it was a Jaeger-LeCoultre, an *original*. Some silver bits – pill boxes, a christening spoon. A ring; Lalique. My gran's too sweet – she blames it on being doolally, which doesn't explain why cheap things aren't going missing, too.'

I look up. Nod. 'I'll consider your case, James. But this level of investigation, if undertaken by the police, would last weeks. I'll probably need more money. That said, I guarantee you the best job in the shortest timeframe possible. Now go home and consult with your family.'

James shakes his head. 'Proceed with haste,' he says. 'When you've *considered* the case, that is.'

He's far too excited about what lies ahead. That level of buoyant anticipation doesn't last long – mine is too dark a world. Soon enough, the kid remembers this plan involves the happiness of a real-life loved one.

'For Gran's sake, we have to be sure he's a good man.'

I give him some advice: 'Never lose sight of that primary goal, James. There's something very addictive about hiring a PI. Don't get too nosy or lose focus of your primary goal – that's dangerous for both mind and pocket.'

'I understand.' He shakes his head, fascinated.

'And our goal here is to discover if Alan Knight is marriage material, right?'

'That's correct.'

I put a hand out. 'You have officially hired a private detective.'

His handshake is limp but ever so grateful.

Theodolite

Operation Lovejoy. *Day One*

James's grandmother's house. A large detached chalet with a panoramic outlook over the Radipole Nature Reserve. You can see Weymouth Bay and, beyond, to the Isle of Portland.

It's a neck of the woods that makes both Michael and I nostalgic. Our father was a devotee of the enrichment activity; many a day – some damp, some blistering, all exhilarating – spent hunting the wetlands. For waterfowl, Jersey Tiger moths, bitterns, dragons, injured Nazis, treasure and *Stig of the Dump*.

'You'll thoroughly appreciate it one day,' Dad assured us. 'I'm honing your skills of critical thinking.'

He must have known we appreciated it even then – being away from the cottage, forgetting that everybody else had a female role model, except us.

The property's prime location makes surveillance problematic. It is the middle house of five and is situated on a private road – there's no need whatsoever for strangers to loiter, unless it's for nefarious reasons.

The rear is entirely off-bounds, every back window staring out at a thousand acres of marshland – undeveloped and unpeopled, the grassy goop appears flush with the English Channel beyond. James's grandmother doesn't even have a back fence – the garden ends and a Site of Outstanding Natural Beauty begins. That unabated view provides quite the moat. There's nowhere for a private investigator to hide.

In cases such as these, the surveillance operative has no choice but to show themselves – a dangerous approach that must be undertaken with great care and an unabashed degree of theatre.

Here, Michael's car boot comes into play. Business cards, hats, clothing, shoes, surveillance equipment and props – you name it, he's designed a niche for it. Having parked in an adjacent road, I choose our disguises, which makes him antsy.

'You're messing it all up.'

'We're on a mission. I don't have time to fold things.'

'Why would you do that, though? *Why?*'

'Michael!' I whisper-roar. I need to focus him. 'Remember *Mr Ben*? He had the shopkeeper to tidy up after him. That's what you are. The magic shopkeeper.'

'I'm not. I'm the boss.'

'Yes, you are. But during this bit of the job, the bit where your car boot gets disorganised, it's best you have firm guidance.'

'You're right.' He nods. Points at his boot. 'But why would you do that?'

I sling a safety helmet and high-visibility jacket at him. Michael likes dressing up, so stops sulking once I've given him a tripod and photo ID to hang around his neck. Today, he will be playing an apprentice of the National Trust. His name is Rob Sweet.

I wear the same personal protective equipment, but carry a file. And wear glasses and my own lanyard that reads: *Sophie Kindle, Assistant Cartographer, Ordnance Survey*.

A note about identification: It's your Get out of Jail Free card. Always have options so you can pander to your audience. Here are some of the cards currently strewn across Michael's boot:

- J. Bridgewater, Transport Planner, Balfour Beatty plc

- Karli Kendall-Jones, Senior Sales Negotiator, Winkworth Estate Agents

- Jules Hill, Midwife, Nursing and Midwifery Council (UK)

- Drew Roberts, Photographer, Time Out Inc.

Warning. Don't get lazy – your business card/photo ID is half the story. You must inhabit each persona as though you have a personality disorder: be conversant in your area of expertise, have a full personal backstory and adopt idiosyncratic physiological quirks. This is *not* schizophrenia; it's self-preservation. Your success rate will depend upon it.

Michael and I walk the length of Kestrel Lane, pitching up at the farthest end, by a cock-eyed telegraph pole. Two houses separate us from Woolloomooloo. My laser distance metre tells me that's 3,690 centimetres.

House-name fact: *Woolloomooloo* is a strange one. It's actually an Australian suburb in Sydney in which there's an iconic pie cart called Harry's Café de Wheels.

While measuring arbitrary things with my distance metre, I remind Michael of his motivation. 'You're here on a work-experience day. It's a requirement for your NVQ in Conservation and Environmental Issues.'

Michael nods professionally. 'Can I be heterosexual?'

'Whatever you think works best.' I do an impression of what I imagine Alan Knight sounds like, i.e. Welsh. 'Well, hello there. What are you folks up to in my neck of the woods?'

'That's too Indian.' Putting his hands on his hips, Michael points his groin menacingly towards me and shows me how it's done. 'Waiting for the thalidomide to turn up.'

'*Theodolite.*' I punch his chest. 'Michael, do not mention the equipment. I'll do the talking.'

He pushes me back harder. 'You always do the talking.'

'That's because I'm better at subterfuge.'

Michael fact: he hates having to talk his way out of a situation. Give him a script, and he'll blag it. Without one, he is clinically honest.

'I am the boss,' he reminds me.

'OK, OK, there's no arguing with that.' I sigh. Hand him my lanyard. Motion for him to give me his. Then I give him the gen. 'You're a thematic map-maker, have a personal interest in cartographic transliteration, and are called Sophie Kindle.'

'She's a girl.'

'And a conservationist. I take it you read the *Dorset Wetlands Monthly*?'

'You didn't say I had to.'

'You're in charge.'

Michael stops listening to me. Instead, he furiously juts his eyeballs to the right.

'Are you trying to tell me things with your eyes?'

'Yes,' he says.

Now I hear it – the sound of crunching gravel. Only one drive has gravel in Kestrel Lane. The Woolloomooloo's.

I don't glance behind me. I smile widely at Michael, gesticulate enthusiastically, and say, 'I am being engrossed in conversation about theodolite-natured work. Now, who's approaching us?'

'The gardener,' he says, with a Welsh accent.

'Shit. Already? How do you know it's him?'

'He's wearing wellies.'

'Remember your training, soldier.'

He drops the Tom Jones impression. 'Five nine. Dirty grey hair, bushy sideburns, moustache, thick and impressive. My conclusion, he looks like the Dolmio man.'

Sounds like a fit. My brother has an acute memory for faces; I trust him implicitly. Nonetheless, I ask the million-dollar question: 'Ears?'

'Yes. Two.'

'Details?'

'Massive. Especially his lobes. They're long and fleshy, like sundried tomatoes that have been ironed.'

'That's him,' I point at something behind Michael. He turns to look at it, too. 'Buddha had extremely slack ear lobes. It indicates spiritual development. Can I make a suggestion? Go and look busy somewhere down that end of the lane, because he cannot get a proper look at you. Your position as boss and second eye will be compromised.'

'I'm going somewhere down the road.' Michael returns my lanyard. 'I can't be compromised. You stay here and get a psychological profile.'

'Yes, boss.'

I turn. Watch Alan Knight approach. When my brother and he pass one another, Michael salutes. 'All right, chief,' he says. And I decide to give him a back pat later – he's playing a heterosexual Welshman brilliantly.

'Hello, there!' I use my own accent.

Alan's is soft and chipper. 'Council work?'

'National Trust. We won't be bothering you for too long.'

'National Trust?'

We stand opposite one another. I'd compare Alan Knight to a homeless Cary Grant; a smaller, more ruddy-complex-ioned one.

'We're making maps.' I glance at my vibrating phone. Vee; it's the second time she's messaged me today.

'How do you do that?'

'I wait for the theodolite to turn up.' I put a casual hand on my hip. 'It's stuck in traffic. You definitely need one of those.'

He's put a hand on his hip, too. 'Don't they use satellites these days?'

I laugh through my nose. 'Sometimes, there are anomalies.' I don't go into them, because they're beyond his comprehension. 'Most importantly, we have to make sure we're accurate, or we could be sued.'

'Who'd do that?'

'Ambulance-chasers.' I genuinely hate them. See how I fold my arms?

Alan follows suit, because we're on the same page. 'They're hyenas in suits.' When he touches a saggy ear lobe, I scratch mine, briefly. Alan won't realise it, but we're making friends.

I even tell him my life history. 'I'm just the CAD person. Computer-aided design and drafting. It's replaced manual drafting. All automated now.'

'A brand-new world,' he says sadly.

'Not this bit.' I show him where he lives. 'They like to keep things just as they are here. Lived here long?'

'A while.'

Liar, liar, pants on fire. The client's questionnaire confirms that Alan lives seven kilometres away in Chartwell. 'How long you lot around for?' he asks.

'Assuming my boss turns up, an hour or two.'

'Well, if you need anything . . .' He does a little bow, then issues a warning: 'It's cold as a witch's teat. Need a cup of tea, you give me a knock, you hear?'

'That's kind.' I smile, then watch him return to the house. First impression: Alan Knight is a liar, but nice with it.

Pulling my phone free, I see a third message has arrived. This is what all three together say:

Tonight 7 p.m.
Rick Stein, Sandbanks
Table's booked x

I don't feel sorry for her. She is unfeasibly cool. And

terrible with money – wooing me with a Michelin-starred restaurant when her mortgage repayments are through the roof – I've a good mind to tell her off. In fact, I do:

You're on, but make it the King's Head in Poole. The drinks are on me.

My motive: ulterior.

I wait in the lane for another twenty minutes, pretending to talk on my phone, appearing incensed by other people's disorganisation. Finally gathering my folder and tripod, stomping past Woolloomooloo, out of Kestrel Lane, all for the want of a theodolite.

Michael and I wait, out of view of the lane, for another five hours.

This is the downside of investigation: too much time to think and not enough places to piss.

Six p.m. I ask to be excused.

'No,' says Michael. 'The client has paid for forty-eight hours.'

Human Resources fact: 'Ten hours I've been on, and I've not had a toilet break. That's illegal.'

He's horrified.

Genuinely, I mean it when I promise I'll be back for the night shift.

The King's Head, Poole. 19:00 hours.

When I enter, I don't show off. Avoid a show-stopping walk – the one where you elongate the neck, flattening the stomach and making saggy babaloos pert. Especially, I don't pretend I'm French – the last thing I want to do is toy with Vee's emotions. I scrub up well; it can be confusing and addictive.

Arriving first, I grab a large sauvignon blanc. I don't buy her one because that's too romantic. I jump a mile when she approaches from behind, grabbing my shoulders, burying her nose into my *komata no kereagatta hito* (the triangle of the neck's nape that looks like a fu-fu).

'You smell like porn,' she says, falling into the seat opposite me.

Schoolgirl error. Rodriguez Narciso is an overtly lustful composition of musk, orange, osmanthus and amber. 'I'm sorry.' I cup my neck.

'Don't be.' She grins, surveying the pub – its secret corners, oak fireplaces, crowded bookshelves; the fact we're hidden around a corner by a door marked 'Private'. 'This is very cloak and dagger. Is your imaginary husband on the rampage?'

I smile. Come clean, sort of. 'I have a confession. My brother and me used to have a secret gesture, back in the day. The "rescue me" gesture. Michael thought I'd done one. I hadn't.'

'He thought you wanted rid of me?'

I squint. 'Michael has a condition.' And I just used it for evil.

Vee doesn't ask what he's got. 'What's the gesture?'

'A Vulcan salute.' I show her one.

'That's not very secret.'

'It is if you incorporate it into an elegant stretch.'

She laughs. 'Well, he's the most loyal brother I've ever met.'

'And he's tidy,' I tell her. 'That balances us out, I think.'

'He looks after you.'

'*Puft!* We might as well be conjoined.'

'Most importantly, he's hot.'

'Runs in the family,' I accidentally flirt. She's being kind about Michael. She also said, "You smell like porn." I'm single. She fondles my ego. Which is allowed.

'Another?' She stands up, heads towards the bar.

'Go on, then,' I shout after her.

She has quite the aura as she hip-flicks her way to the bar.

If I could see chakras, I'd bet hers is hexadecimal code #C5B35, also known as James Bond Girl Gold.

Single. That makes my heart heave a sigh. I wasn't a few weeks ago. In my mind, I haven't been since the first time I saw Tommaso Bellini.

We first met at the Coliseum. When I say 'met', we clocked one another. The guy has one of those faces you have to see again as a matter of urgency. The type that does something peculiar to your synapses. He'd felt it, too. Synchronicity was at work, which is physics and actual proof that Tommaso and I were destined to meet. On our first proper date we didn't even kiss. Instead, we shared Roman delicacies, vintage wines and our deepest secrets, on a terrace encased in a giant birdcage and adorned with fairy lights.

Vee returns with a bottle of Baron de Ley Rioja Reserva, which is exactly what I fancy, even if I hadn't known it until now. While she pours two hefty glasses, I admire the beauty spot on her neck – a centimetre right of her outer platysmal band. Give or take an inch, it adorns the same spot as Tommaso's.

She misconstrues my stare; smiles, drinks, maintains eye contact. How I long for her to be the actual him. But there's no getting away from it: she doesn't make me hum, not in the way he did.

'You know I've just broken up with someone?' I cradle my wine glass.

She's sympathetic. 'Yes, love. How can any of us forget?'

I like the way she says that: 'any of us'. Like I have a ton of friends. Like there's more than one of her.

'Vee, I know this is boring and not fun, and not what you want to hear, and it's certainly not something I want to say. It's just as inconvenient for me, because you are unequivocally beautiful and, in another life, you know . . .'

I'm ashamed at my lack of eloquence. Girls like a full and

lucid explanation when being rebuffed. We may not agree with the explanation we're given, but we need the chance to argue the point.

'The truth is, Vee, Tommaso was attractive in all the ways you are. The two of you share an aura, sort of. That makes this – *us* – too weird.'

'Yes, it does,' she agrees, filling her glass.

'I understand if you're pissed off. If it were me, I'd be insulted.'

She doesn't see it like that. 'Maybe you have a type.'

I show heaven my palms. 'And you, Vee, are it. But my head's lost in action; prisoner of another moment in time.'

She pats my hand conclusively. 'One which is exclusive of me.'

'A bit.' I pat her hand back.

This makes her laugh. 'Thank you, Florence. Your frankness is appreciated.'

'Your personality is spot on,' I'm quick to add. And because I'm on an honesty roll, I say, 'I'm also not sure how gay I am. I am definitely a bit gay.'

'One way or the other, we're all on a spectrum,' she reassures me, standing up, tweaking my nose playfully. 'I need the loo.' Watching her hip-flick to the Ladies, I find I feel deflated – she got over me very quickly.

It takes a good ten minutes to dawn on me – Vee has done a runner. The Ladies has a door leading to the beer garden. And I salute her fuck-you exit while feeling unexpectedly empty, even though my plan is to pick up with her as friends in a few weeks' time. Because, first and foremost, Vee is a coroner.

I'm gathering my things to leave when she returns with the menu.

'I've interrogated the bar staff, all of them,' she says. 'The consensus: monkfish with lentils and black-cabbage salsa.'

I wrinkle my nose. 'Don't they do proper pub food?'

'That's what I said. I got us fish-finger sandwiches and chips.'

I love fish-finger sandwiches. 'What are we celebrating?' I grin.

'Friendship,' she states. 'I don't do lipstick lesbians. But I do do candour.' She pushes her glass at me; I'm to refill it. See how chivalry dissipates when a shag's out of the question. 'Now, you're to tell me all about yourself. Dee from the sauna bar tells me you fucked Scat Delaney.'

I spit my drink out.

She tells me off. 'Stop it. You are ridiculously fantastic.'

Then she gives me a palm clap. I can't tell you how long it's been since I last had one of those.

When procuring a contact, you should tell said contact something genuinely secret, maybe a little sacred. It shows you come in honour and definitely don't play games with another person's livelihood.

My peace pipe is a precious collateral: my most personal information.

'We didn't do it. Just kissed.'

'Yeah, right.'

'On Michael's life.'

'Dee said it looked steamy in the papers.'

'I'm a steamy person.' I shrug. 'Plus, it meant something at the time. Quite a lot, actually.' Hired to test an A-lister's fidelity, I became too involved. Who wouldn't? The guy was sensational. His singing voice was like a melted sunbeam. I sigh, 'The case was a set-up. Hence it ending up in the papers. Professionally and personally, it was an unmitigated disaster.'

'So you went to London to seduce men?'

I shake my head. 'To be a proper PI. The city, the job – it proffered anonymity. I liked it.'

'How many men did you seduce?'

'Loads. A footballer, a tree surgeon, a bank manager, a plasterer, an oligarch, some politicians.'

Her eyes are massive. 'Too funny.'

'I had a strict moral code.' I say it like it was a hundred years ago. 'My mantra was five seconds, tongues, case closed.'

Vee folds her arms. 'When was the last time you had a shag?'

I reassure her, 'Over the last year, I've had everyone I want. Just not carnally.'

'None of them?'

'Neither of them.'

Vee bangs the table, I've proved her point, which is not at all clear. 'So what cases are you working on at the moment?'

'I can't speak about them. Number-one rule of private investigation: it's unswervingly confidential.'

Vee nods, respectful of my enigma. Nonetheless, I find I want to share things with her. I know better than to be impetuous with these urges.

Always enlist a Psychologically Based Credibility Assessment Tool – with one question, to a frighteningly accurate degree, you can decide whether someone is being truthful or not.

I lean forward. Move our drinks out of the way. Put my elbows on the table and say: 'Did you know who I was, when we first met?'

Vee sees it as the test it is. Puts her elbows on the table, too. 'Not a clue, love. My intentions were entirely sexual. You're beautiful and strange. I was drawn to that. And your tits. You have gravity-defying tits.'

That was the right answer. Liars leave out sensory details, exclude the flourishes; cognitive overload manifests itself in them thinking too hard and too slowly. They also fidget, protect their truth portals – the eyes, the genitals, the knees.

'Anything else you want to know?' Vee's so relaxed, she rests a breast on the table.

Yes, I don't say. *Swear on Shruti that you won't fuck me over. Because, update on my friendship status, I've not had one in a long while. The reason being, I'm not good at them.*

For which I blame my mother.

She went and gave me the best start in life. Made me feel the epicentre of her existence. There was nothing, in my mind, not to adore about me. Then she 'committed suicide'. An eternal dreamless sleep was preferable to life with her firstborn. I took it personally. My adolescence was spent being suspicious of my gender. How easily they gave, then took away. I watched them from too much of a distance. Lost touch with my own kind.

Despite my professional instincts, I begin to talk. Objectivity, from the outset, is a struggle . . .

'Twenty-six years ago, a man and a woman killed themselves. The woman's body was never found. The man was identified as a local businessman. My client has reason to believe the body was, in fact, somebody else.'

'Who?'

'A bad man.'

'What type of bad?'

I tell the table. 'The type that's a paedophile.'

'Are you suggesting he was murdered?'

'That is the likeliest option.'

'And the missing woman?'

'Abroad.'

'She's not dead?'

'Not yet.'

Memories distract me. Too lucidly, I remember her – specifically, the coldness she had shown me at the airport.

Losing control of your micro-expressions is very unprofessional. I've certainly leaked a few. Vee's whisper is too gentle. 'Florence. That's heavy.'

'Heavier than you could ever imagine,' I whisper too gently back.

Over the years, its weight has stone-rolled me. Now – especially now – I battle to lift my chin, pull my shoulders back. There's been no one to talk to. The girls at school were wary of me after it happened. Uncertain of what I was capable. Murdering a mother, for instance. Then hiding her body so successfully it was never discovered. I was eight, for Christ's sake.

'Where did the deaths occur?' I hear Vee say.

'A car in a clearing on Twisted Acres Farm.' I look up at her. My eyes say too much. 'That's Dorset.'

She nods, slowly. Then downs her drink in one. 'The answer to your question is, yes. I can help you.'

I've no idea why I'm arguing with her. 'No, Vee. Absolutely not. How on earth could you?'

She's not in the mood to be patronised. 'You know how. I assume your client is an oligarch?'

I smile at my knees. 'How much are we talking now?'

'A couple of grand would be a steal.'

'For a photocopy of a coroner's report? I don't need an expert going through the post-mortem with me.'

'Yes, you do. Now, can you get me a spy camera and a sexy pistol – I'll need both of those. A grand – take it or leave it.'

Take it, take it, take it! 'I'll give it some thought,' I tell her earnestly. 'But thank you.'

'Well, don't take too long. The photocopy guy goes on paternity leave next week.'

'Confidentiality is essential, Vee. Nobody can know anything about what I've told you.'

Deadly serious, she says: 'I'm a Fellow of the Chartered Institute of Legal Executives, and I intend to keep it that way.'

'You're also skint. People should never compromise themselves for cash.'

Her grin is effulgent. 'Don't get deep about it, Florence. This is the most fun I've had in sixth months.'

I wonder where in DABDA she's at. The second D, at a guess. See how she sips her drink, curtly – tight lips, small gulps, small eyes, distracted by the memory of her ex.

'What was her name?' I ask.

'Rebecca,' she says. 'She wasn't *the one*. Which is why it makes no sense at all.'

I get it. Take my notepad from my bag. Write the following down:

Eric Steensen. 13 February 1988. Twisted Acres Farm. Carbon-monoxide poisoning. Signs on the window – *Warning: toxic gas*.

The gs look like 8s. I point at them. 'That's how she did them.'

'How *who* did them?'

'The missing woman.'

I write one final thing: Bambi Love. Then I tear out the page. Hand it to Vee. She studies it for some time. If she notices that the dead woman and I share a surname, she doesn't let on.

And I'm grateful for it.

Slipping the paper into her bag, she exhales thoroughly, then makes an executive decision. 'Whisky chasers.'

While she's at the bar, I consider stealing back my note. I don't want to know any more. Especially not the identity of the dead man in Mum's passenger seat. My suspicion: I knew him uncomfortably well.

Mile High

I loathe flying. Usually, the flight is spent mourning loved ones, should I die, and wondering what they might say at my funeral. And reminding myself of emergency procedure. Like, not opening the lifejacket while inside the plane. And that it comes with a light and a whistle, which you could forget, bobbing shell-shocked among debris and sharks, which I would suggest is not the time to start alerting attention to yourself by blowing a bloody whistle. Traditionally, that's how it goes.

Not today.

Today, I drop, devastated, into the seat closest to the window, wiping away a sweat moustache and getting my breath back. Today, I have never wanted to get on a plane more.

Michael sits back down beside me. 'The whole plane has been waiting for you.'

'Gynaecological emergency,' I say loudly.

It's breakfast, technically, yet I order myself two miniature Merlots. They dull the fretful throb in my tummy. Then I shut my eyes and rest my head against the plastic window frame. Within seconds, its smooth edges dig into my temple, rude as granite. I don't care.

I pretend to sleep for an hour and a half, consumed by too many thoughts. They tumble into an exhausted blur. Amid the tangle, I catch a glimpse of Tommaso – he loved me, then didn't. I spot my mother – she loved me, then didn't. Mostly, I see my father.

He loved me and still does.

If Annie has so much as bruised his feelings, I will assassinate her. This is not something I say flippantly. I've planned it exactly, how I'd commit the perfect murder, if ever the need arose. *Death by Love*: I've even given the technique a name.

Again, my father invades my mind's eye.

Until Darcie, he'd not had a girlfriend since my mum. His life had been about sheltering us. There was no need: the worst had already happened. Pity gets my stomach in a vice. It demands I stop thinking about Dad as a real human being.

Ping! The seatbelt sign has illuminated. I open an eye, slyly. Glance at the English Channel below, then at Michael, who stares straight back at me; he probably has been for the last hour.

'What are you going to say to Sebastien?' he asks immediately.

I rub my face, sit upright and tell it as it is. With Michael, there's no need to work up to a sad story.

'I've found something out about him, Michael. Something bad. So, because of that, the engagement's off. It has to be. And you are in no way implicated, so never have to feel guilty. Understand?'

Michael shakes his head. 'What's happened?'

'Sebastien has a love child.'

'Shut. The. Back. Door.'

'He's ten years old and is called Louis Tremblay.'

Michael shakes his head. 'No, that's his nephew.'

I squeeze his wrist, too tightly. 'He pretended that Louis was his nephew.'

'That's fraud.' Michael yanks his arm free.

'He had a one-night stand with a girl when he was sixteen.'

Michael's lower jawbone drops. 'A girl?'

'That's how babies are made.'

72

'I know how babies are made,' he snaps, then we look to his right – the air hostess hovers with an open black bin bag. I drop in the wine bottles and plastic cup. Michael takes the opportunity to deep-clean the seat pocket in front of him. He retrieves detritus from many flights before – a piece of unchewed gum and an earplug. This goes down well with the air hostess, who flirts, because, on first glance, my brother's tall and golden, with a fabulous physique and a strawberry-blond surf wave that's not overtly homosexual.

Then he wiggles his hands at her, disgusted. 'Have you got a baby wipe?' Holding his fingers aloft, he asks me again, 'A girl?'

'Here's the clincher, Michael. Annie's been holding it over Sebastien for God knows how long. I reckon she pulled him into a false sense of friendship, or drugged him. But I got him to confess in the end. Technically, he confessed to you. He thought he was texting you. It wasn't you, because I had your phone at the time. So I was undercover as you.'

The hostess returns with a baby wipe then checks our seatbelts. We present her with our groins and she thanks us for it. I then take his phone out of my bag. Pass Michael the handset.

'Take a look,' I say gently. 'It happened last night.'

Michael reads the text conversation ever so slowly. It's not until the landing wheels screech open that he turns to me and says, 'He doesn't love Louis? That's not very nice.'

'Well, you've seen him for what he is. And you're the victim.' I grab his hand. He doesn't wriggle it free. Instead, he cooperates with me – holds my hand back properly, using palm, fingers and thumb. The grip's not limp, but shows commitment.

I have a tear in my eye. We kangaroo jump on to and along Bournemouth airport's runaway, and I hold his hand

73

so hard I can feel a heartbeat in his palm, refuse to let go until we're told we're allowed, legally, to unfasten our seatbelts.

'Are you OK, now?' he asks maturely, patting my hand. Placing it back on my lap. 'It wasn't that bad was it, the landing?'

'I wasn't paying attention.'

'That's because I'm magic.' He shows me his palms, then pats my head like I'm his child.

Michael practises his passport face as we queue for Passport Control. He told me once this was because, with his dextrous facial muscles and acting abilities, they might not recognise him otherwise. It was why he was such a good actor.

'I think I made the right decision,' he decides, still-faced. 'To not want to get married any more.'

'You did.'

'I know.'

'We just need to make sure Dad is OK now, Michael.'

He turns to look at me, remaining in passport pose. 'Is he not OK?'

'You know how Annie's a bitch? Before we travelled to Italy, she made it clear to me she wanted to split up her mum and our dad. I think she might have just succeeded.'

His eyes become huge and animated. The rest of his face, though, remains relatively inert.

'Do not look around,' he says.

I'm motionless as a mannequin. 'What?'

'You will never guess who's behind you.'

'Who the fuck is it?' My heart starts to beat fast at the possibilities.

'Aljaž out of *Strictly*.'

And *that* is my brother moving on.

Cross-dominance

Prior to firing up the Dacia Logan, Dad engages in a lot of knob-fiddling. He drives like one might pilot a plane. That gives even mundane journeys a sense of anticipation. This one's not mundane, however. Excitedly, I pat my thighs in the passenger seat.

Love fact: making a memory for another human being is the most thoughtful thing you can do.

I point at the car freshener – a Yankie candle one, coconut musk. 'Who got you that?'

'Darcie,' admits Dad.

'Today's number-one rule: all talk of exes is banned.' I entangle it from the wing mirror. Throw it out of the window. Ask questions of my dad. 'Who's driven this car since the last time you drove it?'

'No one,' he says conclusively.

'So why are you adjusting the mirrors?'

He puts both hands on the steering wheel. Plays footsy with the acceleration pedal, listens to the revs. 'Displacement. Basic physics. Now, where are we going?'

'It's a surprise.'

Michael means it: 'The suspense is killing me.' Curled in half on the back seat, he's fashioned a bed. His rolled-up jacket under his head, a picnic blanket over his knees.

'What's your problem, sleeping beauty?' asks Dad.

Michael sits up straight, talks directly into his ear. 'If you must know, I was in bed having a brilliant dream, then she jumped on my head.'

'He wasn't waking up.'

'Because of the dream. Now I feel burgled.'

'OK, OK.' I shut him up. 'It will involve an element of competition.'

'You and competition is not fun.'

I stamp a foot. 'Michael, you are completely spoiling it.'

'And you're spoiling my case.'

'Case?' says Dad.

'You wanted to be the boss,' I remind him, then tell Dad. '*We* have a case. I'm being encouraging, giving him responsibility. I can't tell you anything about that case, due to client confidentiality.'

'She's not investing,' Michael complains. 'I always have to invest when she's the boss.'

I shake my head, even though he is entirely correct. Since meeting Vee a few days ago, I've been distracted.

'I'm dying of sleep deprivation,' he states.

'Son,' Dad advises, 'go to sleep and try and re-catch that dream. Florrie, this all sounds bloody grand, but I'm not as telepathic as you – what's the address?'

I tap at the satnav, then give Michael the stink eye for a good ten minutes. This is supposed to be the best and only day out I have *ever* organised. It will not end up a lost memory accidentally re-remembered in the future. It will be a day of moments entrenched in our communal psyches.

On the upside, my dad keeps winking at me, telling me with his eyes to ignore my brother. In the end, I initiate paternal bonding. Because today is *all* about George Love.

Paternal bonding. Best achieved via the discussion of unloaded topics. Examples include: politics, finances, fishing and horticulture.

'So, floating the Royal Mail, eh?' I shake my head. 'That's been a shit-storm.'

Post-office fact: I am the sole beneficiary of one. This year, I should have been all over the broadsheet business pages, scrutinising what will happen to the family business once the government has finished selling us off. Instead I adorned the front pages of the tabloids.

It's ungrateful, I know, but I hate the little box of a place. Serving behind that counter, doing the accounts, auditing the stockroom. Apart from the shop door and a clerestory wall, there's not a window in the place. No view. Certainly no future you could be bothered to chase.

Dad mentions the Communication Workers Union and Vince Cable; that's as much as I can tell you – I'm already breaking the rules. Accidentally remembering my ex . . .

Tommaso had been unimpressed when I'd told him I'd not wanted the post office. 'You should respect your father more,' he'd said, strictly. I'd asked if he was afraid of his. That's when I didn't know who Rocco Bellini was.

I'm on a slippery path – wondering what Tommaso's doing now, at precisely this moment in time. I imagine he enjoys breakfast with his mother in her Renaissance villa in the Dolomites. Maybe Howard, her fiancé, is there, too. Whatever, Tommaso will be in a rush, gulping an espresso, kissing his mother on each chiselled cheekbone. The day ahead will be busy.

I close my eyes.

Hear his blakeys on the oak staircase, momentarily smell the pheromones in his saliva, see him jump into his car; a car in which I sat; a car in which there'll still be traces of Michael's DNA – he'd accidentally bled all over the upholstery.

It's a twenty-minute ride to Portopiccolo Sistiana – the hub of the Bellinis' business empire. Their office being a six-star coastal resort attended by football stars and politicians.

I ask the silhouette of last night's moon: *Are you thinking of me, too, Tommaso?*

But the moon's forgotten its role in our love story: *Maybe he is thinking of someone new – Italian men fall in love at the drop of a hat.*

That destroys me. The thought of him loving someone else, ever. The certainty that I cannot share him. The stabbing realisation that I'm stuck in a grieving process destined never to end. It's worse than death. It's also the reason people murder their exes. The name for this condition is limerence, and I have a nasty bout of it.

'This is quite the trek,' says Dad.

Michael agrees. 'How much longer?'

I don't fucking know. I feel too sad. Because of the limerence. Because they're both coming across as very ungrateful. 'What bit of "It's a surprise" do you not understand?'

'The bit about it being fun.'

'We're here,' Dad tells us both, crossly.

Lower Grinstead Farm.

We park up. Gingerly surround a guy with a clipboard. Not just us. Others follow. If I'm honest, there's an air of trepidation. I suspect some of the other participants are recipients of an unwanted birthday present. That those who'd willingly booked themselves on the day now feel judged and silly. The vibe is piss poor – like we're attending our own alien abduction.

Ticking off our names, the SAS wannabe gives instructions:

'No dicking about. You'll be handling lethal weapons designed to maim and kill with maximum pain. Follow me in single file.'

Michael asks the person behind him, 'Is this the actual *Hunger Games*?'

'It's better than that,' says Dad, patting his back, encouraging him along a trail through the woods and into a field.

There, a haggard Mad Max awaits us. He stands astride a Mini Moke and says, in a tortured Newcastle accent, 'Welcome to Winterfell. I go by the name of Lord Brian. My job today, to train you to be knights of the Kingsguard.'

We laugh, good-humouredly. Ten strangers on the same page.

Apart from Michael.

And two others; Lord Brian points at them, he's not one for truck. 'For those who thought they were on the Apocalypse Day, this is exactly the same; our aim united – to survive in the face of hellish adversity.'

Dad and I do an unscripted 'Hooray!' That makes the others giggle.

'So, men' – Lord Brian rubs his hands – 'your job is to protect the whole of Westeros from the White Walkers. Lucky for you, we have crossbows and AK-47s.'

I don't care that he's sexist. I do a Tim Henman fist pump and tell Dad, 'When you play the *Game of Thrones*, you win or you die.'

I explain the basics to Michael . . .

'Westeros is where *Game of Thrones* is set. It's a landmass that looks like the United Kingdom on a map. Think of the White Walkers as the Scottish. We – the Black Knights – are posted on Hadrian's Wall to keep them out.'

'That's racist,' he says.

He's wrong. 'The White Walkers actually have no Scottish in them at all. They're an ancient race of humanoid ice creature.' I point, because there are some pitted around the field, randomly, like scarecrows. Anatomically, they're near enough. Ten feet tall, sinewy and mummified, made from a mixture of shop mannequin, Halloween mask and infrared eyes.

Michael tells Dad, 'They don't look Scottish.'

Lord Brian blows a hunting horn, then introduces us to a neat row of lethal weapons – knives, double-edged axes and spears. 'Your training, men, begins here.'

Michael raises a hand. 'I don't like this.'

Our leader nods. 'Then you'll not last long in the *Game of Thrones*.'

'I do not like this,' Michael tells Dad, seriously.

When Dad puts an arm around his son's shoulders, I think he's going to humour him, tell him it's just a silly game, that he can just watch if he prefers. Instead, Dad does a better Newcastle accent than Mad Max:

'How can a man be brave if he's afraid? I say that is the only time a man can be brave.'

'Series two, episode eight,' a student type tells his girlfriend. 'Ned Stark to Robb Stark.'

I am *so* proud of Dad.

Michael sits out the knife-throwing, because he's morally opposed to stabbing. Though throwing a double-sided axe is fine, because that wouldn't happen in real life.

Soon as you know it, Dad is coaching a completely contented Michael.

'That's it, son. Feet shoulder width apart. It's not in the wrist. That'll mess with your accuracy. Your starting point is perpendicular to your body. Now . . . follow through.'

It gives me a chance to trounce the other blokes, because I have an advantage over men in sports. I'm a girl. Their masculinity rides upon being able to trash me.

Crossbow.

I'm excellent at it. Our targets are a selection of zombie heads with apples on top. I have no qualms about slicing them through the neural cortex. Michael's almost as good as me. Dad is so awful I perform the Miles Test on him.

The Miles Test:

1. Extend both arms.

2. Make a circle using both thumbs and index fingers.

3. Keeping both eyes open, look through the hole and focus.

'Concentrate on my nose,' I say.

'I am,' Dad complains.

'Yep. Thought so,' I tell the student couple. 'He's left-eye dominant. But right-handed. He has cross-dominance. I've got it, too.' I tell Dad, 'Cross-dominance is advantageous in sports requiring side-on stances. You just need to use left-handed stances from now on.'

'Really?' he asks.

'It's not all good,' I warn. 'It can lead to neurological disorganisation.'

But Dad ignores me. And I fall silent, because I watch him do something I've never seen him do before . . .

He mimes a right-handed forehand, then a left-handed forehand, then performs a double-handed backhand.

Double-handed backhand fact: people with cross-dominance have a very good one.

Mum's not the only one with secrets. My father was a county tennis player. I never knew that until I saw his name on a championship board. Because Dad has erased certain parts of his life; won't talk about them. Specifically, the time he spent in Lymington, fifteen miles down the coast – it was where he met my mother, a protected person. Her protection officer, Noah's father, was friends with my dad.

My dad doesn't know I know that.

Pistol shooting.

Having diagnosed his eye condition, Dad is a decent shot. Still, I give him pointers. 'I become meditative when I shoot.

Take a couple of deep breaths, empty the lungs, pause, take the shot.'

'You've done this before?' he asks.

'I'm trained to kill.'

Dad laughs. Michael doesn't; tells him, exasperated, 'She is.'

'I did a course. Tactical pistol-shooting. It's a dangerous world out there. Especially in my world . . .'

Dad stops me there. 'Do you own a gun, Florence?'

I stop him there, too. 'That would be illegal. But it's not illegal to do a five-day programme designed for military special ops and SWAT operators.' I nod. 'Paper, steel, man on man, high-speed drills, moving targets, shooting on the move – you name it.'

My dad doesn't drag me by the ear back to the car, banish me to my bedroom and ground me for a year. He states, 'You never fail to surprise me.'

I smile. 'You'd think you'd be used to me by now.'

He turns to Michael. 'Son, have you fired a gun before?'

'No,' he nods.

'Then, what are you waiting for? Shoot the ruddy White Walkers.'

Michael is sensational. He hits all nine tiny targets. Can't miss a thing. None of us can. We're like *The Indestructibles*.

Hands down, this is the best day out I've ever organised.

Supple as a giant cat, Michael has curled himself into the back seat.

'Next time, arrange something *House MD*-related,' he states.

Nothing, however, can burst my bubble. I want only to remind Dad of the wonderful memories I've made for him.

'You and me were like the group's double act. We made the day for everyone else. It's because we're so interesting.'

Once Michael's snoring in the back, I unscrew a bottle of Rioja I'd stowed under my seat and take a gulp.

'Rehydration?' I offer Dad a slug.

When he actually takes it, I'm staggered. That is *crazy* behaviour for him. Yes, my father is a functioning alcoholic; his golden rule, drinking must accompany a meal or nibbles. But never when navigating machinery. It's what separates him from the morbidly addicted.

He whispers, 'Not a word to your brother. He's so definite about the law.'

The drinking whilst driving, conspiring against Michael, the whispering – it makes me feel shy, like he just did a moony.

'You're naturally ever so sporty,' I tell Dad on the A31.

'Was when I was younger,' he nods. 'Football, rugby, you name it.'

'Tennis?'

He doesn't nod. 'You name it.'

'Why don't you play any more? Tennis, I mean.'

Rather than answer, he opts to wash the windscreen. Silently, we watch the spray. The wipers perform four swift sashays. The air is infused with a citrusy antifreeze.

'Because you did play, didn't you, Dad?'

He points at the bottle. Unscrewing its lid, I check either side, then pass him it. 'A long time ago.' He takes a generous swig.

I jog his memory. 'The years 1977, 1978, 1979 were probably the pinnacle of your career. Hampshire doubles champions. You and your schoolfriend. You were quite the team. Then there was Elaine.' He's about to take another gulp, but I gently lure the bottle free. 'She won the mixed doubles in 1977.'

'I believe so,' he says.

'She was married to Eric, right? The Steensens. It's just

you said you didn't know Mum's suicide buddy, but you did know him, really well.'

'You've always had a wacky imagination,' he tells me, weakly.

'Not really. I saw your name on the championship board at Lymington Lawn Tennis Club. You worked at the post office there, too. Dorset born and bred, you said. Lymington's not Dorset.'

Here's the thing: he's not denying it. Dad has never not denied anything. Neither does he shout *no*, or demand I stop talking about the past. He forgets entirely to repeat his go-to warning in a cautionary and unnerving timbre.

You're dabbling in events that are extremely dangerous. You must not get involved. Do not look for your mum. I will not help you or talk to you about this again.

He also looks ready to weep – that's a killer; usually, it stops a conversation dead.

But I'm on a roll. 'Lymington's very pretty. There are saltwater baths, the Yacht Haven, the smuggling caves – all just around the corner. Are you listening to me, Dad? Michael and I *loved* smuggling. We never went?'

He adjusts the wing mirror so he can see Michael snoozing in the back. 'Sometimes, things are too close to home.'

A chink in his defences. I take the opportunity to tell him off. 'I suffered from travel sickness. Going via Lymington to the Isle of White would have been quicker. You *always* went the longest route.'

Finally, he stares at me. For too long. Twice, I remind him to look out of the windscreen. He then decides to indicate left. We come to a gentle halt on the hard shoulder. Pulling up the hand break, he puts his forehead on the steering wheel and does an unfamiliar emotion.

He cries and laughs at the same time. '*The things we do for love . . .*'

'Season one, episode one.' I can't look at him any more. Not now I've pushed him over an edge with my inability to put old ghosts to rest.

'Who was the dead guy?' I ask the glove box quietly. 'He was your brother, wasn't he? Fergus.'

My dad stops laughing. Just cries and stares at a woman using a pedestrian bridge. She has stopped to watch, too. I'm a breath away from telling him I found his wife in Italy. But blue flashing lights illuminate the plastic of the Dacia's interior.

A brief burst of police siren.

Michael wakes up, quick as a robot. I sit on the wine bottle. Dad wipes his nose with a sleeve.

'We've received some dreadful news,' I tell the policeman's chest.

'Oh no!' Michael shouts at me. 'Don't say it. Just don't say it.'

I put a hand on Michael's knee. Reassure him: 'I will not say it.'

Loophole-in-the-legal-system fact: genuinely distraught old men never get breathalysed. The rest of the car ride is spent defending our motoring decisions to Michael.

'You're properly banned from stopping on the hard shoulder,' he states. 'It's really dangerous. You could have killed me.'

But Dad's too dazed to lie convincingly. 'My badger died,' he mutters.

'What badger?'

Oh, I have an inkling what he's talking about. If I'm correct, my father is mentally banjaxed.

I wave an angry hand at Michael. 'He looks after a couple of badgers.'

'They are *wild* animals.'

'Phone the badger police.' I pull free my beeping phone.

The text I've received makes me whimper. It's one I do not want – not yet. It's too soon – *way* too soon.

Panic arrives with jazz hands.

I hold it together until we arrive at the cottage. Then I go for a run. Fast-twitch muscles deplete adrenalin and stop you from dying of unspecific fear. Only when my lungs scream do I lean my face against a tree and breathe in bark. A blurry beetle trots past my nose, and I crave a moment in his world. Because, in mine, there's a text message that says:

You owe me a lot of squid x

Vee's wrong.

Until I contact her, I owe her nothing. She has no evidence I've read her message. The crux of the matter: she was too quick. Less than three days – the woman's uncommonly efficient. Her timing, however, is so pertinent as to be insensitive. Today, for the first time ever, my father used the power of grief to confirm he'd been involved in murder.

Uncle Fergus.

I'm allergic to the thought of him. Not for kissing me when I was seven. For what he might have done to my brother. Noah's sister was acquainted with Fergus's penchants, though Noah prefers to sidestep his own personal experience.

I fall into a sitting position, my bottom cushioned by a crisp padding of leaves. Winter especially reminds me of him. The smell of November is identical to February's. Cold air causes nasal receptors to retreat; they can't cling to odours, which is why life smells simpler in the winter, allowing bad memories to clang with deafening clarity.

I stay here for an hour, then switch off my phone, walk home, decide I'm not ready for Vee's findings – you can tell too much about a parental unit by the way it kills.

Libido

Yesterday was to be the best day I'd ever organised. But I made too many memories, too permanently engrained in the psyche, too definitely never to be forgotten. How grateful I am for the change in light a new day brings.

Waking Michael at 7 a.m., I tell him to arrange a meeting with James Jardine asap – to sum up the last three days' findings, to most of which I've been a sporadic attendee. Truth is, there's nothing much to report. Too loved up, the grandma and her lover didn't go much beyond the front garden. Now and then, the Ocado van arrived. Speaking bluntly, they're engaged in a love-in.

St Thomas More's Secondary School . . .

We wait for James outside the sixth-form block. Michael talks to himself in the rear-view mirror. The inspiration for his current role: a policeman from *The Bill*. His demeanour: suggestive of heart-breaking news.

When James's face appears too close to my window, I point an urgent thumb at the back seat. Once he's inside, I ask, 'Is there somewhere where we're not on prime-time CCTV?'

James directs us out and on to a dual carriageway. The next junction is a small and unexpected turn-off signposted 'Works Access'. The road, flanked by woodland, twists unpredictably for a kilometre or so, then the tarmac peters out. We park up at a padlocked gate.

I squint beyond it. 'Where are we?'

'It belongs to the garden centre,' says James. 'Nurseries, stock, seasonal fixtures, toilet paper. I'm missing assembly.'

Michael turns to face James. His aim: eye contact. This is very difficult for him; it's why he practises his words before he does talking for real. Their noses are too close, not that James notices – he's suddenly beside himself with excitement; personal space is neither here nor there.

'James,' says Michael. 'Me and my assistant have been doing surveillance, day and night. Between us, that's a hundred and forty-four hours and twelve minutes.'

Excellent. I make a note for our appraisal later. Michael has insinuated that I've been on it full-time, too. Clients hope, rightly, that we go above and beyond the call of duty. Yes, I've been mentally errant. But I'm here now, and there's no truer moment than the present.

'In fact,' Michael says gravely. 'I concentrated so hard, I've strained a tendon in my eye.'

That's bad. Never give the client a whiff of medical information about yourself.

'What can you share with me?' asks James maturely.

Michael opens his notebook and clears his throat.

'Posing as mapmakers, we were able to move freely along Kestrel Lane. Our first discovery: Alan Knight is a nosy parker. At 11:43 hours, he approached my assistant.' He points at me, like I'm a magician's sidekick. 'I went into the shadows and did other stuff. In real life, Alan Knight looks like the Dolmio man. Ear-lobe recognition proved this was our target.'

'*Target?*' James looks concerned.

'We will not shoot him,' says Michael.

I laugh, because he kills me. 'He's joking,' I clarify.

'I'm not. I won't.'

I take control. 'James, I was the one who actually spoke to your grandmother's fiancé. He likes to give the impression he lives there. Offered to make me a cup of tea.'

'He doesn't live there,' James interrupts. 'He's just the gardener.'

Michael takes back control. 'He's your future step-grandad, and he does live there, actually.'

'Err. No.'

'Err. Yes.' Michael has the evidence. 'The porch contains six sets of shoes. Three belong to your grandmother – wellies, a pair of crocs and her pop-to-the-shop shoes. Three belong to her lover – wellies, crocs and a pair of brogues. *Brogues*,' he repeats.

James shakes his head, none the wiser.

Michael points. 'A smart shoe with ornamental perforated patterns in the leather. It's a shoe for every occasion.'

'He's good,' I warn James.

Michael agrees. 'Surveillance continued all night. I hid in a bush. Alder Buckthorn – it scratched my face.' He shows us a cheek. 'They drew the upstairs curtains at 21.20. The lights stayed on until 23.05. I saw no movement until the postman knocked. Your gran answered. This is what she looks like: tall and the shape of a barrel. Dull brown hair tied tight into a bun. She's *definitely* in love – the bun is an old-fashioned pretend one. She didn't have it on in the photograph you showed us. She's dug it out of a drawer.'

'Excellent,' I tell Michael.

'She also has a disgusting rash on her legs. It could be lupus.'

'We're not doctors,' I interrupt. 'James, they're cohabiting.'

Neither male looks at me. James has forgotten that the guy might be stealing and selling his grandmother's valuables. He's got an uncomfortable picture in his head. 'But, she's, like, a hundred,' says James.

I shake my head at him. 'He spent the night. We didn't see them have sex.'

Me just saying it out loud makes him shudder.

'Maybe they cuddled,' says Michael kindly.

'But that's not our focus,' I state, because the elderly have

89

sex drives just like the rest of us, but society deems them too repulsive to satiate it.

Sex fact: it's more subliminal than that.

I say, out loud, 'There's a village in Italy where one in ten residents reaches a hundred years old. The secret to their longevity? Rampant sexual activity. Acciaroli, it's called. Look it up.'

That was *bad*. Don't say your thoughts out loud unless they're relevant to the case.

'My conclusion?' I move on quickly. 'Your gran and Alan are virtually shacked up. She's aware of your concern about her choice of boyfriend, right?'

'God, yes,' says James.

'Then, if I were her, I wouldn't tell you either. You aren't made of money, so we need to remember our focus, i.e. is he marriage material?'

Michael asks, 'How many more days can you afford?'

This is a good question.

'Another week,' says James.

Michael holds out a hand. The schoolboy shakes it. 'Now I'm going to return you to assembly. I have to get back on your case, because I've got a very lot of leads.'

Michael and I agree to restart the *Lovejoy* case the following day. In the meantime, on the pretence of meeting Vee, I get him to drop me at the Travel Inn.

Room 117. My knock is impatient.

'In the shower,' Noah shouts from inside.

I tell the hinge, 'I've got your forty-five pence.'

Silence. The pad of wet feet. The door unlocks. I wait five seconds then hurry in, past the bathroom, towards the window, which I open, the weighted nets and blackout curtains around me providing a fume barrier. I light a cigarette.

When I hear Noah emerge from the bathroom, I push my head back in through the curtains. He's dressed in matching leisure wear – grey T-shirt and the type of shorts that make a pleasant banana of his willy.

I concentrate on his face, on its long hair, wet and loose; he has a hint of Thor about him. 'They charge a hundred smackers to Febreeze the soft furnishings,' I say.

'Squeeze over.' He joins me, shoulder-wedging me rudely into the space. 'I don't remember you being a morning person.'

I feel spatially violated. On the plus side, he smells of Listerine and Lynx. 'I have breaking news,' I tell the car park below.

Noah snatches my cigarette, flicks it away and disappears back into the room; I am to follow him. There's a plethora of moulded surfaces on which to perch, yet we stand, gladiatorial, on opposite sides of the bed.

'I spoke to my dad yesterday. Sort of, in a roundabout way.'

He inhales deeply, pushes his hair out of his face. 'OK.'

'I told him our theory. *My* theory – he doesn't know you're involved.'

'What bits of the theory?'

'How they lived in Lymington. The tennis club. It's where our parents became friends. Your dad being a witness protection officer.'

'This is massive,' mouths Noah.

'Yes.' I agree.

It takes a while for Noah to ask, 'And?'

My headshake is childish. 'He didn't deny it.'

Noah elbows the wall behind him – in triumph or frustration, I don't know. 'Did he say anything?'

'No. He just cried.'

Empathy makes his eyebrows collapse inwards. He hates thinking of my dad sad.

But here's the weird thing. I have barely any memories of Noah, apart from the time we kissed, and another time, maybe. Whereas Noah considers me much more significant. Maybe because he moved away, so mourned different bits of the old life to me.

Listen to him now. 'Han and me loved your mum and dad. Especially your dad.'

I certainly don't remember his sister, Hannah. She lives abroad, their parents having passed away. Noah, however, is unable to trudge free of their secrets. What I do remember is my mother. In fact, she's all I remember; other moments were deemed so irrelevant I forgot to commit them to memory.

Something comes to me. 'Did Dad used to let you drive his car?'

Noah's smile is nostalgic; his small neat teeth; at odds with his machismo. 'I'd sit on his lap. George was in charge of the pedals and stick. I'd do the steering wheel. I came up to your room once. It was flowery.'

'Californian buckwheat.'

'I tried to hold your hand. You elbowed me in the neck.'

'I thought that was Darren Corpe.'

He stares at me blindly. 'Fuck, Flo. We were right.'

'Yes,' I say.

A realisation makes him alert as a meerkat. 'Fergus. Were we right about him?'

I shrug, because my dad's not a murderer; he can't be. 'He just cried.'

Noah sits down on the edge of the baggage shelf and rubs his face roughly. 'He didn't deny it?'

'You want the icing?'

He motions for a cigarette and the lighter. Ignoring EU smoking legislation, he draws puff after puff. The ash is long and pointed before he nods, 'Go on.'

'I have a friend. She's a coroner. She's got hold of a post-mortem report. Not any old post-mortem report.'

Noah turns to face me. 'No?'

'The very paedo.' I say this quietly. The mention of Fergus's name tends to make Noah monosyllabic and furious. 'I guess it will give us clues, you know, to which of our parents likely planned it.'

'All of them.'

'Not the actual murder bit.'

Noah stands up, puts his hands on his hips. 'Don't start wriggling your blood relatives out of this.'

'I have an open and receptive mind,' I assure him.

'So what happens next?'

My suggestion is too lacklustre. 'We go and see my friend?'

Noah enlists his frontalis and frontal belly at the expense of his mandible – his facial muscles form the stock micro-expression for 'surprise'. I have involved him in a major development. Urgently, he pulls on jeans, a sweatshirt, grabs a jacket, leaves the room before me.

'Have you arranged anything?' he says, closing the door behind us. 'No, of course not. Call her now. I'm free all day.'

I lengthen my stride to keep up. 'You're quite chatty when you're excited. I should get you excited more often.'

'Have you phoned her yet?'

I nod very sarcastically. 'Yes, she's here downstairs, waiting in the Ladies, coroner's report in hand.'

'Good. You go and see her. I'm going to attack the break-fast buffet. When you're done, we can hatch a plan.'

'There's nothing to plan. We turn up, she talks us through the report, we leave.'

Noah stops. Tells me, sadly, 'You really don't get it. Life cannot be the same once we see this report.' He knocks on my head. 'In here.'

I put my hands in my pockets. 'I'm ready.'

Noah swiftly continues his march along the corridor towards the stairs and the breakfast buffet. 'We're going to hear home truths. So, first things first – *a hungersome wame haes nae lugs.*'

'I'm not Scottish!' I call after him. 'You're not even Scottish.'

When I reach the stairwell, his voice echoes from a flight below. 'A hungry belly has no ears.'

Modus Operandi

Midday. Barton-on-Sea.

It has a microclimate of its own.

Noah pulls into the car park of a cliff-edge café. Engine off, the wind jiggles his Fiesta. The view ahead: a leaden sea, kicking up a paddy, spitting and frothing. Beyond it, nothing but steely cloud – the Isle of Wight, Bournemouth, the rest of the world are concealed somewhere within.

Once outside the car, the wind hits us like a paddle. Our necks whip back. I pull my hat down, forge forwards. It feels like the end of the world.

Our destination is the Beachcombers Café. Its stark fluorescence is achingly welcoming. Inside, the weather is replaced by a vacuum-packed racket; the culprits, a heave of old people and their accoutrements – walking sticks, aged mongrels, bags for life.

When I spot Vee in a corner, I weave a route towards her.

This is an inspired location – its customers have hearing and memory loss, so are not reliable witnesses, legally. The elderly also have a gung-ho attitude to coastal erosion. Barton-on-Sea is falling into the sea. Five thousand kilometres of fetch, a suzerain of a prevailing wind, spongy cliffs that totter on a clay slip plain. This November day certainly brings with it an air of Armageddon. Perhaps they enjoy the drama – they won't be staying long.

Vee half stands as I approach, bends towards me, kisses me on the lips. That's a pleasant surprise. I'm especially glad Noah is seeing it. We're not just contacts, but friends. Friends so at ease with one another, we overstep sociocultural lines.

'Love what you've done with the place.' I point at her excellent choice of location.

Vee ignores me to grin at Noah. He does himself no favours, forgets to soften his eyes or talk.

'My partner on this case,' I tell her. 'Noah.'

Noah nods. 'You all right?'

'Named after the saint?' she asks.

'He wasn't a saint, actually,' I say.

'Noah Howard,' he tells her. 'The jazz saxophonist.'

I look at him. 'I did not know that.'

He ignores me. 'Vee? What's that short for?'

'Veena,' she nods. 'After the plucked string instrument.'

I want to compete. But Florence and the Machine weren't around in 1979. Parents without a scientific background would never have named me after Florence Sabin, biologist, immunologist, educationalist. Nor was I named after the social reformer and founder of modern nursing.

'You're Scorpio,' I tell her instead.

Delighted, she asks, 'Have you been investigating me?'

People always ask that. Like PIs have nothing better to do then reconnoitre every soul they meet. In this case, however, I have. Just a rudimentary credit, address and occupation check. Contacts must never be taken at face value. 'I'm magic.' I wink, then turn, quickly, to Noah. 'Do not take your hat off.'

He lowers his hands, slowly. 'I'm perspiring.'

'That may be the case. Your hair, however, is the colour of Lucius Malfoy's.'

Vee grins. 'I want to see it now.'

I shake my head at her. 'You shouldn't have taken yours off either. Covering the hair fucks with recall. Especially amongst the aged. Our main aim is to make it impossible for anyone to do a conclusive ID of us together. Especially you, Vee. Your anonymity is crucial.'

'I hadn't realised,' she tells Noah, with big, piss-taking eyes.

The fucker smiles back at her. Unlucky for him: she's *my* friend. So when she pushes the coroner's report across the table, I make her feel indispensable. 'You are a total legend.'

Though I don't examine it. I'm too busy tapping the table.

'Do you want me to look?' Noah says softly.

'No, I do not.' As far as Vee's concerned, this is a bone fide case. He's making me look personally involved.

Who am I kidding? Vee's position permits her access to a whole other level of intelligence. If she's half the woman I suspect she is, she'll have apprised herself fully of the Bambi Love case. See how she, too, lowers her octave. 'Shall I talk you through it, love?'

'It's all good,' I reassure her, turning over the page.

But I'm transparent as a jellyfish. All I can focus on is the first line.

Name of deceased: Eric Steensen.

It's a whopper of a lie. I have to remind myself to respire. Whereas Noah breathes too heavily beside me; is too transfixed on his father's name, picking up the paperwork. I don't snatch it back.

Vee reassures us. 'It's creepy at first. Especially the horrible deaths . . .'

'Was this one horrible?' asks Noah.

Her smile is thin. 'I wouldn't fancy it.'

When a fry-up arrives, Vee takes a triangle of toast, then offers us the plate. I shake my head. Noah picks up a sausage with his fingers, not to eat, just to hold aloft. He fails to notice it again until he's finished reading the report, when he puts the sausage back.

'Eric wasn't six feet two,' he tells Vee.

Vee points her fork. 'The height discrepancy is the first thing I noticed. 1987, the year before Eric's supposed death, he registers with a private doctor in Poole. His personal details there state he's ten and a half stone — there's no data on his height.'

'Did someone delete it?' I ask.

'Of course they did,' snips Noah, pointing at the report. 'The dead dude was massive. Fifteen stone. Eric was lithe, a runner in his day.' He explains his own genetics. 'His wife had the tall gene.'

Now, I take the report, a disappointingly dreary-looking document — no tape recordings or photographs; no brains, gaping torsos, close-ups of waxen lips and unstaring eyes; just lots of things measured in parts per million.

'Stomach contents,' I read out loud. 'Lasagne, chips, iceberg lettuce, crème brûlée.'

'Eric was allergic to eggs.' Noah stares out at the churning sea. 'Most puddings made him puke.'

Vee focuses us. 'And so we come to the modus operandi,' she says. 'Suicide by detergent.'

Are you having a laugh? The wretched irony. Suicide by detergent sounds right up Bambi's street. Just like her son, cleaning products were a passion. Dad said it was her Latin temperament. The medical journals erred towards obsessive compulsive disorder.

'Go on,' I tell Vee.

She puts her toast down, places her elbows on the table and clasps her hands as if in prayer. 'One litre of drain cleaner mixed with five hundred centilitres of anti-dandruff shampoo. The result, a lethal hydrogen-sulphide soup. An airtight space is best; ideally, a stand-alone venue. A car is ideal. To be on the safe side, affix friendly warnings to its windows.'

Warning: toxic gas.

I remember those handwritten notes as though I'd seen them myself . . .

'A Tupperware jelly mould in the back footwell was found

to contain the deadly gloop. It still had a dessert spoon digging from it.' She unknits her fingers. Points. 'You may ask, why didn't they just attach a hosepipe to the exhaust?'

No, I hadn't got that far.

'Carbon-monoxide poisoning would have been nicer,' she adds.

'Unless they wanted it to hurt,' murmurs Noah.

'That's too premeditated,' I argue.

'First-degree murder tends to be,' Vee states. 'This is how it went – the last six minutes of his life. Initially, he'd have smelt an unpleasant odour. Followed by a strong, offensive odour. Followed by a sickeningly sweet odour. Very unpleasant – especially the conjunctiva pain – but not fatal in itself. Then things take a turn for the worse: acute respiratory tract irritation, olfactory paralysis . . .'

I despised the man, yes, but I don't revel in the details of the last throes of anyone's life. Expiration is too irrevocable. I prefer death's minutiae to remain an enigma.

Vee's not employed to do enigmas. 'Fluid accumulated in the air spaces and parenchyma of his lungs, causing laboured breath and a bloody froth. Finally, his central neural system failed, though unconsciousness wouldn't have arrived for a minute or two. It's more likely he experienced complete neural paralysis and a terminal heart attack in the meantime. Whoever bumped him off was bloody furious.'

'My,' I say weakly. 'How was this missed?'

'They chose the identity of the dead man well. Eric Steensen had a history of depression and previous suicide attempts. Four of them.'

I glance at Noah. He doesn't look at either of us. He looks outside, past the weather, back in time.

That puts a different angle on his parents being keen to move on.

'But it wasn't suicide,' says Vee. 'There were sleeping tablets in his system. Three times the highest recommended dose. Why not go the whole hog, quaff the packet, take a rain check on the carful of poison?'

'Who was the coroner on this case?' I demand.

Suddenly, she's protective of her profession. 'Suicide victims often soften the blow of death. Drink, drugs.'

'But that didn't happen.'

'No,' she admits. 'The dead man was lured to his death. Suicide victims rarely polish off lasagne, one of their five-a-day and a pudding before inhaling hydrogen sulphide. Most people's appetite would be on the light side prior to that.'

Noah grabs his sausage back from Vee's plate. 'How the fuck did they positively identify this guy as Eric?'

'The wife, Elaine Steenson, identified him. There was his wallet, too. More significantly' – she leans, conspiratorially, towards us – 'the report is in a folder marked NCP.'

'Meaning?'

'Eric Steensen was a protected person.'

I don't tell her she's wrong. That it was the female in the car who was in witness protection. That the body belonged to my uncle. That Eric Steensen was a depressed witness protection officer who wanted out of something. That the two people sitting opposite her are made from the same DNA as people who committed pre-meditated murder.

I slide her an envelope of money, kiss her brusquely on the lips, then tell her I'll be in touch.

Noah and I have to battle the wind to get to the car. Its doors yanked shut, we look at one another, silently.

'You OK?' I ask. 'That stuff about your dad being depressed?'

'Makes sense,' he says, without elucidation.

I wonder if he knew that his father had tried to take his life. I hope so; otherwise that's quite the kicker.

My gut instinct . . .

Bambi fed Fergus his last meal. That's all. Eric and Elaine bullied her into making hydrochloric sulphide. Eric, especially, wanted it to hurt. Dad was out – at church, probably – and had no idea what was going on.

Noah puts his key in the ignition. 'The sleeping pills in his system – that's interesting.'

'I bet Bambi secretly laced Fergus's food with them – so it didn't hurt too much. She certainly wrote the signs to stick on the windows of the car so no passers-by were harmed.'

'Is that back in the day when she gave a shit?' Noah looks at me as though I'm deluded. 'Come on, Flo, they drugged Fergus because he was hench. He'd have killed my dad if they got in a fight.'

'They still had to get him to the car?'

'He and George did exactly that.'

I shake my head, because that won't be how this happened. We're silent for the rest of the journey. When Noah drops me in the village, we're too preoccupied to say goodbye.

Beelzebub

Michael and I dump our luggage in the hall. My head swirls. About Mum. About Dad, and what Annie has done to him. About my brother – limping, broken-toothed, the startling facial haematoma. I'm in so much shit. All made inexorably worse by a freezing cloak of truth: I will never see Tommaso again.

'Dad?' Michael calls; searches the cottage for him. 'He has to be here. His car's outside.'

My torso fizzles with electricity, fear so manifest it threatens to hood me. That somewhere in this house, my father lies dead. Poisoned, suffocated, stabbed. Mostly likely, hanged. The reason, ultimately, my inability to let the past rest where it fell. I need to get out of here. I can't find his body. I won't. There are too many other explanations, before I settle for that one.

Michael suggests searching the garden. 'Maybe he's in the greenhouse.'

Yes, where he's had a heart attack. Midnight gardening. Death preventable, but for hypothermia, what with his children having buggered off to Italy.

'You've been to Annie's place before,' I say. 'You'll have to drive me there now.'

'No,' he states. 'She scares me.'

I grab both his shoulders. 'The last time Annie and I fought, I destroyed her. She lives in Winkton, right?'

'You had a fight?'

'Yes. I punched her in the solar plexus.' I pull his arm towards the front door.

'I don't like her at all, Flo.'

'I know, but if you don't drive me, I'll have to drive myself.'

Michael does not say, *That is so illegal.* So, at a loss, I take Dad's keys from the bowl and stomp to the car port. The Dacia's interior smells sweet and musky – it turns my stomach. I'd open the windows if I could remember where the ignition is and how to do signalling, but mostly manoeuvring – the crux of my failure to obtain a licence. Clutch control especially; biting points are an enigma to me, never mind reversing out of a car port.

The car kangaroo jumps and stalls. My scream is pitiful, because nothing is in my control.

That's because you couldn't leave anything alone, my Dad would be saying. He'd also be saying, *You're unlicensed, uninsured and over the limit. Get out of my car or I'm calling the police* – were he not dangling by the neck in the garage.

This isn't melodrama. It's my baggage. Suicide leaves behind children saddled with a certainty – that self-slaughter will pick off all your loved ones in the end.

I return inside. Michael's still looking lost in the hall.

'Where's reverse?' I ask. 'And I'll be needing the address. Michael, I'll walk if I have to, but we have to face facts – what if she's killed our father?'

'*Who?*'

'Kathy Bates.'

Michael shrieks, 'The film actress?'

Every time.

Annie's house is exactly as expected – chocolate-box sickly, the type infants draw. Four windows, apex roof, central door, path leading to the picket fence. Apricot walls strewn with evergreen creepers. In the square front garden, hydrangea bushes hibernate in straight lines, like a dead vineyard.

Her front door is frosted glass and has a lot of things taped to it. A local newspaper article about RAF Winkton cut out with shrimping scissors. A handwritten note: *No junk mail, menus, charity bags*. No charity bags – who actually writes that? A certificate stating that Annie is Winkton in Bloom's gold-prize winner. She's also a member of Neighbourhood Watch.

The woman thinks she's the hub of the community, insinuating that people pop by all the time, even when she's not in, just to admire her existence.

Annie fact: she hasn't got any friends. She hasn't even got a doorbell.

My knock is so hard the glass drops into its sash. She and I dispensed with etiquette some time ago. When there's no answer, I bang on the front window, peer inside. The lounge is an ode to floriculture and chintz – flowery sofas, foot rests, wallpaper and lampshades. It's difficult to see past the visual mayhem, to focus on the patio doors and their view into the garden.

At last I spot her. In the far corner of the garden, barely visible in a russet-and-green camouflage cagoule. My heart falters when I see that Annie is digging a hole.

To the right-hand side of the house is a gate. Using a furious shoulder and hip, I force it open, ripping my jacket on the shards of wood. Wild-eyed, I arrive in the garden. Rather than bury a body, however, she shovels dead leaves and is entirely unaware of my cacophonic entrance.

I sit on a patio bench, lean my elbow on a concrete Cupid and imagine pointing a Beretta M9A3 (with silencer) at her fat head. Its lank brown hair slapping her ears as she works. How easy it would be to pop her off, if only I'd planned ahead.

Lighting a cigarette, I take a look through a back window.

A small office, its walls cluttered with books; hardbacks, mostly. And files with handwritten labels: *User Guides – White Goods*; *Our Lady of the Saints – Minutes*; *Winkton Neighbourhood Watch*. A large desk, empty apart from a spotlight and a furry pencil – orange and black; it looks like a hornet. On the wall above, an over-sized alchemy cabinet; its endless nooks are filled with unlabelled spice jars, the contents of which suggest sorcery and deviltry. Dust, hair, soil. Annie is an actual witch, I conclude.

'Florence? Florence, is that you?' I hear her call; turn to see her march across the lawn as though I'm the loveliest surprise.

I shout back at her, 'How old are you? Forty-five, fifty?'

She shakes her head, pulls headphones from her ears. 'Sorry?'

'I was just saying, you're too young to be wearing an A-line skirt of sensible length.'

She comes to a standstill before me. Puts her hands on her wide hips and fakes compassion: 'How *are* things, lovey?'

'You tell me.'

'Well,' she sighs sadly, 'Mum is in mourning, as you can imagine.'

I show her my canines. 'Where is he?'

'Your dad?' She shrugs. 'If I had to guess, the post-office stock room, but you didn't hear it from me.'

I hold my stomach – the post office was his life's work. Its purpose – to ensure I always had something to fall back on. I couldn't have been clearer in my disdain for it. That would be some message, finding him dead there.

How to remove somebody from the ground using your hand and their neck:

Hook the throat while controlling their dominant arm. Squeeze in and up simultaneously – a forty-five-degree angle is ideal – and thrust. The victim will raise themselves on to the toes, shifting their weight backwards; now perform a close-step with your back foot.

Annie's a solid woman. I'm unsuccessful at getting her off the ground, but she gets the drift. 'What is my father doing in the post-office stock room?' I demand.

'Harm, harm,' she rasps.

'Harm, harming – what have you done?'

'Harmony. Website.'

I drop her, sort of. She gets her breath back, rearranges herself, straightens her cagoule.

Her tone remains unapologetic. 'George is on them a lot. Dating websites. Nothing perverse. Elderly man looking for companion. It won't land him in serious trouble with the other parishioners. He always ticked the Normal box, sexual-preference wise.'

I poke her hard in the left atrium. 'You set up a fake profile for my Dad on Harmony?'

Annie holds her heart, like she's about to arrest. 'And Match,' she complains. 'But it was Tinder that did it for my mother.'

To help her heart attack along, I aim my second poke at her left ventricle. 'Have you deleted his profiles yet?'

'No, because I didn't set them up.'

'Dad's a techno-twat and you know it.'

'Perhaps the special-needs kid helped him?'

My jab is a corker – her lip instantly bursts. It brings a tear to Annie's eye. Still she refuses to lay down or retaliate. Instead, she does a few gasps, dabs her lip with an ironed handkerchief and tells me, strictly, 'Now we're quits.'

My laugh's hollow. 'We will never be quits.'

Annie points up at the guttering and says, 'I beg to differ.'

A little red light blinks excitedly, because her security camera just saw action.

*

A dead weight, I walk towards Michael's car. The humiliation makes my cheeks burn. When I get into the passenger seat, Michael is especially disappointed in me.

'You had another fight.' He pokes my grazed knuckle as though it's a dead mouse. 'Did you win?'

'I did.' I rub the broken skin. 'If somebody had filmed it, it would be the coolest fight scene ever. So cool, you'd think she'd stage-managed it.'

'Is she dead?' he asks.

I shake my head, because *why* didn't I look to see if she had CCTV? I'll tell you why – I'm not a thief. Neither was it premeditated. Neither would I be a very good murderer, because good murderers always check for cameras. Now, there is unequivocal proof that I, Florence Love, did break and enter; point an imaginary Beretta at her head; attempt to strangle her, then – finding her too unwieldy to asphyxiate – did punch her in the mouth.

Murderers also refuse to leave DNA in the victim's mouth, or fibres on their A-line skirt, or more saliva on the discarded butt of an Italian cigarette.

'Christ!' I shout at Michael, because I am a dick.

'What?!' he shouts back.

'I left my phone.'

I did not. Nonetheless, I walk back to the front door. There's no CCTV outside Annie's cottage, I note – just a security light, standard make, standard range. Cameras are mounted on the side gate and back garden only. At the front door, I look under the mat and around the stoop and front garden for a spare key.

Nothing.

So I look in through the letterbox. Spot a key box is screwed to a wall.

Shout, 'OK, Annie, you have a deal. It's over. I'll keep my family away from yours, especially my dad. In fact, consider it my sole aim in life. We are officially out of each other's hair.'

That's how Annie had phrased it the first time we met. *We despise each other. We can pool that hatred. Fingers crossed, we'll be out of one another's hair in no time.* I'd agreed. I verge on complicit.

I add, 'And you're sacked.'

Returning to the car, I give Michael instructions. 'Let's get back home and phone around his friends.'

I don't tell him to go via the post office. I rub my knuckles and watch Annie flicking me the bird from an upstairs window.

Lair

Michael's car is outside, and *House MD* is paused on a still of someone having a lumbar puncture. Yet I can't locate my brother. My overwhelming need: to do anything other than think about Death by Detergent. I look for distractions, am staring from the lounge window, playing the alphabet game with myself (man-made waterbodies), when I spot the door to the tree cabin is ajar.

The Yellow House, we called it. Snuggled in the trees at the far end of the garden, it felt cosy and safe when we were kids – it came with an excellent view of the cottage and a pair of red binoculars.

I walk up its ten steps very gingerly, yet thirty years have failed to weaken its construction. My father is health-and-safety conscious – the Boy Scout type who audits his electrical appliances, then issues home-made Portable Appliance Testing certificates.

The last time I came up here, it homed a galaxy of cobwebs and insect corpses. A swift elbow to the treehouse's door and it swings open halfway. Poking my head around it, I see my brother sitting on an upturned fire bucket. He scrutinises the walls and gable. They're covered with pieces of paper, in the middle of which is a smiling A4 photograph of Alan Knight.

'It's very symmetrical,' I say. 'Half police incident room, half psychopath's lair.'

'I know.'

'You're a chip off the old block.'

His head turn is histrionic. 'Not off your block. You are a slut.'

'That's harsh, and entirely the wrong word. Room for another?'

'You'll have to make yourself small.' He shuffles to the left.

Cross-legged beside him, I survey the evidence – a neat mosaic of newspaper reports, webpages, handwritten lists, a map of the south coast. And the odd meme. Were Michael capable of Machiavellianism, those memes would be issuing me the middle finger.

Team = Together Everybody Achieves More.

Divide the work and multiply the success.

Teamwork makes the dream work.

I glance at my brother's profile and wish I hadn't. He looks shattered.

I used to have a saying: *The day I don't deliver professionalism, empathy and guile is the day I retire.* Over the years, I've had a lot of sayings. Most of which I've stopped actually saying nearly enough.

I sniff the air. 'You've had a deep-clean?'

'One hundred and twelve antibacterial wipes. Flo, I've stumbled across deceit.'

'OK, boss. What you got?'

Michael acquires a new persona, one who has a transatlantic drawl. 'Alan Knight is a goddamn liar.'

'Is he?'

'Yes.'

'How?'

'He was not in the Welsh Guards and he did not serve in the Falklands.' Michael shrugs. 'Everybody lies.'

'Who is he, really – Alan?'

Michael picks up a sawn-off broom handle. Points it at a newspaper article on the ceiling. 'A roofer who fell off his ladder and married his nurse.'

We crane our necks at a page from the *Brighton and Hove*

Weekly. March 1980. A black-and-white photograph of Alan Knight and his new wife, Angela, at the registry office. Beneath it: *Local roofer Alan Knight marries Angela Herbert, the NHS nurse who saved his life.*

Michael clarifies things: 'Alan looks small, because he's in a wheelchair. He broke his back. Even his wife's name was a goddamn lie. Margaret isn't called Margaret. Margaret is called Angela.'

'The wife – is she definitely dead?'

'Yes. I found her Facebook page. Lots of people wrote "RIP".' He has a moment's silence. 'That means rest in peace.'

'Christ, it's still accessible?' The data-protection travesties that occur in the name of social media. Yes, it's great for the likes of me, but the dead have no say.

'Hold on,' I squint. 'The older generation didn't do social media, not back then. How old was Angela when Facebook launched?'

'No age,' he sighs. 'She was deceased.'

I frown. 'Who set her page up then?'

I'm confusing the issue, so Michael bangs the broom on the wall. 'The photograph of Alan and Angela was taken two years before the Falklands War. The British Army did not send people with broken backs to the Falklands.'

He points at a piece of paper on which he's handwritten: *The British Army did not send people to the Falklands with broken backs.*

Michael leans too close to me. When I turn to face him, I can't focus successfully on his eyes. 'Everybody lies, Florence. *Everybody* lies.'

Finally, it dawns on me. 'You're being Hugh Laurie out of *House MD*.'

He nods. 'I'm concentrating on achieving his grating monotone and ruthless approach.'

'It is superb,' I smile.

'I know.'

Yet the wicked truth is this:

Michael doesn't have a fucking clue. Not that his mother is alive. That his parents are murderers – the premeditating sort who found comfort in a cruel death. He doesn't know the convoluting extent to which everybody lies; he just knows the catchphrase.

'May I make a suggestion, Michael?'

'No.'

'Get a copy of Angela Knight's death certificate. But first we should break into Alan Knight's house – the one in Chartwell. It's the least we can do.' Putting yourself in personal danger is an excellent diversion from your own shit. 'Now, go to bed, on medical orders. You're to sleep for nine hours, at least – that's six ninety-minute cycles. The secret to being a good boss is a happy circadian rhythm.'

Michael looks relieved. 'I have been dicing with death.'

'And now you can stop. Because I'm here. Got it, boss?'

'Got it.'

The treehouse's window on the inside is cleaner than my face. On the outside, it's a birds'-shit camouflage – I peer through the gaps. Watch him fake-limp back to the house, now and then flicking the decapitated broomstick roguishly. I'm sure I see his mouth move – my bet, he's addressing his imaginary medical team.

Michael takes my word as gospel. Goes straight to bed. Leaving me to wait for my dad to come home.

Nota bene. Curiosity is rarely a well-meaning friend.

Yet I need to see Dad's face. To see what he's capable of.

My father, however, doesn't return. When Michael's alarm sounds at 2 a.m., in order for him to continue his investigations, I lack the professionalism, empathy and guile to join him. Too furiously, I send text messages.

Where the hell are you?

And, *Ignore this text ONLY if you're dead.*

And, *If you're not dead, I'm putting you in a home.*

At 2.37 a.m. my father replies, *All fine. Will tell u all in the morning. Dont worry about me i'm a bog boy x*

A *bog* boy. The appalling punctuation. His bastardisation of the word *you*. Do I fume. No, he wasn't aware that I was waiting for him. Yes, he's almost seventy, so allowed to be drunk somewhere else, with someone else. Trouble is, given the lack of people with whom he spends the entire night, there's only one option as to his whereabouts.

I am right.

At 7.30 a.m., I watch him from my loft-room window. Manoeuvring the Dacia into the car port. Flattening his hair, before performing the walk of shame to the front door. I listen to him making tea in the kitchen below, whistling 'My Funny Valentine', which is intense and too emotionally ambiguous for a dad to whistle.

How *could* he? Anyone but Darcie. The deal was: we were in mourning together. Him, Michael and me. The Muska-Loves, united in interminable grief. Now he's ruined it.

Nine hundred hours.

Michael and I are currently moseying through Chartwell. The sun is on full whack yet fails to dissipate the cruel nip. I tie the hood of my cagoule so it's tight about my cheeks and examine the surroundings. Identical houses – small, detached, thatched, plonked willy-nilly; the road that winds around them appears an afterthought. The house numbers are in all the wrong order.

I note my bowel's reluctance to perform a nervous tickle.

Another saying I don't say any more: *If surveillance no longer tickles the bowel, it's time to throw in the investigative towel.*

'It is the actual twilight zone,' Michael mumbles into his scarf, because he is not digging his moustache. 'There's no rhyme or reason.'

'The house numbers were based on the order of rent collection, back in the day.'

'But we're *here* in the day, Flo.'

I put a reassuring hand on his shoulder and nod.

What I know about Chartwell . . .

A late-Victorian concept village, it was created by a minted philanthropist; his goal, a little utopia for his minions. Inside toilets, agriculturally self-sufficient, a sense of community, while paying homage to the Arts and Crafts style.

Number 20 is nestled between numbers 34, 19 and 35. Less loved than the other cottages, its wooden door peels blue paint. The sash windows need restoring. Alan's front garden is a piss-poor advertisement, given his line of work – it's a tangle of brown thicket, the deadwood of a previous owner's creation.

Breaking and Entering 101 – Tip #1: make sure the house is empty.

I approach Alan's front door, and knock, loudly.

Michael hisses from the pavement. 'He might be in.'

'No, he won't. He'll be at church, as he is every Sunday. Trying to ingratiate himself with his future son-in-law, the vicar.'

Michael makes big eyes. 'What if he has swine flu?'

'Then he won't be in any fit state to recognise us from the last time we met. Now, re-stick the side of your moustache and get over here.' Remembering my place, I do a salute. 'Boss.'

Once beside me in the doorway, I pass Michael some Scandinavian-style specs. My glasses are olden-day NHS ones with a pink frame.

'Who are we?' he asks.

'The type of people you don't want to see, even when you haven't got swine flu.' I pass him a pamphlet.

Michael squints at the title: *Does God really care about us?* Looks up at me angrily. 'You know he does.'

I pat his chest. 'Keep that passion.'

The house is empty.

Breaking and Entering 101. Tip #2: never damage the woodwork. That's bad manners.

Too eagerly, I pull free my Brockhage semi-automatic 2-phase bump gun. You *have* to get yourselves one of these. This particular model leaves no sign of jimmying, picks a lock in a true vertical direction (as opposed to the traditional, curved shape), has a soft rubber trigger for comfort and boasts fifteen needles. In reality, the private investigator uses, maybe, three or four needles throughout the course of their career. Nevertheless, it's rude not to have the full kit, especially when you're an anorak like me – its shiny accoutrements are one of the few things I like to polish.

'That is so illegal,' Michael states.

'I'll tell you what should be illegal.' I point the gun at him. 'The price of bump-free locks.'

And there's a truth. It's illegal to own one of these guns unless you're a locksmith or a Special Services agent. Their storage and use are as litigious as owning a shotgun. That's sensible in Never-Never Land. In the real world, it's draconian and leaves the locksmith on quite a bunce. Take my advice – cut out the middle man and get yourself one off the Darknet.

Alan's home security is older than me, so my gun works a treat. *Bang!* It bursts the driver pins out of the lock cylinder, leaving them fleetingly unobstructed. A second *bang!* We're in.

Breaking and Entering 101 – Tip #3: when skating on thin ice, speed is your friend.

Lethargically, I wander into the living room – a disappointingly dingy space with low ceilings and small windows. The predominant colour theme is burgundy, which usually gives a room an air of 'womb'. But there are too many cardboard boxes, littering the floor space and furniture – I spot a sofa, two old-fashioned armchairs, an occasional table and a stand-alone computer. A sliver of sunlight slices through the murky space, displacing dust motes in *Matrix Reloaded* slow motion. The place hasn't seen a cloth in months.

I use a pen to flip open a cardboard box.

Michael pulls his scarf over his mouth and asks, 'Is it a severed limb?'

I look down at the contents. 'Yup. His wife's head.'

'No. Oh, dear God, no.'

'My bad.' I look up at him. 'It's just comics.'

Immediately, Michael takes a look in the box. The contents delight him. Fifty or so pristine publications, each in a plastic cover. He flicks through them.

'I goddamn don't believe it,' he's saying. '*Amazing Superman. Captain America's Weird Tales.* These are worth millions.'

'That's pushing it,' I say, looking through the other boxes. '*X-Men*, *Fantastic Four*, *The Avengers* . . . Alan's certainly got himself a healthy pension pot, though.'

'He's got to be a thief.'

'Or maybe just a collector. It's amazing what you can pick up at a house clearance. Where's the kitchen?'

You can tell a lot about a man by his fridge. His financial position. The fat content of his internal organs. Whether he's organised, sociable, environmentally conscious and/or well-travelled.

Unfortunately, we don't get to see Alan's refrigerator. A cough from the front garden stops us dead in our tracks. The tinkling of keys, metal on metal; there's no time for either of us to run or hide. Before I've time to summon an excuse, a man appears in the doorway to the living room, blocking our exit.

Twenty years old, a cubic-zirconia earring, low-slung jeans

and designer skivvies. 'Oh, fuck!' He takes a step back when he sees us.

Michael puts his hands up. I slip mine in a pocket, finger my bump gun. Yet the lad doesn't lunge at us, or demand answers, or run away, or call the police. He apologises for startling us.

'I didn't know anyone was here. I'm Nico's mate. Just popping in to, you know . . . Excuse me . . .' He winds a route around us. 'Sorry. Thanks. Great. Sorry . . .'

My brother doesn't move or blink – he's the Marvel anti-hero Chameleon. While I push my pink glasses up my nose and look peeved, as though this lad's the one in the wrong, because that's the impression he's giving me.

The boy-man knows what he's looking for. Goes to a box marked *I/H*. As he bends over to open it, I see the twisted head of a pre-rolled joint in his back pocket. Taking out just one comic, he says, 'Bingo.'

It has the Incredible Hulk on the front. Which makes me think of my dad and 'The Lonely Man' theme. My shoulders drop.

'Thanks, sorry . . .' As he passes me, I pickpocket his spliff. It serves him right. He just stole a classic comic from his mate, Nico.

The door slams. Number 20 is silent once more.

'Whose bloody house are we in, Michael?' I whisper. My brother shrugs.

A reminder as to *Breaking and Entering 101 – Tip #3*: when skating on thin ice, safety is in your speed.

'You've got thirty seconds. Pop upstairs. See if there are clothes, undies, blood-pressure tablets – old people always take medication; check the name. I'll keep lookout down here.'

'Why can't you do it?'

'You're the boss now,' I explain, while checking out

Rightmove on my phone. The website confirms this cottage is up for sale, billed as vacant possession.

I order the property's Title Register online. Fifteen pounds and moments later, they're in my inbox.

'He's on the pill,' Michael shouts down.

I shout back, 'Alan Knight doesn't own this place. An Eastern European couple do – Nico and Aneta Novak. In the history of mess-ups, this is a contender. May I suggest we get our arses out of here?'

We park up in a lay-by off the B3059.

Michael taps the steering wheel. 'Alan might rent a room there.'

'No one's living there. Why have we stopped?'

'I'm calling an extraordinary meeting,' he says.

'Good. You've chosen the spot for it.' I show him my doobie. 'Can I smoke?'

Michael agrees, because he knows my views on drugs. I don't do them. Not unless there's a really good reason. Professionalism being one of them, and I'm not exhibiting enough of it today.

'First on the agenda – your ineptitude,' I say. '*Why* didn't you carry out the paper checks? The Land Registry, Zoopla – more importantly, the electoral roll. It's so basic –' I disorganise his glove compartment.

He pulls at my elbow, trying to stop me. 'Why would you do that?'

'To find this.' I show him a pink Clipper. Spark up the joint. When the smoke hits my tonsils, my bowel performs an instant jig.

There it is . . .

I don't exhale until Michael slaps my thigh and demands I breathe out now.

Cross-eyed, I admire the blue smoke stream from my lungs.

Twisting and dancing around the rear-view mirror, it hunts for air. Shoots free when Michael opens my window.

'Cripes,' I tell him. 'That's strong.'

Then I cough twenty-two times. Michael uses my momentary incapacity to lean across me and re-tidy the glove box.

Sitting back in his seat, he says, 'You're right. I'll strike myself off.'

'Fortunately for you, your profession is unlicensed. Put it down to experience. But remember, a circuitous route is expensive for the client, which is tantamount to fraud.'

He nods solemnly. 'I'm so putting it down to experience.'

'I think you could benefit from an NVQ.' I take another puff. 'It's a qualification, with lots of rules to learn. You'll love it.'

'OK,' he says, putting a hand over his mouth to ward off antioxidants. 'We haven't found out if Alan's stealing any antiques yet.'

'Maybe he's not.'

'Maybe he is. We *have* to find out.'

'Why?' My next puff is more restrained.

'It's what James asked us to do.'

'The family wanted to know if Alan Knight was nice and trustworthy. You've got *brilliant* evidence that he's not.'

'Flo, stop smiling.'

'I can't. It's a side effect.'

We watch a lorry park up ahead of us. I'm thinking what an effulgent yellow it is. Yellow being a shade you should never take for granted. Flies can't see it, colour being a figment of our imaginations, an evolutionary trick enabling the assessment of external information via refractions of light.

That's beautiful.

I look up and say to Michael, 'I'd forgotten you were there.'

'Maybe he's a career criminal?'

'Maybe, maybe, maybe . . .'

He drops the hand from his mouth. 'Flo, I don't like your attitude.'

I make a concerted effort to stop smiling. But there's a little pocket of joy in my gut. A pocket inside of which a light-footed Morris dancer performs a jig. That's too lovely a feeling.

Taking a final toke, I become very serious indeed. Think of less frivolous styles of dance. Krumping, for example. An ireful street dance evolved to release frustration in an aggressive yet non-violent way. That does the trick.

My squint is ominous. 'Maybe Granny Jardine's the one with something up her sleeve. A double-crosser, like Janet Colgate in *Dirty Rotten Scoundrels*.'

'I *love* that film. It has Michael Caine in it.'

'And Steve Martin.'

'He's my hero.'

'No, he's mine. *The Man with Two Brains*.'

'*Dr Hufffffuuffffffuffer* . . .'

We both have a little competition, whereby we try to out-*Hufffffuffffufer* the other. This goes on for some time; because I'm stoned and Michael's got Asperger's. To refocus myself, I have to squeeze the hot end of the joint with my thumb and index finger.

Michael shrieks when I throw the remainder of the spliff into the glove compartment for later.

'OK. Facts. Your client and his family cannot afford to be chasing maybes.'

'Kathleen Turner,' says Michael. '*The Man with Two Brains*.'

'How *sexy* was she?'

'Not very,' he frowns.

'She said being a sex symbol was an attitude.' I do her husky, American drawl: 'Most men think it's looks, most women know otherwise.'

'I definitely go for looks,' he says.

I can barely contain myself. 'Sebastien was hideous-looking. I mean, I don't want to be unkind, Michael, but he was really, *really* ugly. I mean, *ugly*.'

'Not to me.' He puts a hand on his heart.

That darned Morris dancer revisits my tummy. Softly, I say, 'You're being very good with the break-up and all.'

'Work's helped.' He nods.

'Let's give James a ring. Tell him you've solved his case.'

'What about the antiques?'

'It's knowing when to stop. Now stop behaving like one of *House MD*'s medical team – all over-enthusiastic and wet behind the ears, spouting shit they've read in textbooks. Where's your ruthless monotone?'

'It's here,' he says. And it is.

The Morris dancer makes a twist of my innards.

'Extraordinary meeting ended,' I declare. 'Let's get you back to your incident room. Tonight, we'll meet James. In the meantime, prepare everything you're going to say. Provide documentary evidence a prosecution would be proud of. Always remember, however, your job is not to imply or infer, just to present the facts. And check those facts – double- and triple-check them, because relationships depend on them. This is your big moment, Michael.'

'You're giggling,' he says.

'Yes.' I perform a spontaneous and hearty love sigh. 'It's because you make me proud.' A mother never told him that, enough.

The C-Bomb

Yurtspuddle Garden Centre. 6.02 p.m.

James and Michael sit opposite one another. James hasn't changed out of his orange T-shirt. He was too impatient for our news. Michael wears a suit and looks too plagued. Pulling his paperwork from a designer document holder, my brother checks it's in the right order, then places it into small equidistant piles on the table. Like a newsreader, he waits for his cue.

James says, 'So?'

Michael acquires a frown. 'How are you?'

'I'm good, thank you. How are you?'

'I have the beginnings of a cold. My office doesn't have a radiator.' Why Michael is looking at me is beyond me.

'Buy one – you're the boss.' I get the meeting rolling. 'We wanted to talk to you urgently, James, because we've closed your case.'

That fills him with disappointment – the possibility that we've found nothing and that Alan is an honourable man.

Michael's quick to put his mind at rest. 'I have to warn you, James. Our findings are extremely concerning. Your family will probably want to go to the police.'

I kibosh James's exhilaration. 'This is a problem for you.'

Michael talks over me. 'The police don't like it when victims interfere in their own crimes.'

I put a firm hand on Michael's shoulder. 'It hurts their feelings. Plus, your family will look a bit crazy.'

The reason PIs never get involved with the police: our methods are illegal, as the rozzers well know. But we manipulate the system, and that pisses them off no end.

An example . . .

Should a policeman ask me: *Do you have a contact in the prison service – an officer for whom a hundred quid will cover a quick check on their system, providing a target's entire criminal history, including court dates and prisons attended?* I would say: *How dare you. I am able to provide a comprehensive list of crimes, court dates and prisons attended via means accessible to all. Mostly, officer, I use Google.*

Court dates are publicly available. Fact. You just have to search every court in the land. In addition, there are a bounty of local newspapers, and hundreds more that have petered out over the last fifty years; most have archives and all love to report a crime.

That's what the general public pay us for, I'd tell that policeman. *Our patience and dogged determination while using extremely legal routes.*

'Suffice to say,' I tell James, 'The police don't like us or those who employ us. We need to bear in mind your dad's a vicar. Your mum's a vicar's wife. It will get in the papers. I would like to avoid them looking unhinged.'

'How will we do that?' Michael asks.

I frown at him, briefly, then tell James, 'We will give you our findings and explain how they can be sourced, legally. You will then tell everybody you did it yourself. You know, of an evening, like a proper computer-obsessed schoolkid geeky type . . .' I do a wave in the direction of his imagination. 'You were frightened for your granny. So, in between ethics homework and *Runescape*, you became an amateur sleuth. The local papers will be all over that story. You're a kid. You'll be lauded. Your parents aren't implicated in anything. It's a win-win situation.'

James becomes serious. 'Is it a win-win situation for my gran?'

I nod. 'In the long term, yes. In the short term, not so

much. You take it from here, boss.' I give Michael the floor.

He opts for the personal touch. Makes me move out of the way, so he can manoeuvre himself around the table, to sit beside James.

PI tip: never, ever do this – it encroaches on personal space and a whole host of other grey areas.

Now Michael opens his little black book, clears his throat, reads his opening statement.

'I cannot prove that Alan Knight does not love your gran. I can prove, though, that he's a total liar. In love or not, Alan's history, *criminally*, suggests he is very good at fraud.'

He stops so that James can react.

James is as much of a drama queen as my brother. A hand flies to his mouth. 'Fraud?'

'*Fraud.*'

Fraud? I don't demand.

'Has he been to prison?'

'Yes.'

'Are you sure?'

'I have the evidence.' Michael pats a pile.

I grab it – they're newspaper articles downloaded from the internet. He's cut them out and pasted them on to plain paper. Annotated them. Given them handwritten titles, which he's underlined with a ruler.

'What did he do?'

Michael returns to his notebook. 'He's guilty of being a thief. Over the last forty years, he's done bird eight times. The last time was two years ago. He's part of a famous gang of old men.'

Shut the fuck up? I don't say out loud.

'Like in *Lovejoy*,' he tells James.

'*Lovejoy?*'

'A TV programme from the eighties,' I interject.

'He liked to break the fourth wall,' Michael tells us. 'That's where an actor reveals his thoughts and motives to the camera.'

'A gang of old men,' I remind him.

'Yes. Alan pretends to be an antiques expert – one who knocks on your door and offers to value your ornaments. Only he's not, he's casing the joint. Later, he returns with the other wrinklies and steals your stuff. The Brighton Knockers they're called.'

Examining the articles, I am blown away. It was a big case, well documented. I vaguely remember it. There's even a photograph of Alan.

'Is he still a gang member?' asks James.

'That I don't know. But I do know other stuff. He doesn't live at Number 20, Cottage Terrace. It's owned by people of ethnicity.'

Given this new information, I want to shout out other things. Like, of course the comics are his, or part of a communal bootie. Reward for years of house-lifting. But I don't – it's not our job to infer or imply.

We drop James Jardine at his father's church in Poole.

PI tip: never do this. We're not a taxi service.

But Michael's a worrier, waves James goodbye like he's losing a brother. Once he's disappeared into the cloister, Michael turns to me and nods. 'What a guy.'

I pat his knee. 'You did good, Michael.'

'I know. I based my summing-up on The Hero's Journey. That's not something you'll know about.'

'No.' I sigh kindly, because The Hero's Journey, also known as the Monomyth, is a pattern of narrative that appears in drama, storytelling, myth, religious ritual and psychological development. First identified by the scholar Joseph Campbell, it's a common template of tales – a hero who goes on an adventure and, in a decisive crisis, wins a victory, then comes home transformed. And although I'm unsure how Michael incorporated The Hero's Journey into his closing statement, I do know a truth: that was the quickest and most efficient case ever, neatly tied up with a bow.

A PI no-no: telling your dad about a case. You swore an oath of confidentiality.

But Michael chats so animatedly, recounting our day nigh-on verbatim. Of course, I don't tell him off. I stand, back to the sink, and examine my father's face, body language, linguistic foibles, looking for clues I've missed in the past – the ones that indicate he's capable of killing his own brother.

Dad gives me nothing to go on. His stance is too relaxed and receptive. He executes no micro-expressions whatsoever, simply wears his heart on his face. Biochemical fact: a contented psyche is difficult to penetrate.

The reason he's happy – he and Darcie are in the early stages of *giving it another go*. I know this because he's had a bath before bed yet blow-dried his hair; the pyjamas he wears are fresh from the packet, creases and all; his ears are fuzz-free.

This was not supposed to happen. What about the oath he pledged to Michael and me – that we'd mourn our losses as a trio? More prevalent, there's Annie, who has my labia in a nutcracker.

I interrupt Michael. 'You're seeing her again, aren't you, Dad?'

'Darcie? No, love.'

'But you were with her last night?'

I hate the smile he does – it's one entirely exclusive of us. 'We have bridges to build.'

Michael puts his hot chocolate down with a clatter. 'Flo, you said they were out of our hair.'

Dad frowns at me. 'What's Darcie ever done to you?'

'She gave birth to the Antichrist.'

'Annie's all right.'

I'm flabbergasted. 'Are you having a fucking laugh?'

Michael says, 'You said "fucking".'

'Language, both of you!' he snaps.

Fuck language. 'Annie *bullied* your son.'

'And Michael will never have to see her again. We're just talking. It's allowed. And I do not appreciate you cussing in front of your brother.'

'He's thirty.'

'Twenty-nine,' says Michael.

Now is as good a time as any. I pull out a chair. Join them at the table. 'I know, Dad, why you and Darcie broke up.'

'Why?' Michael asks me.

Dad looks momentarily panicked, behaves badly, like a cornered bully. 'Because of your sister. She and Annie clash, so I can't have a life.'

I become motionless. While Dad juts his eyes at Michael, trying to insinuate that my brother's the reason he betrays me. 'You're actually quite selfish.' I frown.

Dad looks hurt. Argues weakly, 'You know there are other people in the world apart from you?'

'Too much so. It sits heavy on my shoulders every day. The mother who will not be spoken about; I'm especially aware that she couldn't give a monkey's.'

Michael leans forward, intrigued. 'Whose mother?'

Dad's eyes get huge. Frightened I'll blab, he goes for my Achilles . . .

'Getting yourself in the papers for being sexual with men.'

Humiliation makes me blush, as he knew it would. His having seen me half clothed in a tabloid is kryptonite to my self-worth.

'I always stopped her before it went too far.' Michael makes me sound like a nymphomaniac.

'Getting your brother involved.' He diverts the conversation from Bambi. 'Arriving unannounced, always with a maelstrom of tribulation. Flitting off abroad with Michael without so much as a goodbye note. The chaos you leave behind. Your need to constantly live in the past.'

I tell Michael, 'Dad broke up with Darcie because Annie put him on dating websites. The woman hates us all. And, actually, Dad, you lost your *companion* because of a twenty-five-year-old scandal, one where a man expired. So, *if* I'm unhinged, I have a very good excuse.'

Dad glowers. 'Go to bed, Florence.' My laugh flat, I refuse to move. So he pulls out his phone. 'It's time I spoke to Annie.'

Christ on a bike.

He instantly regrets this decision, too. 'If you'll excuse me,' he states, leaving the kitchen to make the call in private.

'Think you'd better go to your room, Michael. It's going to kick off. I need to deal with this.'

He holds tightly to the side of his chair. 'I don't want to go.'

I rub my face. 'No talking then.'

Dad is gone for ten minutes. On his return, he sits down heavily. Examines my face. 'For the love of God. Tell me you didn't, Florence?'

I lift my chin. 'The likelihood is, I did.'

He pushes his phone's screen at me. I see words like *side gate* and *strangled* and *lacerations*.

'You *texted* her?' I frown.

He slams the hand piece face down on to the table. 'What have you done?'

'What does she say I've done?'

'You broke into her home.'

'It was the garden,' states Michael.

'You were there, too?'

'I didn't want to be. She made me.'

'It was when we got back from Italy. We came home and you weren't here. Annie had told us to hurry back – the insinuation was sinister.'

'We thought she'd murdered you,' nods Michael.

'You what?' Dad asks me. 'Have you lost your mind? You committed grievous bodily harm. The woman went to A&E.'

'Of course she did.' I stand up, at my wits' end. 'And it was *actual*.' Pointing at them both, disappointed, I don't know which of my family I got my balls from. 'I'd love somebody to attack somebody else on my behalf. I'd see the romance in it.'

'You strangled, punched her, caused criminal damage—'

'Dad, you're still refusing to hear a thing I'm saying. You haven't even asked why Michael hates Annie so much, not properly.'

'I know Annie's forthright, but, you know . . .'

'No, I don't.' I'm sick of his spinelessness. 'She's been sending your son insidious texts. She broke up his engagement just as she destroyed your relationship with Darcie.' A whirl of fury, disappointment and frustration, my voice rises three octaves. 'And do you know why you haven't listened to his concerns? Why you refuse to take them seriously? Do you?!'

WARNING: some may find the language ahead extremely offensive. My father certainly did. He's about to throw me out.

'Because, Dad, you are cunt-struck.'

Michael spits hot chocolate at the table.

Wilderness

Day 1

I do exactly as I'm told. Leave. I don't bang the front door behind me, I'm too emotionally disembowelled. When, halfway down the lane, I remember I left my book on the bed, I'm done for – sit on a verge and have a power cry.

I have never felt this hard done by.

The novel I left behind: *A Pair of Blue Eyes*. Tommaso had been reading it the day we first spoke. The day I noticed his unfeasibly symmetrical face. And his grandpa reading glasses – like he'd borrowed them on the hop, having realised his far-sightedness only that morning. I was captivated.

Homeless, my plan was to go live in his mind for a few days.

In the absence of the book, I score some weed. As retribution to my father, who chose Darcie over me.

Half an hour later, I spot full beams in the distance. They wind their way up the lane towards me, disappearing sporadically behind tree trunks and hedge. The local dealer's name is Red. Because he's ginger. And Chinese. Though there's no need for the pseudonym – it's common knowledge his real name's Dan and his parents own a chippie in Lyme Regis. It's called The Codfather II.

We talk through the window. Swap congenialities. He tells me he's carrying some old-school hash, which is serendipity gone mad – that's what I smoked at Tommaso's mother's engagement party. I buy a small bar, then pat his bonnet.

Red does a three-point turn. I turn on my torch and disappear into the trees opposite.

The undergrowth is manageable, this time of year. I kick a path through it while smelling the bar of Nepalese brown, its aroma taking me straight back to the day I spent in a Renaissance villa on a mountaintop in Italy.

All that nostalgia makes me ditsy. There's an oily moss on the stile. I stack it; sustain a bastard crack to the right glute. To spite my dad, I try to enjoy the pain; because we had just bloody well bonded. I felt it. And now we've unravelled again.

I am going to murder Kathy Bates.

Perfect-murder tip: stick to complete strangers, and ones that don't have incriminating video footage. And kill only one person ever – so as not to develop an MO. An MO is as telling as a polygraph test. Which, arguably, can be beaten. (When asked the calibration questions, you should think of sexually exciting imagery and/or tense your sphincters, all of them.)

A low-lying branch stabs me in the cheek. I swear, the woman's a voodoo witch. I make that branch promises: my revenge will be even better than murder.

Using the moonlight, I weave through the thicket. My destination is a squat fence. Old as a longboat, its being held aloft by steely determination and ivy. At my feet is the evidence of previous visits, detritus destined to outlive me – cans of Shandy Bass and chipstick packets. It's been a few years since I last hopped over this fence – my landing's not pretty.

As a teenager, I came here. Pretended I had a mum. That she was looking for me *everywhere*. Should she find me, she'd be heartbroken at my vulnerability. Dragging me home, her emotions a mixture of fury and relief; tickling my ears for two hours afterwards; telling me there's not a thing I couldn't share with her; that everybody has their foibles and I'm as sane as her.

In her absence, I had a father. One who didn't understand the importance of humouring my methods, so thought me living rough was self-indulgent and a branch of self-harm.

I see it as being like Glastonbury. An endurance test, from which you always return changed. If nothing else, you bring home a refreshing perspective. Not that I've done Glastonbury. It's on my things-to-do list, though. Just as soon as I've got myself a friend.

In the meantime, this is my festival. An unpeopled one with no music . . .

It's essential neither Dad nor Michael sees me from the cottage. I scurry gently up the wooden steps into my home for the foreseeable future.

The Yellow House.

Michael has removed his case notes and given the treehouse another dose of CIF. It smells bathroom fresh. An airbnb for campers.

First things first.

How to keep warm in a wooden box as insulated as a pergola:

- Wear a base layer of merino wool, your choice of mid-layer and an insulating synthetic layer on top; a fleece hat and neck warmer; a thin pair of thermal socks, and a pair of wool ones for the top.

- Double up your sleeping bag, putting one inside the other.

- A blanket below is worth two on top.

Second things second.

When running away from home, create a better option than the one you just left. I look around, make an alteration. Position *The Handbook of British Garden Birds* beside me on the floor. Push the upturned bucket – my spy seat as a child – towards the window. I hear a rattle from underneath. My plastic binoculars.

I sit on the bucket and pull the lenses as wide as they'll go.

The living room. My brother watches the TV. Hugh Laurie scowls back at him. I told him I was never returning. That's always worked in the past. He'd followed me to London, because of his need of me. I'd taken him to Italy without Dad's permission, because he'd cried like a bereaved fox when I tried to get into the taxi. He joined me on my honeymoon, the second one, because – his words – *I don't feel well without you.*

Sometimes, I wonder if, under his veil of innocence, is a man as manipulative as the devil himself. Look at him, sitting in the Angel's Seat, swaddled in guest duvet, drinking a glass of red, like Jennifer Jason Leigh in *Single White Female*.

Then there's my father, who gives even less of a shit. Pacing the kitchen, he talks animatedly into his phone. It's Darcie, I suppose. And his posture is saying this:

The C-word, I know. Unforgivable. Rest assured, I've thrown her to the kerb. Yep, I told her to get out. Michael's not even bothered. He's completely satisfied with the outcome.

'The C-word was your Get Out of Jail card,' I mutter, replacing the binoculars under the bucket.

Third things third.

I perform fifteen push-ups – girl ones – to get warm. Then eat a packet of Brie – fatty meals metabolise slowly, increasing your mean night-time body temperature. Pulling a V-cushion from my rucksack, I get into my sleeping bag.

V-cushion fact: they are ergonomic and a lovely blast from the past. Just the ticket when you're alone and feeling profound dejection. What's not the ticket: a joint. Solitude is too fickle a creature – its manifestations range from serenity to unexpected harrow. Instead, insert earplugs and employ diversionary tactics – *The Handbook of British Garden Birds*, for example.

As payback to my father and the rest of my blood relatives, I read the hardback from cover to cover. Memorising each species, Latin names and all. While so doing, my shoulders lighten, forget the baggage they labour to lug. Learning stuff has always been my retribution.

Day 2

Dawn. I am awoken by Dendrocopos major, aka the great spotted woodpecker. Length: 23–26 centimetres. Wingspan: 38–44 centimetres. Black and white; the males' genitals are a flashy scarlet. This one currently pisses on his territory – not by pissing but by enlisting a Chinese torture technique known as drumming – the treehouse's timber providing excellent resonance.

What hacks my nerves the most, though, are the wild parakeets. Psittacula krameri. They're having a right old wrangle in my tree. It's not their fault they're here. But now they are, I wish they'd just assimilate, instead of screaming like drunken chimpanzees.

How I long for a croissant and the *Daily Mail* online.

Yes, the *Daily Mail* is a travesty. Everybody in the world, including the *Daily Mail*, agrees. Yet it's addictive. Ask Kim Jong-il. North Korean fact: there are two unidentified users there. Go figure. Like Kim Jong-il, I'm in its snare. Especially, I'm prone to leaving chopsy comments.

The reality of last night hits me afresh. I turn on my

phone. No messages or voicemails from my family – I'm a distant memory to them.

Though I do have a WhatsApp from Veena.

HAVE to see The Theory of Everything. You on for it on Sat?

That makes me feel loved. And shy. Then, nervous.

Going to the movies with a new friend is more stressful than a first date. First dates allow you to use your powers of body language; your personality deficiencies are white-washed by sexual charisma. Initiating a friendship, on the other hand, is brutal. Your partner doesn't care if you're pretty or sexy. All they care about is you being a nice person.

Look at me, worrying already. What if there are gaps in the conversation? Because, BFF fact: neither of you can get a word in edgeways. Another BFF fact: comfortable silences are indigenous to the territory. I am terrible with silences. The clown in me comes out.

Any initial joy at the prospect of friendship soon dissolves. I remind myself of the rules – *never become emotionally embroiled with a contact*. Tap my finger in time with the Dendrocopos major and wonder, is it too early for a joint?

Yes, it is.

If you do it every day.

The Handbook of British Garden Birds serves as an excellent tray on which to whip up. The hash's distinct aroma evokes the exact memories I knew it would – a few puffs in and I lie, looking out of the window at dead leaves, reliving my Italian love story in Technicolor.

We were so connected, Tommaso had insisted Michael also attend his mother's engagement party. I hadn't told him I came as a twin-pack. His house was a castle in the Dolomites. His mother felt like home. When Michael took a tumble and lost his tooth, they nursed him as if he were their own. I even shared a joint with the fiancé, Howard – a secret smoker from Bermondsey. I giggle to myself. We'd bonded on that mountainside. Then he went back inside, leaving me with compromised spatial awareness, hence my ending up stranded on a cliff face.

Who the hell *was* Lancelot?

I watch the cottage until 7.20 a.m. Dad's routine is set in stone. Plate and cup in the sink, brush hair using the mirror on the kitchen sill, disappear into the hall to collect coat, keys and mobile. Then say out loud, 'Coat, keys and mobile.'

I hear the Dacia fire up. Eventually, a slow crunch of gravel. The rude clatter of the cattle grate. I count to one hundred before treading stealthily to the shed, internet booster in hand.

Nosiness is a prerequisite when private investigation is your game. Ex-boyfriends, girls I went to school with, arbitrary strangers – I'm helped by a powerful search tool. A CD-ROM – UK Info People Finder V14 – mandatory office equipment for a one-man band like me.

Back in the treehouse, I fire up my laptop, insert the CD.

Twenty-seven million electoral-roll names and addresses, fifteen million Directory Enquiry listings, two and a half million company records and a whole bunch of classified search facilities.

I punch in 'Lancelot'.

The beauty of this software: it doesn't need a location, a date of birth or even a surname. The search options are as expansive as your creativity.

Within a few seconds, I'm provided with an address for every adult Lancelot registered to vote. It is a ridiculous name; still, there are eighteen in the UK. Only one lives in Reading.

'Lancelot Edward Shaw,' I say out loud. 'Thirty-eight years

old. Still lives with his folks in a two-hundred-and-eighty-grand bungalow on Wessex Drive in Whitley.'

I type his name into Google – it is *fascinating*.

Facts about the man who rescued me from a mountainside: he was once a gymnast, quite a successful one – part of the national squad up until five years ago, when he became a coach at a prestigious gymnastics club in Woodley. His previous grammar school had invited him back as guest speaker on Speech Night. I find his blog – a bland one; the man lacked talent for keeping an audience hooked.

However, his final post gets my attention.

He tells his followers he's leaving gymnastics to join the army.

I input every connotation of army job and rank into the search bar, along with Lancelot's name. I check online military records. Nothing comes up. He abandoned his twelve followers, just like that.

I could give them an update, though . . .

Someone is paying Lancelot Edward Shaw to watch an Italian crime family.

'Who do you work for?' I muse. Then, 'That's not the point. The point is, Lancelot could be an *assassin*.'

What a wonderful bolt of electricity that sends through me. Morally, should you have *any* suspicion that someone is going to be killed, you should tell them. Even if that involves dicing with danger yourself. Returning to a country, for example, that wants you dead – that's always OK when done in the name of love.

The long and short of it: Tommaso deserves to know he's being stalked by a trained killer.

And I deserve to know who my mother is.

The Morris dancer performs a Mexican wave. And I tell him, cockily, 'It's the tenuous leads that give rise to unexpected finales.'

Day 3

When I'm sure Dad and Michael are out, I enter the cottage, pack a rucksack, then cycle full pelt to the Travel Inn.

9.40 a.m.

Noah's not in his room. Reception confirm he's not checked out, so I wander into the restaurant. There's quite the crowd; the breakfast buffet is a bun fight.

Don't get me wrong, I'm a vocal advocate of the queue. But waiting in line for every individual element – each egg option, sausage, spoonful of beans – it's no wonder most guests have the same attitude as me – I'm starving and I'm never going to see these people again. I jump straight in at the eggs. My intention to pay, if anybody asks. They won't. Not now I've spotted a friend – not the one I was looking for originally, but she will more than do.

'Vee,' I squeak, then clock her guest.

Noah and Vee sit opposite one another, reading their newspapers, plates wiped clean in front of them.

'Did someone forget to invite me to this party?' I dump my bag on a spare seat.

Noah looks up, surprised.

Vee confides, 'We had a drink last night. One thing led to another. You know how it goes . . .' She does a mortified frown.

So do I.

Noah's not mine. But neither is he hers. She's a lesbian – a bona fide one who doesn't flit niches; not a sexual flibberti-gibbet, like me. I respected that in her.

It sounds like I'm boasting when I tell Noah, 'I met a man in Italy. I can't remember if I told you about him?'

'Nope,' he says.

I did. 'We were very much in love.'

Vee nods earnestly. 'This the guy you told me about?'

'The very one. I'm a bit worried for his mum.'

Vee shakes her head like I'm incorrigible. 'You've been doing some digging, right?'

'You know what I'm like. I can't help myself.'

'She can't,' Vee tells Noah.

Noah silently watches my every gesticulation.

'While digging, I chanced upon some information he needs to know about.'

Vee shakes her head. 'You are so flying to Italy to tell him.'

I take a dramatic breath. Put a hand on hers. 'I'm sorry. It's top secret. You understand?'

'My lips are sealed,' she swears.

Finally, Noah pipes up. 'Professionalism, first, Veena. Excuse us, will you?' Then he makes no attempt to move.

Vee is the most accepting woman I've ever met. 'Bastards,' she says, gathering her things. 'I'll meet you in the bar.'

Smiling, I watch her leave. The minute she's out of earshot, I say, 'Did you *sleep* together?'

'No.'

'Then why are you having breakfast?'

'She's taking me to her cousin's place. He has a room to rent. I can't stay here for ever . . .'

'She said one thing led to another?'

'It's called a joke. That's when you talk humorously or flippantly. *Your* friend arrived half an hour ago. We had time to kill.'

'When did you swap numbers?'

'The café. Are you usually this possessive of your pals?'

I point, noiselessly, because I'm way too inexperienced to say.

Vee currently sits in reception, holding court with an elderly couple. 'She is a blast,' I warn him.

'You were telling me about your love life,' he states.

'Why do you need to rent a room? You live in Inverness.'

'Landed a job down here. Too good an offer to let go.' I

frown. Am about to ask about his wife and child. Noah taps the table impatiently. 'What's going on?'

'I was telling you about a man with a secret. Remember I got stoned on the mountain in Italy and was rescued by an acrobat?'

'King Arthur?'

'Lancelot.' I pull my laptop from my bag. 'I couldn't print anything up because I've been living rough.'

Noah laughs. Stops abruptly. Looks me up and down, then takes the computer.

But he's taking too long. 'In summary, Lancelot's working undercover, watching Tommaso's home.' I put a hand in the air, keen not to jump the gun. 'He's probably an assassin.'

'And you care, because?'

'It's his mother's place. Jolana might be in the firing line. Tommaso held great store in protecting a mother.' I talk mainly to myself. 'I know I made a promise not to go back, but these are extenuating circumstances.'

'Err, email him.'

'What I can do is hang around the borders. Italy shares borders with a few countries, and nobody has banned me from the whole of the EU. And then there's the fact that you haven't been banned from Italy at all.'

He smiles. 'You want me to go and save your ex-lover's mother from an assassin. Leaving you to live happily ever after?'

I lean forward. Make my eyes bigger. 'Leaving Tommaso Bellini personally indebted to me.'

'You're a piece of work.'

'That's impossible: I'm a Cancerian. And Tommaso Bellini has something we both want.'

'Information?'

I don't blink. '*Answers.*'

For a while we stare one another out. Until I win, and he

pretends to examine his palm. 'I'm still getting my head around the coroner's report.'

Picking at my cold egg selection, I tell him plainly. 'Well, do it quickly. Life's ever so short.' I grab his hand and prod at his lifeline. 'Look. What is it, four inches long?'

His smile is tired. 'Tops.'

'That's no time at all. Noah, we need closure. *Both* of us. He knows what my mum did and who she is.'

Noah takes several deep breaths before resuming stare-out mode. This time, however, he has a weapon; the twinkle in his eye.

'So you're in need of a wingman?'

I break eye contact. Because there he is – the Noah that made me tremble when I was eight and struggle to converse naturally with him. It made me lean towards defensiveness, back then. Though it's not just the twinkle. It's the fact he's become a sexual being, what with me imagining him at it with Vee.

Suddenly, a memory arrives. I point as though I've just woken up, 'Did we go to Longleat on a school trip once?'

'Nope,' he says.

I flap a hand. 'You're here now. And you're right, I need a partner. Especially if I'm going to avoid getting killed by Italy.'

It's a swell of emotion, I think, that makes his voice break. 'Go on, then.'

Relieved and grateful, I bang the table too hard.

Burglary

Noah let me stay in his room – on the proviso we pull the twin beds as far apart as they go. Tomorrow, we will hatch plans for the final phase of Operation Bambi Love. In the meantime, I have essential business.

3 a.m.

I've been listening to Noah's breathing for forty-five minutes. Using my phone light to monitor his eyes, I'm able to conclude that Noah is in phase four of the circadian cycle. Deep sleep. In this stage, there's no eye movement or muscle activity – the result of the brain producing a squillion delta waves. The body busily regenerates itself; the mechanics of sleep require that you're good as a broken robot. For the criminally minded, this is a useful window of opportunity.

I slip to the bathroom to get changed.

When committing a crime, wear clothes that don't shed. Tightly woven fabrics are preferable to loosely knitted ones, as are filament yarns to spun yarns. In an ideal world, I'd wear a paper boiler suit with hood, mask and latex gloves. Tonight, I wear a lightweight shell suit made of UV and water-resistant high-tenacity polyester.

The cycle ride to Annie's house takes forty minutes. Sweating like a glassblower's arse, I hide the bike in a hedge, then walk down the lane to her front garden. Her bedroom window is ajar; her snore, a methodical grunt, like a contented bull mastiff.

Avoiding the security light, I enter by hopping over the fence on the right-hand side of the property. I land in the dead-end alley in which Annie stows her bins.

My aim: to obscure her security, because revenge is best dished out in the absence of recording devices.

How to obscure a camera lens.

An all-frequency jammer – I had one in London. A pocket-sized gadget, it disarms every camera and mobile phone within a thirty-metre radius. However, while my plan is in its infancy, I cover all bases. Standing on the bench, placing a foot on Cupid's head, ensuring I am out of view of the security camera, I use an atomiser spray to mist its lens. I've opted for a sugar solution. Over time, it builds up, making the image increasingly blurred. If you're in an absolute rush, use Duck tape or radiator paint.

Annie's snoring would normally make me murderous. Tonight, I'm grateful for it, especially as I can hear it from the back of the house, too. I look up to find the upstairs bathroom open.

It's too good an opportunity – the one I've been waiting for.

I tighten my shoelaces. When breaking and entering, always wear shoes that are too big; and, if possible, borrow a stranger's orthotics – that scuppers footfall recognition.

Parkour is a blast, as long as it's low down. Three storeys is tops for me, and only because climbing the wall to my loft room was my party trick as a teenager. See how I hoick myself on to the kitchen's flat roof, then up on to the bathroom sill.

Opening the window fully, sliding inside, I swiftly ascertain the reason why she's left the window open. Rotten inside and out, Annie's bathroom is a mixture of stink bomb and air freshener. I also guestimate that her snoring falls within the eighty–ninety range – that's not far off a howler monkey.

Her bedroom door is ajar. Quickly and silently, I get downstairs, swinging a right then a left, shutting the room's door behind me.

The office. An eerie space. The light of my torch reveals her hardbacks, a hundred of them – all biographies. Elizabeth Taylor, Angelina Jolie, Brigitte Bardot, Kate Moss, Grace Kelly . . .

Christ, the woman lives her life vicariously through the most beautiful women that ever lived. When you have a chip the size of Annie's, this library can only feed her wrath. That explains a lot. I'm not big-headed, but realistic – I am very fit. Being faced with me as a stepsister must have been unbearable.

Now I peruse her apothecary wall unit. Shining my light at each recess, I can confirm the spice jars don't contain basil, turmeric or star anise. Unless they've putrefied into dust, which is what appears to be in most jars. No, some have other things inside, too. Gravel, chips of rock, a beer-bottle top, fluff. I pick one up – shake it; its contents are grey and course, like bath salts. On its bottom, there is a home-made label. It says 12/12/98. The others have labels, too. Some recent, some as far back as the eighties.

I take pictures of them, because it's likely to be proof she's insane. Then I sit at her desk.

Security tip: never have a book in your desk drawer called 'Finances'. Especially don't write a list of all your passwords on the second-to-last page. Though Annie has this covered – she's written all her secret codes in *very* small letters. That always stops a felon. I take a photograph of it; open her laptop and smile.

Password protected. I squint at her list.

Computer – *Hulagiri*

'There's not a hula hoop large enough,' I mutter. Then don't breathe for a minute, because it's suddenly quiet as death.

When Annie's grunts resume, I study the screen and its little yellow folders. Open one called 'QT Series DVR'. I'm tempted to rename it 'Please Delete All My CCTV Footage Here'. I pull up a calendar – the dates in blue have recorded footage. I select the lot. Everything that's been recorded ever. Then I check to see if Annie's backed up the files. Of course, she hasn't – my air pump is silent but violent.

When I leave I do so via the front door, using a spare front-door key from a cabinet that says 'Key Cabinet'. I use it to ensure the door shuts noiselessly behind me.

I leave the key in her front garden among her hydrangeas and return to my bike, bloody elated. Pedalling fast feeds my excitement, each foot rotation a step closer to tomorrow morning and planning for Italy.

Noiselessly, I slip back into my bed. Noah sleeps, none the wiser, in exactly the same position as I left him. And I can't stop thinking of age-old adages; my current favourite – *the measure of a superhero is always her nemesis* – I struggle not to snigger out loud. So I assume the recovery position and bury my nose in a fresh and full pillow.

Sleep hits me like an anvil.

Part II

Part II

Putting Old Ghosts to Rest 101 – Tip #2: Seek Full Disclosure

A note to mankind . . .

Enigmatic goodbyes leave a girl insane. Forgive them; they cannot grieve until they have the colonoscopy results of a duck's arse. This is *not* being desperate, it's the by-product of being a deep thinker.

A note to womankind . . .

Men's inability to overthink was once fundamental to the propagation of the species – women should be more deep thinking about it; accept that men *cannot* give every reason why you're chucked – they've forgotten them already.

For closure's sake, a brief period of stalking is permissible. You are not a bunny-boiler, so stick to the rules:

• Don't get spotted – your aim is to shadow then corner your ex. (Read *Stalk and Kill: The Thrill and Danger of the Sniper Experience*, Gilbert, 1997)

• When he can't escape, unload your list of questions. Be thorough – this is the last conversation you will *ever* have.

• Wear a pinhole camera in your lapel. You'll want to pore over his answers, body language and micro-expressions when you're back home.

• When sick of the sight of him squirreling free of meaningful conversation, have a burning ceremony and move on.

Base Camp

Until recently, my knowledge of Slovenia was poor. I was vaguely aware of it as a spatial entity. According to my research, however, there are actual people living there, valid as you or I, going about their business of running a country very well. Of course, I knew that already, but it's something else actually seeing the proof.

Ljubljana Jože Pučnik airport. Noah and I smoke outside in a designated area, admiring the country's modernity and a bright-blue slice of foreign sky.

Noah inhales the air. 'It's clean as water.'

'It's why Slovenians live to an old age.'

'How old?'

'A hundred and twelve.'

'All of them?'

I nod. Another fact: 'Ljubljana translates as "the loved one".'

He takes a thoughtful puff of his cigarette. 'That's nice.'

I can see right up his nose. 'Why is it so difficult to empathise with people until you've actually met them?' I ask his nasopharynx. 'Then again, it's difficult enough understanding the motives of family members, never mind grasping the essence of every living being.'

'Aye,' he says, gravely.

'It's the animal activists I don't get. They take on the woes of every living species. A survival tip, Noah. Pick and choose where to invest emotionally. You'll go mad otherwise. People-pleasers suffer the most. I'm one. I know.'

This is, apparently, hysterical. 'You, a people-pleaser?'

I do not have to explain myself to him. But I do. 'It's a by-product of my job. I have to be everything to everyone. Seriously, Noah, how can any of us be rounded when we have a gnat's cock of a clue what goes on in the collective mind?'

He shrugs, changes the subject, which is rude. 'I read there's a vineyard for every seventy people.' He smiles. 'I like that in a country.'

Noah's been doing a lot of that today: smiling. It's unexpected, given the gravity of our journey, but a huge relief, given his usual cynicism. Plus, he's much better looking when he's not looking murderous. I wonder what we look like to those who pass by. Whether they think we're a couple on a weekend break; whether we match; whether we exude a certain presence.

A snapshot of Noah . . .

Tall, built like a knight. His hue, a sandy Scandinavian. Skin tone on the hex colour system: #342, also known as Bleached Beech.

Me . . .

Tallish, too. But darkish. It's difficult to guess my ethnicity beneath the beanie and hood, but my T-section is Hex Code #564, also known as Light Oak. I could be half anything – Persian, Hispanic, Indian . . .

Once upon a time, I thought that made me alluring. These days, I err towards absolutes. Like, where the fuck was my mother actually born and who were her parents? Because they certainly weren't the imaginary Nonna and Nonno she'd waxed lyrical about when I was small.

I stab my fag into a bowl reminiscent of a holy-water urn, pull my scarf up and around my jaw, accidentally put an arm in Noah's.

He doesn't shrug me off; he tramples over my well-laid plans. 'Let's get a cab. What is it, thirty-five kilometres?'

'Eighty.' I show him my map – I've given this a lot of thought. 'We'll get a train from Ljubljana Tivoli to Povir, then walk to Lokev. Twelve euros each and two and a half hours later, we're at base camp. Job done. Leave me to it, OK. This is what I do.'

'Plan roundabout routes?' He leaves me to join the taxi queue, turning once to tell me off. 'You get there how you want, but I'm not on a bloody gap-year.'

Lokev

Like other countries of the world, there are lots of towns and villages in Slovenia, one of which is called Lokev. My research suggests it's the perfect place in which to disappear.

Situated on the outskirts of a medium-sized town, it enjoys a steady trickle of tourists. Outdoorsy couples in hiking boots, woolly hats and ski jackets; they traverse mountain paths and cycle well-organised routes around the Slovenian Karst. Which is beautiful. A rugged limestone plateau. Rivers and lakes vanish into the ground; magically, they resurface via funnels and sinkholes.

When undercover, place yourself within a small yet fluid population. And always have your backstory sown up, which means sticking as close to the truth as you can, though with dramatic flourishes.

This is ours.

Noah and I are childhood sweethearts, who lost touch then were reunited recently when he stalked me relentlessly in London. He is a motorcycle courier for Santander. I was a dancer with the Cirque du Soleil. Retired, due to meniscus issues, I now illustrate comics. Note: the best part of being a female private investigator is the fact that you can and should reinvent yourself, regularly. Having chosen a fascinating backstory, however, be ready for a cross-interrogation. Especially from other women, who are not stupid.

Noah is certainly doing an excellent job of making our relationship look authentic. 'Could we not have got dropped off at the hotel?' he bickers.

'Yes.' I shake my head. 'I want to get a feel for the place. To do a recce.' Which is tricky in Slovenia. Everybody owns a dog. As we walk through the village we are followed by a chorus of barks, most of them from breeds as small as gerbils. Houses nestle, higgledy-piggledy, in a jagged landscape. The people's optimism is palpable – their houses are yellow, terracotta and orange; their geraniums are a luminous red; they're partial to rainbow-coloured windmills.

'Look, a shop,' I say. 'It's really enchanting. And there's an architect's. And a *lovely* primary school. I read that the ruin on the hill was once a church called St Clement's; he's the patron saint of sheep!'

'The miraculousness of human civilisation,' sighs Noah. 'Do you always have to be so dramatic?' He puts an apologetic hand in the air, though doesn't change vein. 'Or explain everything that's going on in your head; which is a lot, at any one given time?'

'Are you going to be analysing me out loud for the rest of our mission?'

'Probably,' he concedes.

'Then this is not going to work.'

He marches in the direction of the hotel, safe in the knowledge that I need him more than he needs me. 'Oh my God.' He points at the hinterland. 'Some hills. A tree.'

'Tommaso's mother is Slovenian,' I call after him. 'She was a very classy woman. Jolana was her name. She owns Castella di Friuli, which is just over there. Look, that's where Tommaso lives.'

Noah turns around. We look west towards the Italian border, towards Trieste and the foothills of the Dolomites.

'Good, we're back on point. I take it you've got a postcode for Tommy-boy, or should I just ask for directions at border control?'

The most important reason I chose this town . . .

According to my map, it's five millimetres right of the Italian border. The Italian commune of Trieste and its peripheries lie directly left of that border. Making Tommaso's office and home within cycling distance. Should you have the luxury of a car, it's a twenty-minute journey. The cherry on the cake: movement between the Slovenian and Italian border is as organised as a sneeze.

Before we enter the guesthouse, I remind him: 'For the purpose of this mission, you are going to have to be nicer to me. We can't both be the boss. And refrain from discussing border-control issues in public. Now, let's get booked in. I've a PowerPoint presentation lined up.'

Hotel Krasna. Lokev, 78

A stone guesthouse painted a deep sunset yellow. Inside smells brand new. The guests' written comments are glowing, but barely fill a page. If I had to sum up the aesthetic, it would be: Adriatic chic with a splash of the Von Trapps.

Ours is an airy, twin-bedded room. Its view, verdant hills and snowy peaks interspersed with silver shards of rutted limestone.

We decide to eat dinner in the restaurant downstairs, though I make it clear I'm not paying.

That reminds him, 'We need to talk expenses.'

'*Expenses?*'

He bows, insistent I enter the restaurant first. 'I might be your skivvy, but I'll always have my dignity.'

'Misers have no dignity.'

We choose the table furthest from the two waiters, who stand poised; eager to facilitate our every culinary wish. We're the only customers. There's no background music. Our words bounce crisply from double-height stone walls that funnel them towards the roof to loiter in the eaves, like cigarette smoke.

I whisper, 'The address of this place – Lokev, 298. It could be the film title for a horror film set in an abattoir.'

Noah ignores me to order everything on the menu.

While we wait for our drinks, I touch my phone screen too often. No missed calls or texts from Michael or Dad.

'You're not their mother, you know.' I'm about to argue with him, but he's already moved on. 'Let's talk strategy. When do we get started?'

'Now.' I put fingers to my lips.

I've called the PowerPoint presentation 'Operation Bambi Love (Phase II)'.

Slide #1: *Travel.*

This slide outlines how Noah is going to get to Tommaso. I mutter him through it.

'Use this taxi rank in Sežana, the closest town to here. It's a twenty-one-minute walk. It's called Taxi Tiric. Your destination, Trieste bus station. Expected journey time, seventeen minutes. There's a taxi rank – always take a legitimate taxi. Your final destination, Portopiccolo Sistiana. Twenty-four minutes, tops.'

'I thought I was off to a castle in the Alps.'

'Tommaso lives in the castle. You're going to where he hangs out.'

Noah's snort is weak. 'He lives with his mum?'

I flick to the next slide.

Slide #2: *Portopiccolo Sistiana – Facts.*

Beneath are publicity photos I've copied from the resort website. Silently, we read the spec.

The entire resort is an ode to six-star opulence. Situated in a snuggle of cliff, it overlooks billionaire's yachts and the Adriatic. Its epicentre is a bar, restaurant and infinity pool that will take your breath away . . .

'This is the Bellinis' playground and Tommaso's office.'

Noah frowns. 'He sounds like a complete tit.'

'You sound like a complete tit.'

The first course arrives. I push mine to one side. Noah demolishes his in four mouthfuls. Flaps his napkin for me to continue.

Slide #3: *Cover Story.*

We lean in.

'Getting access to a mafiosi's diary is impossible. We may have to play the long game. But the longer the game goes on, the trickier it gets not to arouse suspicion. *Unless* you're a tourist. So, this is the ruse – you're a tourist. You can go there every day and evening, just waiting for Tommaso to turn up. You've got your cover story – just stick to that. You're holidaying alone for an indefinite amount of time. Having just split up with your wife.'

His cheeks drop. For a moment, I think he's going to cry.

'Like Shirley Valentine,' I add, confused.

He gulps his wine greedily.

I slide him a piece of paper. 'Give this to him. Say a close friend from England gave this to you to pass on to him. A secure email address. That friend is desperately concerned for his safety. At no point say my name or tell him a single thing about what I know.'

'I get the drift.' Noah hurries me along, orders another wine.

Slide #4 is a succinct, but unimpeachable rule.

Do not tell anyone where you are staying.

'Where am I staying?'

'Three options. I recommend Le Falesie. B&B. Sixty

euros – winter rates. He must not follow you back here. Base camp is our safe place.'

I draw his attention to slide #5. There's a photograph of a mobile phone on it, and a close-up of the voice-memo app. It's the most important slide of all.

Slide #5 – *Record everything.*

This is especially important when relying on a man. They relay events too succinctly, lacking the dramatic flourishes that unveil glaring truths; unless that man is Michael – his eye for detail is pathological. I check my phone, missing him with an unexpected urgency.

'And that's it?' he says snippily, nodding his thanks to the waiter, who refills his glass.

'That's it. Noah, are you OK?'

'I'm bushed and starving. I get hangry.'

'Good.' I take his full glass away. 'One's enough, given the danger of your journey ahead.'

'Be gone with you,' he snorts, as though Tommaso is small fry. Then he eats his next two courses like it's his last supper.

Noah leaves the next day after breakfast.

'No contact,' I tell him, strictly. 'Not unless it's an emergency. He mustn't link us.' I shake his hand goodbye, warmly.

'Understood, hen.'

But he doesn't have a Scooby as to what he's letting himself in for. Trust me, I want to be doing it myself. If I was, I'd have included other slides in my PowerPoint presentation.

Secret slides, for my eyes only . . .

Slide #6: Tell Tommaso: '*I think about you a hundred times a day. I've even considered turning a blind eye and becoming a gangster's moll.*'

Swiftly followed by slide #7.

'*But I can't.*'

158

Morally. And because I have a mother who tucked up a Capo di Tutti Capi, or two – let's face it, the probability is that Bambi was an informant. What better reason for the Bellinis' unwavering hatred?

Should this be the case, her case will be documented. Today is the day, therefore, I decide to investigate mafia informants – female ones, specifically.

First, however, I make a call. Michael picks up within one ring. 'Flo. You are never going to guess what?'

My whole head relaxes. 'I am not.'

'Guess.' He doesn't give me time. 'I've got another case.'

'No,' I say, strictly.

'I have.'

'No. You're not ready. You need micromanaging. I'm not there.'

'That was your choice.'

'It was not!'

'And, guess what?'

I say this, flatly: 'You're missing me?'

'Nope. I've solved the case already. And, guess what? I'll give you a clue. My new client's name is James Jardine.'

'Oh, Christ.'

'And, guess what?'

I throw something out there. 'Alan Knight's wife's not dead?'

'Oh my God, Flo. You are properly *psychopathic*.'

I look at the phone. Put it back to my ear. 'She's not?'

'Angela Knight volunteers for Dorset Blind Association. I did surveillance on her. The earlobes are a perfect fit.'

'They're still married?'

'Yes.' Sadly, he informs me, 'There's a name for that.'

'Bigamy. It's one of the mainstays of our job.' If Bambi is married to her lover, his own mother's a proponent of it. 'And the word for me is *psychic*. Michael, you did good.'

'I know. I'm going to have to hire.'

'Do not hire.'

'You're not my keeper.'

Palms up, I lose it.

'Oh, do what you want. Set up a PI firm. Hire an entire team. Do it. But, currently, you're using my software, spyware; in fact, my everything. You don't have a single contact. Never mind a vocational qualification. You've never read around the subject. You don't have a professional email or telephone number. You're living at Dad's, registered on the electoral roll, lacking any enigma whatsoever. Most especially, you don't have a website or any concept of how to drum up business in a world dominated by ex-coppers and security specialists who would laugh you out of the Yellow Pages.'

He has to be told.

'Then there's the clients. They're not all pubescent. Some are evil, most are disturbed. All are tortured at some level. It can be stupidly dangerous and you're not ready yet. One day, but not yet.'

'I so am.'

'You'll get killed.'

We sit in silence. Michael forgetting to ask a single thing about me.

'Anything else going on, apart from that?' I ask.

'Annie dropped Darcie here yesterday. She did a big-tongued face at me.'

'She what?' The bitch makes me bite an actual chunk out of my inside cheek. 'I will kill her.'

'Me, too,' he agrees. 'Have you left me for ever?'

'No.' I smile.

'Good. While you're not here, I can do private investigation as a hobby then?'

'That's a brilliant place to start . . .' I cut Michael short, promise to call back tomorrow, because Noah phones me. Too late, I swap calls. He doesn't leave a message. When I call back, his phone goes to voicemail.

'Call me back if it's urgent.' I leave a message, then settle in at the desk to research hated women.

I read every female-mafia-informant story I can find. *Pentitas*, they're called – it's too pretty a label.

Maria Cacciola, for example. She snitched on her husband regarding arms stashes. Full witness protection, however, couldn't outweigh the pull of her three young children. *Pentita* fact: it's biology that leads to their downfall. Maria left witness protection to return home to her kids. Ten days later, she drank a bottle of bleach. A lot of *pentitas* go that way.

I remember the method my mother used to kill Fergus.

Perhaps, like Maria Cacciola, Bambi missed her child – the other me, a better me, the real me. Her firstborn daughter. Maybe my mother was forced into a loveless marriage – an older man who was imprisoned, leaving her a prisoner of his family.

I give myself a mental slap.

My mother's oldest daughter looks just like Pannacotta Man. He's been on the scene for ever. Chances are, he was always her soulmate.

I feel instant pity for Dad. Crush it mercilessly – how can he let Annie even park on his drive?

My research also tells me that Bambi fled Italy during one of the most infamous Mafia purges of history's entirety. The US Federal Witness Security Program was established, becoming a blueprint for other Witness Protection Programmes within Europe. International cooperation was borne.

The Number-one rule of WITSEC.

Your new life must be an unmitigated lie. When you get married, for example; revealing your prior identity to a new spouse is sacrilege. Maybe Dad doesn't know.

I tell myself off. The problem with maybes is knowing when to stop. Best to stick to facts; I buy the eBook: *WITSEC – Inside the Federal Witness Protection Program*. My plan is to read it all night if I have to.

That afternoon, I shower then doze. I have a specific problem in mind, and in the twilight zone between consciousness and unconsciousness lie a lot of answers. Cognitive neuroscience agrees – while dozing, your nerve cells remain surprisingly alert, making it a lazy form of decision-making.

My specific problem is this: eighty per cent of protected persons were, once upon a time, a horrible human being. Where does Bambi Love sit?

I dream about nothing – my sleep is too heavy. And long – I'm only awoken by a clatter outside my door.

Disorientated, my eyes shoot open. It's jet black. I don't know what day of the week it is. Stumbling upright reminds me I'm not at home; the wooden floorboards are freezing. I knee a side table. For a second, I think I'm in my old mansion flat off Tottenham Court Road. Another bang. Then rustling outside the room. I look left and right for weapons, but it's dark as death.

Too late, the door flies open, light rushing at my retina.

Noah turns the lights on. I pull my T-shirt over my bottom.

'Twenty minutes, door to door. Can't complain,' he declares.

'Noah?! What time is it?'

'Ten forty-five. Case closed in, what, ten hours?'

'You saw him?'

Negotiating a route past me, he collapses on to his bed. 'You been asleep all day?'

'No,' I lie impatiently. 'Tell me what happened.'

'As instructed, I went to the main attraction in Portopiccola. Found your man among a gaggle of women.'

That stings. I sit on the edge of Noah's bed. 'And?'

'And the answer is, *no.*'

'No?'

He shows me his phone. 'I have recorded *everything.* Slide # 6.'

I don't grab it.

I notice his cream jumper. It's splattered with bloodstains. Fuck. *Fuck.* 'You told him I had information? That I definitely wasn't in Italy?'

'Just as we practised it.'

'Verbatim.'

'I'm not a robot. I adapted it according to the situation.'

Excellent PI tip: never sound like you're reading from an autocue. Always adapt it according to the situation.

Yet I say, 'Why would you do that?'

Noah wiggles his phone. 'It's all on here.'

It is not! The questions his transcript can't answer . . .

What did you think of Tommaso – as a person? Was he pleased I was chasing him? Were his gums still pink and his molars effulgent? Did he have his barbered beard? The cheekbones and eyes of a lion? Beauty spots – three discernible ones, big as shirt buttons – one on his cheek, two on his varnished neck.

'You go get a snack at the bar,' I tell him. 'I'll transcribe the recording.'

He doesn't argue. 'If they're still serving. I cannot function on an empty stomach.'

That's a fallacy, I don't say. Human intelligence evolved from the biochemical focus that hunger produces. Being hank marvin should be used to cognitive advantage – it maintains an edgy state. But Noah's too focused on foraging and hunter-gathering.

'Go fill your belly.'

I want to be alone. When he passes me the phone, I fiddle with it too timidly, before saying, 'Give us your password, then.'

Piss-poor

Private investigation and transcription go hand in hand. Detailing infidelity, criminal activity and drug use in film-script form makes for brilliant reading. A professional transcription will pinpoint dates and times, every um, err and pause. Nothing must be omitted.

Key rule: your goal is a complete and truthful record of what was said. Clients especially love them – it makes them feel they've got their money's worth.

3.12.2014. 18.16
Voice record activated
Noah: I'm sitting in the main bar of Portopiccolo Sistiana. Two other patrons – middle-aged couple, drinking coffee. A waitress – black, university age, a weave down to her arse. No sign of the target. [10 seconds of rustling] Fucking thing.
Voice record deactivated

That makes me jealous. That Tommaso might ever be in the same room as another girl. Especially one that has hair and an arse. I wonder if he's moved on already. Is currently making love to a new woman. Then I stop wondering, because it's been over a month and he's the most eligible bachelor in town.

4.12.2014. 19.26
Voice record activated
Noah: A party of 11 has just arrived. [30 seconds of Italian

garrulousness and laughter] I think one of them is Tommaso
Bellini, but these Ities all look the same.
Voice record deactivated

They do not. Especially not Tommaso. Tommaso looks more Italian than any Italian man I've ever met. I listen to this excerpt over and over. Straining to distinguish which voice could be his, but all I hear is a bunch of people about to enjoy an evening exclusive of me. That's a stinger; an ex existing seamlessly without you.

4.12.2014. 19.50
Voice record activated
Noah: The group is well known to the waiters and back-room staff.
    They're eating and drinking. Look to have settled in for the evening.
    On further examination, I can confirm that Tommaso Bellini is
    not among the group.
Voice record deactivated

I'm irritated. Because Noah's not building the scene at all. When did these mystery waiters arrive? What are the diners eating? How can you confirm that Tommaso Bellini is not among them? Have you checked their ears? Very specifically, I described Tommaso's – he has the genotype Ee, so his earlobes are detached and quite fleshy. What about his beauty spots? They're a giveaway. I drew Noah a map of his moles.

4.12.2014. 20.20
Voice record activated
Noah: [Too close to the phone]. The mountain has come to Muhammad.
    The mountain has come to Muhammad.
Voice record deactivated

This would be admissible, yet embarrassing in a court of law. PIs should maintain a neurotically PC code of conduct. To the transcriber – never editorialise or make sarcastic notes in your account. It's not the place for it.

4.12.2014. 20.27
Voice record activated
Noah: I'm going in. [15 seconds of rustling. 116 seconds of indistinguishable male voices. No distinguishable emotion or topic of conversation established. What with Noah having put the phone back into his fucking pocket]
[50 seconds of Italian, cutlery on china plates, a champagne cork. A scraping of metal along the floor]
Tommaso Bellini: Can I sit?
[POSITIVE ID! The rise and fall of his tenor actually made me yap]
[The chink of glasses]
Noah: The Scots never refuse a wee dram.

I pause the recording.
Can I sit? Can I sit? Can I sit?
Tommaso's precise cadence and musical accent bounce around my skull, nothing occupying the cavity, just the echo of him. Maybe this is the place to stop. *Can I sit?* No news is good news.

When referring to an event/issue that is not clear to everyone reading the transcript, use numbered asterisks and footnotes.

I waver before tapping play.

Tommaso: Then I suggest our cultures have a lot in common. [A second clink of glasses] In vino veritas. Where is she?
Noah: [Pause] Not here.
Tommaso: In Italy?
Noah: No. She'll keep her word.

Tommaso: Is she . . . OK?

Noah: That girl will never be OK. [*A considered guess: he's tapping his temple*] Tommaso, you have a mother, right?

Tommaso: [*Silence. Nothing, zilch, nada*]

Noah: Well, I don't.

Tommaso: And?

Noah: I envy you in ways you can't yet imagine. One day, you'll know, though. And when you're where I am, and don't have a mother any more, I hope you get solace in having known her name.

Tommaso: You're starting to piss me off.

Noah: In Scotland, we call it bonding.

Tommaso: How do you know her?

Noah: My story for a name.

Tommaso: Are you lovers?

Noah: [*Sounds bored*] She's moved on from you, if that's what you're asking. I can guarantee she'll never contact you again.

Tommaso: Are you lovers?

Noah: Pal, if you don't mind me saying, it's a bit late now, worrying about that. She fucked off, like you told her to. Yet, despite my advice, she is risking life and limb to help out your selfish arse.

Tommaso: My friend, you haven't got a clue.

Noah: You'd be surprised. For fuck's . . . the woman thinks the sun shines out of your arse, man. Just tell me Bambi Campanella's real name. The one on her first ever birth certificate. Then we'll be gone.

Tommaso: Who's we?

Noah: [*Pause*] Take it in the royal way.

Tommaso: The what way?

Noah: She's a lesbian now.

[*Tommaso sounds like he's spitting liquid at Noah. There's the scraping of chairs*]

Tommaso: [*Unintelligible shouting*] Serviettes?

Noah: I'm fine. Leave it.

Tommaso: [Menacing] You coming here was a mistake. You're not doing your girlfriend any favours.

Noah: Lucky for you, pal, she's about to do you one.

Tommaso: What are you talking about?

Noah: Flo's chanced upon information on a man who wants you dead. I told her you weren't worth risking her life for. *[40 seconds of rustling]* And she's not my girlfriend. *[10 seconds of rustling]*. I've lost my wallet.

Tommaso: [Too flippant] I have enemies. It wouldn't surprise me.

Noah: Right. *[Pause]* That's it? *[Pause]* I'll tell Flo you're as concerned about your own mother as hers? *[Rustling]*

Tommaso: My mother?

Noah: A guy's stalking your castle, apparently. Flo's concerned your mum will get caught in the crossfire. What's that?

Tommaso: Your wallet. It's been interesting meeting you, Noah Steensen. I hope, for your personal safety, you are who your credit cards say you are.

Noah: [Laughs] You for real? I promised I'd give you this. *[Pause]* Take it, man. Her contact details, if you decide to, whatever. She's closed down the private-investigation practice, so you can't contact her through that any more. Now give me my wallet.

[A LONG pause]

Tommaso: Remind me of the name of that?

Noah: Of what?

Tommaso: The private-investigation practice?

Noah: [Backtracking] It was a girly whim. Never got off the ground.

Tommaso: Florence Love – after the urban settlement, not the nurse – is a private investigator?

Noah: [Mumbling] I don't like your attitude.

Tommaso: Jiro! Prendi a Jiro! Ho bisogno di Jiro, ora! Goodbye, Noah Steensen. Consider us bonded.

[Methodical rustling, 1,340 steps, intermittent exclamations of 'Prick!' and 'Total prick!']

Noah: Taxi!
[Unmethodical rustling]
<u>*Voice record deactivated*</u> *[abruptly]*

I am incandescent with rage.

While Noah snores beside me, I lie in the dark, my arms folded so tightly I'm getting cramp in a bicep. We have just had our biggest argument ever.

'Are you totally mad?' His key barely in the door, I was shouting. 'Going in all guns blazing? Do you know who he is?'

'Yes. He doesn't know who you are, though. You forgot to tell him about your job.'

'There are a lot of reasons a girl doesn't tell you about her job. For example, the fact she once specialised in entrapment only to be outed by the red tops.' I stamped my foot – a girl would get it. 'I never told him at the beginning and then it became, I don't know, the norm that I wasn't one. Like he's in any position to be precious – he forgot to tell me he was heir to a crime syndicate.'

'He is a prick,' stated Noah.

'You're a prick. Tommaso was good to me and Michael.' I sounded juvenile, especially when I said, 'To show I could trust him, he told me the hugest secret. The biggest I have ever kept.'

'What was it?'

I flared my nostrils. 'Never.'

This is what he told me.

Tommaso has a secret middle name. Named after his father's best friend, Massimo, who's in hiding for the rest of his life, having enraged the mafia. He preached the wrong tenet – that there were options for the community's children other than joining the Firm. It was too catchy an idea. Rocco continues to secretly protect his childhood friend, despite himself being a working crime lord. When I met Father Massimo, I saw first-hand why. He had the aura of the Pope. He was also the first person to ban me from Italy indefinitely.

Noah didn't push me for any information whatsoever. Took off his shoes and socks as though I wasn't there.

I hate the type of argument where one of you refuses to cooperate. 'And *why* would you insinuate that I was your girlfriend?'

He told a blister on his toe, 'I insinuated you and he were over, which you are, which is the exact reassurance he needed.' He glanced up. 'Giving it the big I Am – what type of arsehole thieves your wallet?'

'The waiter will have borrowed it, and Tommaso *is* the big I Am. Noah, he has your name. Flight records will show exactly where we got off. He'll definitely have a contact at easyJet. He'll know everything about you by now.'

He stood up. 'Why? He's never looked into you. Otherwise, he'd have known about your sordid past.'

He had a point. I've googled Tommaso to within an inch of his life. Everyone loves a stalker when you fancy them back. Yet Tommaso was failing to be one.

'You told him I was a lesbian. That I never wanted to see him again.'

'I put a line under it.'

'You went off script.'

'It was a diversionary tactic.'

'Because you said *we*. *We*. The royal *we*.'

In an instant, Noah's eyes switched colour – their blue flooding with black iris. 'Am I here to help you and the pretty boy get back together? Because you sold it differently. That we were ascertaining your mother's real name. To find out about our parents, once and for all.'

'But we cannot do it without Tommaso's help. He knows

her real name. He also understands what it would mean to me.'

'The guy broke up with you, then threatened your life.'

'Anyone would think you're jealous of him.'

'*What?*'

Yes, I fought the urge to continue arguing. Yes, I was aware that I don't have to be the star of every scene. Yes, my need to have the last word can be counterproductive. Still, I shrugged. 'Unrequited love. Probably.'

'With who? *You?*' That made his mouth laugh. Not his eyes. 'I would rather head-butt a filleting knife.'

There followed an uncomfortable minute. Noah undressed to his boxers, without taking his eyes off me. It was quite the issue-laden striptease. I tried not to look, but he was too nakedly angry.

Once in bed, he warned me, 'Your ego is out of control.' Then turned every light off, using the switch between our beds.

It's not! I shouted at him, using my mind. *It's kooky and over-compensative.*

I'm genuinely telepathic, because Noah shuts my brain up, too. 'Florence. Go the hell to sleep.'

I didn't. How could I?

It's 4 a.m. Still, I clench my arm muscles and stew. Tommaso may be out of the equation, but there are other routes of enquiry. There have to be. Currently, however, they fail to present themselves.

Stalagmite

The next morning, I breakfast alone. My footsteps ricochet around the space as I do slow laps of a table. It heaves with breads, meats, cheeses, granola, homemade yogurts and pickles, freshly harvested fruits and vegetables. There's enough for thirty. It makes me feel sad and guilty. For their lack of customers. For my inability to make a dent in the feast when people starve to death. For the attentiveness of the two waiters who stand poised, excited to see my reaction to their fayres.

When Noah's footsteps gatecrash the silence, I'm a little relieved. 'Why didn't you wake me?' he asks.

'Don't do morning arguing. My mouth takes a few hours to warm up.'

'Thank God for that.' He takes a plate, looks at the options. 'Wow. Where to start?'

It's a rhetorical question. He enthusiastically constructs quite the food mountain. When I join him back at the table, he points his knife and talks with his mouth full. 'You fucked me off last night. For that, I'm sorry.'

'Is that an apology?'

He rocks his neck. 'An explanation.'

This is why it's definitely an apology . . .

He transfers a slice of cured prosciutto from his plate to mine, jutting his chin at it; I'm to try it. He fills my tea – adds a dash of milk. When a waiter asks if we'd like a port shot, Noah nods at me: 'Give her mine. She likes to get her drinking done early in the day.'

'One less thing to think about,' I say.

Noah's smile is sheepish. 'Look, Florence, I've been thinking. A *lot.*'

'When?'

'All night.'

I stop him there. 'No. You snored all night.'

'Not all night.'

'The rest of the time, you twitched.'

He takes a huge mouthful of unbuttered bread. 'In between snoring and twitching, I got some thinking done.'

'You also do a rhythmic click at the back of your throat . . .'

'I was a dick. You need to grieve a little. I get it – you fell for the guy.'

I down the port shot. 'I've decided I'm staying here for a bit. I feel closer to the truth, geographically.' I shrug. 'And I've nowhere else to go.'

Noah stops chewing. Looks at me across the table. His nod is decided. 'Tommaso knows we're here now. Makes sense to hang around.'

'That's too risky.' My smile is huge.

'If you don't want to die, it's the only option. I'll stay, too.' He resumes chewing. 'In the meantime, we need to get out, forget everything; some you-and-me time.'

I tut. 'There you go again.'

'What?'

'Coming on to me.'

Noah is unnecessarily stringent. 'Not now or ever. Think of it as team-building.'

I like the sound of that.

Bonding can be achieved via the mutual participation in a new experience. Clinging to a team mate for emotional support takes a relationship up a notch.

Those who wing-walk together, stay together.

My issue with height precludes the wing walk. Caves,

however, are a definite goer – not ones you get to via a pothole, nor ones in zones of seismic activity. A spacious cave – one through which Indiana Jones could drive out-of-control carts.

Postojna Caves.

The English-speaking tour guide is called Drago. Small, articulate and informative, he has no time for the less agile. The oldies are left out of the factual loop. My deep respect for the elderly means I wait behind. Explain what they've missed.

'Biggest tourist attraction in Slovenia, UNESCO world-heritage site, twenty-one kilometres of passages, galleries and halls.' I chivvy them along. 'This tour is riddled with danger, but they haven't lost a tourist yet. Don't take photos or touch a thing. He hopes we're not afraid of heights, because we'll be crossing a skinny bridge that dangles fifty metres above a raging underground river.' I point, strictly. 'I did not know that. If I had, I'd have plumped for a day at the stud farm.'

They laugh. 'I'm not joking.' I make them aware.

Yet the underground passages and halls are both roomy and cosy, everything drenched in an oily yellow, like chicken skin. The stalagmites and stalactites are intriguing – some caterpillar-sized; others the dimensions of a Doric column.

'This place reminds me of the Penis Museum,' says Noah.

I snort. 'Where's that?'

'Reykjavik – Helen and I loved the place.'

'Did your son go, too?'

'It's an exhibition of cocks.'

'To Iceland.' Clocking a little girl about to fondle the walls, I catch her arm. 'No touching. That's a very strict rule.' Then I turn back to Noah. 'Are they actual human penises?'

'Some. But mostly animal ones – whales, elephants; the bigger the better.'

Now he's said it, every rock looks like pickled phallus.

Drago tells us that some have names, a result of their distinctive appearance. 'Can you guess what we call this one?' he asks.

'The Leaning Tower of Pisa,' says an over-enthusiastic German girl.

'The Leaning Tower of Penis,' Noah mumbles back.

For him, that is hilarious; the kraut certainly thinks so. She swishes her blond hair away from her shoulders, revealing a naked neck, laughing like he's Henning Wehn (the only German comedian I know). Distracted, I fondle a stalagmite's cone – that feels unexpectedly spiritual, handling a rock formation born of the Middle Palaeolithic period, which happened half a million years ago.

'Oops,' I say quietly.

UNESCO will never know. God might, but I suggest, if he exists, he'd be pleased that someone is revering one of his miracles.

We continue walking. Noah tells me about his mum. 'She was just like you. Neurotic or phobic, I don't know the right word.'

'Neither.'

'Let's say irrational,' he nods. 'Spaces, heights, spiders, water – you name it, she was allergic to it.' He smiles. 'She got stung by a wasp on the Eiffel Tower once. Getting her down was hilarious. Not for her.'

'You look happy talking about her.'

'Happy's pushing it. My biggest memory is watching our backs. You feel that tension as kids.'

There's a truth. A child is as in tune to a parent's mood as they are yours, recognising every facial expression exactly as it's meant – fear, loss, confusion, grief.

We've stopped at a mound of bat shit. Drago tells us, 'The droppings are called guano and an entire ecosystem depends on it . . .'

'What did your parents tell you, exactly?' I ask. 'Because you literally left Dorset overnight.'

'Dad did. We followed a few months after.'

'Moving a whole family takes preparation, and the coroner's report is suggestive of premeditation.'

He shrugs. 'I'm not so sure. It was a whirlwind. I remember their faces. Everything changed that night.' He pauses. 'Hannah and I were told Dad was dead. We went to his funeral.'

I gasp. 'That's dreadful.'

'He was depressed, Mum said. One of his business deals had gone sour. We were told he'd invested in new technologies in the Far East. I grew up thinking the Triads wanted us dead. As long as we never told anybody about our old life, we'd be safe. That was life north of the border – my sister and I living in fear. What a crock of shit.'

Noah and I glare at the dunghill until the elderly catch us up. 'It's bats' poo and feeds an ecosystem,' I say. 'Noah, you really need to cheer up. Not at this moment. In general.'

'Sorry?'

I show him a placatory palm. 'Your melancholia's catching. It's not your fault, it's your star sign. Doesn't mean, however, you have to be lumbered with those traits.'

'What are you talking about?' He frowns.

'That!' I point at his eyebrows. 'Virgos are notorious non-laughers. They don't bond easily with other star signs, apart from Librans, who are forgiving of a lack of demonstrable emotion. Tell me about your son?'

Pretending to have spotted something, he tries to march ahead, but I hold on to his arm. 'It's perfectly fine – actually, it's quite *polite* – to ask after people's kids. Now, tell me about him? I'm genuinely interested.'

'Ah, you know, he's just a bairn—'

I interrupt him to point, alarmed. 'No way. *No* way. That's not safe or legal. We haven't got harnesses.'

The jewel in the crown of this particular cave system is a gaping chamber through which the River Postojna runs a raucous route. A hundred metres tall – this hole is ideally suited for a megacity of hobbits, living in its sides, their crooks like homely corporate boxes at the O2.

'I can't continue,' I tell the old people.

'Just look at your shoes,' states Noah.

But too quickly our path begins to weave itself along the cave's sides. The drops are too sheer. There is no way I'm getting out of here alive.

Noah, however, holds my hand like a dad and pulls.

'My son's called Callum. He's like me – hair, physique, temperament.'

'Is he doing well at school?' I demand.

'He's three.'

'That's too young for school.'

I study the inside of Noah's elbow, which is called the cubital fossa. I tell it: 'The outside of your elbow is called the wenis, like penis – that's where the word "wiener" comes from; that and the German sausage . . . Tell me about the car accident – the one that killed your parents?'

I don't know what his face does, but his voice falters. 'There was no foul play, if that's what you're getting at. My mother was driving. She was a liability behind the wheel.'

Drago shouts, 'Please be careful. The moisture from the river can make the paths slippery.'

I whimper.

Noah asks me quickly, 'How do you kill a circus?'

'Go for the juggler. Noah, this place is still too tall.'

'And, yes, I have split from my wife.'

That makes me look up at him. 'All the evidence points towards it,' I say.

'Yes, it does,' he agrees.

'I am sorry for your loss.'

'She's not dead.'

'It's sometimes better if they were. Whose fault was it?'

He takes a moment to admit it. 'Mine.'

I lose my footing, stumble on nothing other than the fear of falling. My scream is pathetic. Noah unlocks our hands in order to put a fierce arm around my shoulder. 'You really do have a fear of heights.'

I don't. I suffer from barophobia, which is a fear of the profound. I zone in on Drago, who's stopped in a cave lay-by. I peer between and over heads to hear him better.

'. . . the reason we can't touch them? The oil and dirt on our fingers alter the surface tension at the exact place the water clings. We're toxic to the stalagmite. Death turns it a startling black.'

I look back, appalled. I've no idea how long it takes for murdered limestone to turn black, but I refuse to be here when it happens. For two and a half thousand more steps, my barophobia is replaced by a more maverick shuffle, and I whisper Hail Mary's, until Our Lady is sufficiently satisfied to beam a thin shaft of daylight at us.

'Glory be to God,' I tell her.

In response, she offers unto us a cavernous sinkhole into which the sun funnels warmth.

'You better now?' Noah checks when we're waiting at the foot of the funicular. I nod, grateful. He leans into my ear. 'Good. Now let go of my arm. It's cramping my style.'

'No,' I tell him, because Noah has noticed the over-enthusiastic German. The sun makes her hair the most golden shade of white. Younger than me, perfect blue eyes, sleekly Amazonian – you'd want her on your side in a fight. I remind Noah, 'We're on a mission.'

'And I'm having some downtime,' he winks, untangling my arm from his.

*

Our taxi driver is called Ludwig and can't speak English, though he can say, 'Hel-*low*, hel-*low*,' in a high-pitched voice, which is amusing, given Ludwig's a bear of a human. He also drives with the speed and precision of a stuntman. The Little Trees pine air freshener barely moves.

Noah has used Ludwig before – they greet one another like brothers.

'For somebody who's tight as a tick, you spend a lot on taxis.' We get into the back seat.

'I'm a courier. I like to get from A to B fast.'

Something dawns on me. 'Was it Ludwig who brought you back last night?'

'Yes,' he says, defensively.

I look at Ludwig's reflection in the rear-view mirror. He hasn't a clue what we're saying; his eyes don't flinch.

I point at Noah's mobile phone, specifically its voice-recording facility. 'You called, "Taxi!" After you left Tommaso, you said "prick" twenty-three times and "Taxi!" once.'

'All right,' Noah confesses. 'I hailed a cab, an Indian guy.'

I should tell him off. 'There are a lot of Indians in Trieste.'

'Apparently, they came with the shipbuilding industry . . .'

I interrupt, 'Forty-five, married, father of three. A ship's engineer by day, a local-studies know-it-all of an evening? What was his name?'

'I don't know.'

Using an earbud each, we re-listen to Tommaso's last words. They're in the background, and spoken in Italian, so we understand little. Yet I grasp one word.

Jiro.

Tommaso says it three times.

In the whole world, I know of only one Jiro – a driver employed by the Bellinis.

'He's from Bangladesh.' Adrenalin makes me laugh:

Tommaso knows where I am. 'Lovely guy. Jiro's a regular cabbie around Portopiccolo Sistiana. I've had him before.'

On arrival at Hotel Krasna, Noah shakes Ludwig's huge hand with both of his and alights the car without paying. I settle up – give the driver twenty-five euros in return for a handwritten receipt.

Though Ludwig holds on to it for a while. We have a polite tug of war, before he lets go. Then he says, in his weird soprano, 'You. You.' Points urgently at Noah's retreating back. 'No, him.'

That evening, Noah and I dine in our room, trays on laps. Noah is doing social media, while I wonder about Ludwig's farewell. Perhaps he was warning me about Noah? I look across at him in his single bed. Mouth ajar, he looks harmless enough. Perhaps it is a message from Tommaso – discovering my job title must have piqued his interest. I chuckle; this could pan out.

'What's funny?' Noah asks.

'Just thinking about today.' Accidentally, I miss my mouth. Red wine drips down my neck and décolletage. I look at it pool in my cleavage. 'What a waste.'

The bathroom. I undress, throwing the clothes into the corner, emptying the pockets of my jeans, put a five-euro note on the toilet seat. Am about to throw away Ludwig's receipt when I notice an anomaly. The date, time and location are wrong.

It says, *Petek, 5 December, 10.30 a.m, Pokopališče, Lokev 12.*

This is definitely my receipt – I watched him scribble it. Sitting on cold tiles, I fire up my phone. Punch *Petek* into Google's search bar. It translates as Friday, which indeed tomorrow is. Next. *Pokopališče.* My fingers tremble a little, my thumb suddenly too big – I hit the wrong letters. When, finally, the translation arrives, I baulk.

Only you, Ludwig had been trying to say. His receipt being one of two things – an invitation or a prediction. My destination is the same, whichever. *Pokopališče* is the Slovenian word for graveyard.

Bora

As instructed, I've come alone. Noah thinks I'm at the Tabor Military Museum, a hundred yards from our hotel. He has no interest in Slovenian history, so remains in the room reading WISTEC the e-book.

The graveyard is a fifteen-minute walk and occupies a small, square plot on a lonely edge of the village nestled secretly among undulating fields, stone walls and sheep.

Apart from necromass and cattle, I am totally alone.

This is what being alone sounds like: a drainage wind. That's the meteorological phrase for the wind that shows no respect for hairspray or elegantly draped scarves. This particular one is called the bora.

If the sky is clear, it's called the bora *chiara*; the light bora. Today, fat clouds dip their bellies at the hilltops. Bora *scura* – the dark bora – is upon us, and she's a witch. Whipping me with my own hair, she makes the strands as vicious as samphire. A frozen wind, expelled by the Antarctic, simply passing through, bora *scura*'s goal is one-fold: the Adriatic.

The jitters threaten to make me vomit, so I sit on a bench and wish I'd worn a hat. And an earpiece. And had Michael looking out for me in a secret corner. Currently, I could scream full pelt and hear myself only vaguely.

When, finally, the bora has gone, be it for three seconds or an hour, it's like the mute button's switched on. You hear the odd car sweeping past in the distance. An eagle's scream. The village church, sending a raucous memo every fifteen minutes, reassuring its congregation: *You're not alone, even if this is the closest you'll ever feel to it.*

Other things going against me:

- There's no CCTV.

- I am the cemetery's only visitor.

- Nobody knows I'm here.

- About to be visited by the mafia; there's an open grave in the corner, covered by plyboard and a shovel.

- My watering eyes wash away eyeliner and concealer applied earlier with such intention – to look irresistible and impossible not to love. Being attractive was the one thing I had going for me.

I'm doing deep breathing when I hear his voice.

A momentary silence makes his cadence pristine – it's as though I listen to him through a telephonist's headpiece. 'So the gap-month girl is actually a private investigator. And not any old one, at that.'

I don't turn around. I ask my knees: 'It took you this long to google me?'

'I didn't think I had the need.'

'Well, you did,' I say. 'Assuming you ever gave a shit.'

Having considered this for a moment, his answer is sincere. 'Florence Love, I am not a masochist.'

I tell my thighs, 'That's something I never get about boys. Their inability to dwell on the past. How they successfully park their feelings then function perfectly well without you.'

'Woman, I did not google you because it would've hurt my heart.'

The relief. I stand and turn to face him, barely avoiding a Victorian half-faint back on to the bench.

Tommaso is more effulgent than I remember. His nose more Roman. The nostrils more equally proportioned. His green eyes more piercing. His lashes blacker and denser. His philtrum more defined.

'Look at you with your hat hair.' I shake my head at the magnificence of him.

He shows me his Vespa helmet and says, 'You look astonishing.'

'It's my deck-of-a-speedboat look.'

'You wear it well.'

'Stop it.' I smile.

'Stop what?'

'Looking at me like that.' Tommaso studies small portions of my face; time has apparently watered me down, too. 'You're making me want to flirt.'

Taking a step back, he rubs his hair, then walks towards a gravestone. For all its power, the bora cannot diminish Tommaso's aura. His gait is a masterclass in presence – currently, it swamps this cemetery, Lokev and all of Slovenia.

I join him. Read the tombstone. It puts a dampener on things.

Andrej, Katerina and Zora are just a few of the Janovicks buried beneath the marble hearth. On top sit colourful glass candle-holders with chains, like a priest's thurible. And a golden urn of blush-pink lilies lies on its side. Tommaso leans over to stand it back up. For a while we look at the bent flowers.

The wind picks up. Tommaso shouts at the Janovicks: 'You hid things from me.'

The wind drops instantly, awaiting my response.

'I'd given up being a PI when we met,' I explain. 'Tommaso, the stuff in the papers was bad. I wanted you to like me for me. Please don't take it personally. I dug myself a hole.'

For a millisecond, we hear the bora before she arrives.

'You entrapped Scat Delaney?' Tommaso shouts through a tidal wave of air.

I place a hand on my heart. Shout back. 'It was a total accident.'

'Like me? Was I an accident, too?'

'*No!*' I shriek. 'You were the most chemically complete interaction I've had with a man. I didn't know who you were then. I still don't.' When the air is quiet, I tip my chin upwards. 'Go on, Il Capo. Let's get it over with. Ice-pick me in the neck. Carrier bag over the head. Whatever it is that you lot do. I'm sick and tired of it all.'

'You're a very dramatic woman,' he mumbles.

I point at the empty burial hole. 'And if that's for me, it's not what I had in mind.'

'No,' he agrees.

'I don't know any of the other dead bodies. Mourners would be non-existent. It's not nearly magnificent enough.'

'I could *never* kill you,' he states.

'Really?'

'I'd get someone else to do it.' I can't be sure if he jokes, he turns away too quickly. Shows me the graves. 'Know why I chose this place, Florence?'

'To scare me, and it worked.'

'*Cavolo!*' He puts a gentle hand on my shoulder. 'Because you *love* a graveyard tour. We both do.'

That makes me feel bad. We spent our first date admiring Hadrian's mausoleum playing Graveyard Top Trumps, trying to outdo one another regarding the celebrity graves we'd visited.

'But I agree.' He nods. 'Considering the context, it looks sinister.'

I reassure him, 'It's romantic, now you've explained it.'

For a moment, I think he might pull me into his chest

and smell my scalp. But he goes back to being a stranger, just like that, just like last time.

'My problem is, when a private investigator doesn't tell me they're a private investigator, I wonder things.'

'Like what?'

'Bullshit doesn't fall far from the arse.'

'Who even said that?'

'My father.'

'About me?'

'No, not you.'

'Tommaso, you're doing it again. Talking in riddles. All the sinister innuendo. You're cleverer than that. I loved you better before.' That hurts his feelings, so I continue. 'Did I make you up? Where's the you who didn't want to follow in his father's footsteps? The you who was a chef, who spent a stag do visiting the Shelley and Keats Museum, who named the angels on the Ponte Sant'Angelo after the Spice Girls. The you who looked after Michael, like he was your flesh and blood. The you who is not you any more.'

The grip with which he suddenly cradles my face is too firm. Whatever his intentions, I won't shut up.

'In the absence of that you, what have I got to lose? I might as well scream it from the rooftops. *I'm Bambi Love's daughter!* It might get me killed. It might also mean I die knowing *something*.'

He mutters, 'Think of Michael. Your father. Your boyfriend.'

'I'm sick of thinking about everyone else. And he is *not* my boyfriend.'

I can't say when our faces got this close; we're an inhalation away from kissing when Tommaso lets go of my cheeks. 'The man's in love with you.'

'Probably. What's your point?'

'Get away from him tonight. Don't tell him we're meeting.'

I reiterate: 'He's not my boyfriend.'

'He hopes to be,' he warns. 'He'll do this by making you feel interesting. Do not pander to your ego. Taking you for romantic walks in the caves. You are not interesting. He just wants to make love to you.'

He had me followed all day. My stomach smiles. 'And that bothers you why?'

'Because *I* want to make love to you.'

My heart purrs. My pitch too seductive. 'What exactly *are* you here for, Tommaso?'

He frowns, his own pitch dropping onerously. 'My mother. Her mortal danger.'

'Of course.' I frown, too. 'And, in return, you'll give me Bambi's name?'

My callousness makes him smart. 'You're using Jolana's life as a bargaining tool?'

I shrug. Mourn the loss of my moral compass. Explain, weakly, 'I'm allowed a mother, too.'

Eventually, he nods, coldly. 'This evening. Nine o'clock. Lipika. The stud farm.' Walking away, he shouts back, 'You'll tell me everything. *Capiche?*'

I don't reply *It's quite urgent, about your mother, I could just tell you now.* Tommaso and I are too decided on one thing – the overriding desire to see one another again is muddying everything.

'*Capiche?*' I shout back. 'You're such a stereotype.'

'She *will* be the death of me,' he yells at the hills.

Noah and I huddle over his laptop in the hotel restaurant. There are four other diners this evening, so we chat with relieved abandon.

'Your dad must have struggled sometimes, with the type of people he had to run around after. I'd be tempted to shop half of them.'

'You get that from your mum.' He smiles.

I'm too light of mood to be snippy. 'We know nothing about anything yet. Bambi may have no connection with the mafia at all.' Leaning across him, I scroll down the page. 'They're a dubious bunch.'

Examples of high-profile women in witness protection:

Lori Fortier – involved in the Oklahoma City bombing.

Gloria Abad – a Portuguese Hell's Angel.

Maxine Carr – provided a false alibi for her child-murdering boyfriend. Free now, she has a sparkling new identity and a lifetime injunction to safeguard it.

'You smell nice,' says Noah.

'I showered.' I brush it off. Take a walnut from a plate of foraged nuts. Tell him my plans. 'You know I practise Ayurveda?'

'I did not, hen.'

'Well, I do. So I'm going to find a quiet place. I need to *earth*, then evaluate and meditate.'

He nods earnestly. 'Very good, Grasshopper.'

My excuse, although brilliant, poses a problem. You do not evaluate and meditate while looking hot. That rules out make-up or any change of clothes in front of Noah.

'Shouldn't be more than a couple of hours,' I say.

'OK, my weirdo friend. Wishing you and your zen well.'

He called me his friend. I feel disloyal. 'I might eat in a local bar, then sit on a hill. Assuming I can get wifi.'

Key to lying: don't over-explain yourself.

'Most importantly, I need to check in with Dad and Michael. Especially Dad. It's been long enough . . .'

Noah saves me from myself. 'Please stop vocalising all your thoughts. If you need me, I'm here. Call me or scream.' Noah nods towards a window. It's opened barely a crack. 'It's a small place, I'll hear you.'

I frown. 'Who are you – Batman? How will you find me in all that dark?'

'I will find you,' he tells me, very definitely.

Make-up, earrings, Chanel No. 5 tester in a pocket, and a KFC wipe to remove make-up on return. A beret in my bag. And a merino-wool throw, a hefty splash of apricot to break up my navy-blue ski jacket.

There's a small church a spit from Hotel Krasna. Its toilet, once public, is now locked and derelict. The door's wood is rotten. Using my torch, I knock out its lock. Inside, I use the ancient mirror to get ready.

Entrance to the stud farm is via a tree-lined boulevard boarded by white picket fences. It's American-looking, like Southfork Dallas. I pad its tarmacked driveway for a kilometre at least. And I'm grateful for it.

I walked here. All the way. Forty-three minutes of tripping through undulating countryside, often as black as death, my mind on nothing other than Tommaso. When I hit concrete, I had to stop myself from jogging.

The rich whiff of manure is comforting. As are the snorts, snickers and neighs. I can't see the horses, but they're out there somewhere in the meadows, defiant as I in darkness's face.

My breast vibrates. I pull my phone free.

Daddy Love, flashes up. A dad in shining armour; I'm unexpectedly relieved to see his name – assuming he has phoned to apologise.

But it's Michael's voice who says in a loud whisper, 'She's got ashes, Flo. Dead people's ashes.'

'Who?'

'Annie.'

'You're in her house?'

'We think she's either a serial killer or a grave robber.'

'Dad's there, too?'

'No. James is.'

'Hello,' says James Jardine.

'Am I on fucking speakerphone? Why are you on Dad's phone?'

'He left it at Annie's. I came to collect it. That's my alibi.'

'Where's Annie?'

James says, 'Singing classic show songs at Christchurch Cathedral. The ashes have dates on them.'

'James, go home,' I state.

'No.' Michael forgets to whisper. 'He's being my partner. It's OK – we're just doing it as a hobby.'

'Doing *what*?'

'Gathering dirt.'

James says, 'Gathering ashes, more like.'

'Tell me you didn't use my bump lock?'

'I did not use your bump lock. We came in through the roof.'

'What *the what*?'

'We think they're trophies,' says James.

'Of her evilness,' adds Michael.

I stop walking. 'Or maybe they're members of her family who have passed.'

'One hundred and sixty-seven of them?' asks James.

'Or maybe they're something completely normal,' I say, strictly. 'James. Go home and straight to bed, and never speak of this to another person. Michael. Take samples and give them to Vee.'

'Why?' they both ask.

'She's a Fellow of the Chartered Institute of Legal Executives and has a degree in death. Her contact details are in the Asset File.'

'OK. Bye.' Michael hangs up.

What the hell? I try to call him back, but the line's busy. Confused, I message Vee to forewarn her.

Just humour him, I ask. Which is disloyal, because Michael's got me thinking, too.

Lipica stud farm is fortified by a tall ribbon of stone wall, acres long; the type that flanks an abbey or a prison. It's too tall to scale, and I've no idea where we're to meet until I arrive at the car park. The farm's entrance is blighted by an ugly hotel – seventies corporate, all concrete and glass walls, cosy as an open fridge.

Not romantic at all.

I shake my hair free of my hat and begin to ascend its steps when a sharp whistle whips my head to the right. Tommaso stands beneath a tree in the car park, the stark light illuminating just one side of him.

I walk towards him. 'You look like the Phantom of the Opera.'

'In a good way?'

'Is there a bad way?'

'Then I shall stand in the half-shade more.'

One metre apart, I stop quite abruptly. He has that combination of features that makes you want to whimper. 'Hello, again.'

He does a little salute, just as he did on the evening we first met. Embarrassed, he pushes the rogue hand into his pocket and becomes formal. 'What did you tell lover-boy?'

'I'm locating my zen. Noah's all right.'

'I hate his name.'

'Well, I love it.'

'I bet you loved the name Scat as well.'

'I love the fact you're spitting jealous. His real name was Scott, actually.'

'Did you love him?'

Not like you. I shrug, nonchalantly. 'I can't really remember.'

'And now you're a lesbian?'

I smile. 'A beguiling mind muddies the sexual waters. You're being very possessive for a man who told me to fuck off and die.'

He pulls me to him, roughly. 'I told you to fuck off *or* you'll die.'

I relax into him. Every muscle, tendon and sliver of cartilage. My face rests on his chest, the wool of his pea coat tickling my nose; Tommaso inhaling my hair with thirsty breaths. This is how we remain for a while.

When I step away, he studies each of my eyes. Then says, 'Come. There's someone I want you to meet.'

We don't enter the stud farm through the iron gates and turnstiles. Tommaso takes us further around the wall to a small wooden door. He rattles what looks like a bunch of jail keys. 'The owners and I are friends.'

'I imagine you have a lot of those nowadays.'

But he's too busy seeing me for the first time. 'A private eye – seriously?'

'Seriously. I'm excellent at it.'

There's not a soul except us, yet it's as bright as a football stadium, and vast. Pristine training areas, stables, stone outbuildings, a chapel and a museum; meadows and paddocks as far as the eye can see.

Tommaso presents the stud farm's inner sanctum with the flourish of a ringmaster.

'It's very Hapsburg,' I say. 'Do you come here often?'

'Only when I'm wooing women.'

'It's quite the venue for a first date.'

'The private breeding preserve of noble families and their Lipizzaner's.' There's a pause. 'The dazzling white horses with the dancing feet.'

'I'm a philistine.'

'If only,' he complains, steering me through a stately maze of limestone stables. Stopping at one to yank open its door.

Inside, four silver horses. They fidget snootily. Tommaso covers the introductions.

'Björn, Benny, Anni-Frid and Agnetha. May I introduce Florence Love After the Urban Settlement Not the Nurse. I know, it's a ridiculous name. But she's a very specific woman.'

Especially, he pets the fourth horse. 'Agnetha belongs to my mother – she asked that I check on her. Who calls a horse Agnetha, uh?' He winks at Agnetha so she's aware he's joshing, then tells me a secret, 'She's *Mamma Mia!* mad. Now, let's sit.'

He lays his coat on a low bench of hay bales and we sit facing one another, cross-legged. He has to palm-punch his knees to kick-start some menace.

'My mother. She's in danger how?'

I pretend he's a client. 'There's a man who's been watching the Castilla de Friuli. I believe he's been spying on your family for some time. He's in Italy under the pretence of being a geologist. Yet he seems very apprised. A bit too apprised. He certainly knows who the Bellinis are. Most importantly, he does not like your family – not one bit.'

I start at the beginning.

'Your mother's engagement party. I went outside to smoke a cigarette and got a bit lost – only for a little while – but out of nowhere, a man appeared. He showed me the way back to the house. I realise now he was spying on you and your family. Back in England, I chanced upon some information. He's a gymnast who joined the army and was never seen again.' Tommaso appears fascinated. 'His name is Lancelot Shaw. Middle name, Edward; hails from Reading. After the event, he broke into my hotel room and left a note on my pillow. It said you were dangerous and no good, and that I should get away from you as soon as possible.'

Momentarily bamboozled, he says, 'I know him. So, how's my mother in danger?'

I squint, 'How do you know him?'

'He's one of mine.' He nods. 'Well, he was until you told me he left a love letter on your pillow telling you to fuck me off.'

'No!' I shriek, because this is terrible. I remind him of Lancelot's good points: 'The guy saved my life.'

'I thought you were just lost?'

'It was quite a slope.' I shake my head. 'If he's one of yours, why was he hiding in the woods?'

'Security and counter-surveillance.' He tells me the cons of being a Godfather. 'My father has had eighteen attempts on his life. Plus, there was a government minister at the party.' He frowns and half smiles. 'The little rat.'

I wait for elucidation. He can hardly be bothered to explain.

'Family holidays in Croatia, he was maybe fifteen and met a girl. Then I met her – I was twelve, it became my party piece.' He explains his beef. 'When he wasn't doing acrobatics, Lance sucked joy from the air, you know?' I do. 'Once, he hacked into my *World of Warfare* account and sold off my weapons stash. I put eight lizards in his pant drawer for that. When his nose outgrew his body, I didn't steal his girlfriends any more – they were too ugly. He blamed me for it.'

'His nose?'

'Everything. Lancelot has Napoleon issues. Lucky for him, our mothers are close.'

'But he's English?' I argue weakly.

'And my third cousin. Italians live all over Europe these days.'

'Don't kill him,' I beg.

He waves an exhausted hand. He has no plans to. His eyes

suggest a more puerile revenge. The type he and Lancelot have no doubt fostered since childhood. The type that binds two alphas for life.

Heat collects in my cheeks. 'He's no danger to your mother, then?'

Tommaso looks sorry for me. Desperation is a woman's worst perfume. I wish he'd say something – the silence is excruciating. As is his facial expression – it's now telling me I'm useless at private investigation. 'Florence. Is that it?'

I become absorbed in my thumbnail and quote God. 'Better a thousand times careful than once dead.'

Tommaso takes the thumb away from me. Using a light finger, he traces a path down to my wrist. Here, he turns over my hand; begs a favour of my heart line:

'Don't make me tell you her name.'

My chin shoots up. I clench his cheeks in my hands. 'You will never see me again. I swear.'

'Then we should make love now.'

'I don't need the details. Just her name. Oh, Tommaso, please.'

'If we don't do it, we never will,' he tells my lips. '*Never.*'

'You're talking about sex?'

'No!' His firm tone unsettles the horses. 'Much more than that.'

I let go of his face so he can stand up and pace. For a while he communes silently with Agnetha, who hears him, all right – her left eye is a wide, ceramic, brown saucer. Their heads gently butt. I wonder what she says.

Mind made up, Tommaso swings around. Going by the look in his eyes, I'm sure he plans to shoot me dead. Especially when his apology is so detached.

'There are no words to describe how sorry I am, Florence Love.'

My heart stops. Completely.

Tommaso takes a deep breath. 'Ruth Andreina. There, I said it.'

'What? What did you say? Ruth And-*what?*'

'She's not who you think she is. You're chasing the dream of a woman who doesn't exist any more. Maybe she never did.'

'Ruth *Andreina?*' I demand. It means absolutely nothing.

'Ruth And-*reeeina,*' he rolls his r's.

'That's it?'

'That's all you will need.'

'Ruth Andreina.' It means absolutely everything. 'Thank you,' I nod, kissing his hand like he's a cardinal, forgetting to savour a thing about his skin. I boil with questions, all of which he's unprepared to answer.

Tommaso wants our goodbye to be heartfelt and certainly more sexual. Pulling me to him. I shake my head. 'I need to do some research.'

'Not now,' Tommaso begs a little. 'Wait an hour at least.'

Yes, I have grieved for Tommaso Bellini for an entire month. Yes, that month of progress has been voided by seeing him again – I will have to start again from scratch. Just not today.

'One of us has a mother to fathom,' I say quietly. 'Find me, if you need me – you have the resources. And the permission to stalk me for the rest of my life.'

An expression – brand new to me – arrives on his face. Momentary devastation; I think he might cry, but the return of his game-face is breakneck. 'Only if you never stalk me back,' he states.

A Biggie

I walk home using more dangerous routes. The roads. They don't have pavements or lighting. I don't jump from view when I hear a car approach, even though I'm a woman alone, and unhinged people are indigenous to all areas of human population, and often have cars. I don't care. Just try out her name on my tongue.

'*Ruth Andreina.*'

I play with the sounds, do a lot of tongue-work. By the time I arrive back at Hotel Krasna, I'm in a deeply disappointed place. Her name doesn't sound like hers. It sounds like a stranger's, which is impossible because I knew her once.

10.42 p.m.

Noah is sitting up in bed, iPad on his lap. 'How're your chakras?' He looks up when I enter.

'Shot to pieces. What are you doing?'

'On the case. What's up with you?'

'I met Tommaso.' I put a furious hand in the air. 'It's a huge secret, of course, like everything else. So, do not get snippy with me or question my motives. It was a roaring success.'

'Lipika,' he nods. 'Tell me he didn't show you his horse?'

I frown. 'His mother's.'

His laugh is forced. 'The man is a ball of cheese.'

It's too much; he isn't. I slide down the wall and sob into my hands. 'I have her name, and I should be ecstatic, but I'm not.'

Noah moves quickly, squats beside me, wipes my snot with his T-shirt, uninterested in my mental stability. 'What is it?'

'You just let me wander off?'

'I've put a tracker on your phone. Her name, hen?'

'You, what?'

'I'm your wingman.'

'That's so devious.'

'And you smell of shite. Tell me you didn't have a tumble in the hay.'

I shake my head wearily. 'Bambi Love was born Ruth Andreina.'

He tries the name on his tongue. Over and over. Its tip fluttering up and down behind undersized front teeth, rolling his r's, sounding too Russian.

'It feels clunky, right?' I say.

Noah stands up, yanking me to my feet in the process, depositing me on the bed. 'You up for an all-nighter?'

I crinkle my nose. 'Not yet.' So he pulls the duvet over my legs and tells me to sleep.

But I listen to Slovenia, which is silent as the moon; and the soft pad of Noah's index fingers on his tablet. Eventually, I'm hoodwinked into a cruel sleep. I don't know what I dreamed about, but I'm left with a brutal sense of failure.

'What's the time?' I ask Noah.

'Four thirty-five,' he tells his iPad.

'Bet there's a hundred Ruth Andreinas. Have you tried different spellings?'

'Yes, hen. And they're mostly Facebook posts or Twitter feeds. Nobody notorious, so far.'

I shake my head. 'She's not a Twitter-feed type of mum.'

'I'm checking them all, just in case. Go back to sleep.'

'No. I need to call my dad.'

He says this softly: 'But you can't.'

'I can. Because I . . . just . . . I don't know how to feel.'

'Me, neither,' he agrees, even though this is my heartbreak and she's my mum.

'Do you think Bambi and your dad were lovers? He did a lot for her. Pretending to be dead.'

'I think that had more to do with him murdering someone.'

I agree. Because it was definitely Eric who did premeditated murder. Meaning Dad's in the clear. 'Can you just turn the light off now?'

'I'm not done.'

'Please. I don't know how to feel,' I remind him.

It's very unlike Noah to obey me. To just turn off his light and to lie awake for as long as me. Too wired, too distracted, the silence brimful of possibilities and question marks. I squash my face and ears under the pillow, and beg for sleep.

10.40 a.m.

Noah lifts his head. One eye open, he looks at our cases by the door. 'Are we off?'

'I've packed your stuff and checked under the bed and in the drawers twice. There are clothes for you in the bathroom.'

'We're going home?'

'Not on my shift.'

That makes him throw his legs out of the bed and push his boner down and to the left. In the bathroom he pisses loudly. Clears his throat, splashes his face, gargles. When he re-enters the room, he's less engorged and more alert.

'Shoot,' he tells me, hands on hips.

'First, we need a taxi.'

'To go where?'

I reassure him. 'I'll pay. And of course, you don't have to come. If you want to go home, that's fine.'

'Where to, woman?' He does an actual stamp.

'Castillo de Friuli, Noah. I'm going back to Italy.'

The taxi drops us at the bottom of a hundred steps that lead to a looming villa on a mountain's jut.

'His mum came out of her divorce well,' says Noah, as we ascend.

'She was Head of Environmental Studies at Bologna University, actually.' My bottle is waning, so I slap my cheek.

'That doesn't buy you a listed villa.'

'Or a field-studies centre. It's got a restaurant, too.' I tell him a truth. 'The Bellinis treat their exes well.'

I'm not sure how well I'll get treated now, however. The guy at reception puts me at ease – he doesn't recognise me from Adam.

'Table for two,' I say. 'Is Jolana around?'

'Yes, somewhere.' He smiles, quizzically. 'I think she made for walk.'

'Great. When she gets back, can you let her know *Florence Love* is here.'

He fails to recognise my name, pull a gun, press a secret button under the counter, instead taking us upstairs and seating us on the stone balcony that overlooks mountains, spruce, rivers and sea.

'Wow,' says Noah. 'The prick is a lucky prick. Why are we meeting his mother?'

'She liked me.'

That sounds tenuous, when said out loud. But the law of attraction is also the law of creation – quantum-mechanical fact. Which means the universe makes people click for a very good reason. Ask the ancient Babylonians.

There are just six diners in the restaurant, the atmosphere is flat, unlike the last time I was here. The eaves had heaved with chatter and mirth. I point through the pillars of the stone balcony and tell Noah, 'Just down there, that's where I pulled a whitey.'

'Classy.'

'And over there.' I wave a finger at a large table inside. 'That's where Michael lost a tooth.'

'Always drama.'

'I never solicit it.'

'No,' he says, smiling.

Immediately, I know it's her – just from the tip-tap of her shoes. Like her son, her presence supersedes her. I spot the top of her head crowning as she comes upstairs – her short bowl of a haircut idolatrising her face, like a halo. Her broad shoulders and straight back. The stretched legs of a ballerina. Her perfume, Evening Rose by Aerin – she'd worn it at her engagement party; distinguishable by a surprising mix of rose centifolia and Bulgarian rose absolute.

She's also preoccupied. Not about me being in the building – the guy downstairs hasn't told her that a Florence Love awaits. Too inattentive, she slips behind the bar to make herself an espresso, failing to clock her customers.

It takes quite the finger wave before she zones in on me.

'Florence?' she mouths, then looks either side of her. Approaching me, she kisses me hard and fast on each cheekbone. Looking at Noah, then back to me, confused, she asks, 'What are you doing here?'

'Thank you so much for seeing us.' I say it like she's Anna Pavlova and we've been granted an audience.

She hasn't granted me anything. 'Darling, Tommaso said you had split up?'

'Ruth Andreina,' I say back.

Jolana's forehead collapses. 'You've seen him? Florence, you cannot be here.'

'There's the problem. Everybody keeps telling me this, but nobody's actually killing me.'

'You might lack regard for your own life, but he's my *son*.'

I shake my head. 'He's not the one whose life's in danger.'

Her eyes suggest otherwise. 'I'm going to tell you a story.' Though, first, she leans towards Noah. 'Who are you?'

'A cousin,' he lies.

'Please leave us.' She nods.

Noah's move to a table inside is unexpectedly obsequious. Jolana leans forward, speaking quietly and at bullet-speed.

'The Mala del Brenta is also known as the Venetian mafia. You may have heard.' I shake my head. 'Based in the Veneto, and Friuli-Venezia Giulia, its structure is like the Cosa Nostra model. Only more violent.' This is delivered bluntly and with a pause. 'In the 1960s and '70s, Sicilian mafia bigwigs were sent to north-eastern Italy to live in solitary confinement; the idea – to isolate powerful Sicilian ringleaders from mafia members. Big names. Horrible people. Underworld figures, bandits, bank robbers, drug traffickers, kidnappers, assassins. These men formed new gangs. The carnage between them was unprecedented, even by Italian standards.'

She sits back, crosses her legs, because it pains her to say this. 'The Bellinis changed that. At the beginning, maybe, by being the most ruthless. Latterly, for an adjustment in work ethic. The job my son has chosen – I hate it.'

'Tell him you hate it; he can change.'

'But I understand it, too.' Her laugh is exhausted. 'Like you, I fell in love with a man from this world. And guess what, you cannot fix them.'

I argue, weakly. 'His father thrust this upon him. He didn't choose it.'

Her nod is cheerless. 'He did. A long, long time ago.'

'He likes cooking and reading . . .'

'And he can cook whenever he likes, buy himself a Michelin star; in fact, Tommaso can do everything and anything he wants.' She puts four long fingers on mine. 'I'm so sorry for you. Your mother. How lonely you must have been, growing up.'

I can't talk. My bottom lip trembles too much. I want to tell her that my loneliness can be referred to in the present perfect and future tense, too.

She continues, 'My son has such a job ahead of him. His role, to maintain peace in the region. Don't complicate this. Too much sits on his shoulders. And he *can* make a difference, Florence. Thanks to the control he has over this little chunk of Italy.'

'I just want to talk to my mother.'

This she says with absolute conviction. 'He is able to protect her better than any police programme. As long as it remains between him and her.'

You what?

Jolana misconstrues my silence for disappointment. 'If the Ferrari group find out, there would be a war. Do you understand? A *war*. I will not have that. He is going against his own father. Do you have any idea how powerful Rocco Bellini is?'

I nod. 'I saw him.'

'The Ferraris and the Bellinis have enough historical beef, without this. On every level, my son plays with fire.'

The Ferraris? 'She's safe, though?' I ask, quietly.

'Tommaso sets great store by a mother. He went to a great deal of effort to move her to safety.' She looks at me for a while. Admits, 'I've never known him so bewitched.'

'Why would he risk so much?' I say foolishly.

She just told me. 'For *you*, Florence.'

The ache of losing Tommaso hits me afresh. Love is extraordinarily simple, yet almost always inopportune. I flick away tears, because where's the fairness in that? 'So, everybody lives happily ever after, except me?'

Shoulders slumped at my naivety, Jolana looks at Italy for answers. I follow the direction of her eyes for the clues as to where she is – north, south, east or west?

'If I was your daughter, I'd never give up,' I say. 'Not until I'd kissed you one last time. What if Tommaso was missing?'

'Stop, Florence.'

'She's never known me as a grown-up. She knows nothing about me at all. I want to have coffee and a conversation with her, like we're doing now. That's what mums and daughters *do*. I never have, though. Please, Jolana, where is she?'

'No.'

I glance at Noah, who watches on, hawk-like. 'Jolana, you have a mother, too.' For a moment, she won't look at me. 'What wouldn't you do for her?'

She says cuttingly, 'My mother is not your mother.'

'Where is she?'

'No.'

'A region – just give me a region.'

I think she's going to slap me. 'You'll never contact Tommaso again. *Ever.*'

Toes and fingers splayed, legs uncrossed, I tell her strictly, 'On my brother's life.'

Eventually, she takes my face. Kissing one cheek, she mutters at my jugular. 'Campo del Ghetto Nuovo. The Jewish quarter. That's as specific as I can be.'

I mutter back. 'I really have to write this down.'

She walks back to the bar. Noah asks me questions with his eyes. My eyes answer: *Tommaso risks everything for no reason other than the love of a girl he'll never have – I am the most ill-fated woman I know.*

Jolana knocks the nail in my coffin. Handing me a slip of paper, she says, 'My son and I will never see or hear from you again.'

'I've given you my word,' I nod, then make her a further promise. 'But I won't stop hating the world for it.'

Part III

Putting Old Ghosts to Rest 101 – Tip #3:
The Parent–Child Resolution

Parent–child relationships are skewed. Mothers and fathers are too invested – this is key to the survival of the human race. Children are perpetually irritated – also an anthropological requirement, it fosters the desperate need to escape.

Parental fact: they are all right. Once you get to know them. Do this by applying the same broadmindedness as you would the rest of humanity.

• Remember, for example, that autobiography is unique – it produces billions of differing frames of reference, none of which can be measured against yours. This doesn't make parent's choices wrong, it makes them not you.

• Never fixate on their choice of words, especially during emotionally charged encounters. Vocabulary is a powerful tool – it can reveal and shroud truths. Yet the quieter you are, the more you hear.

• All possible personality traits sit somewhere between two very extreme points. This means *everybody* is on a spectrum. Don't misconstrue this. It's neither a conundrum nor a disease, but an exercise in acceptance – especially when it comes to blood relatives.

• Most importantly, be aware. The mind is a chump. It can often spend a lifetime accepting what the heart has always known.

Dothraki

Campo del Ghetto Nuovo is a square in Venice. You can get a bus all the way there from Trieste. It costs under a fiver and takes three hours ten. Noah and I use the time to research our destination, Venice's first ever ghetto.

'*Ghèto* means a foundry,' I tell Noah. 'It's where they make cannons.'

He leans his temple on my shoulder. 'I can read. Scroll down.'

I paraphrase instead. 'The Jews did get their freedom back. Venice was considered one of the most liberal and forward-thinking places on earth. Until 1944. All of them deported, most never to return.'

Noah puts a hand over my mouth.

I talk through his fingers. 'They're emancipated and prosperous now, thank God. I worried the place would be a hotbed of . . . I don't know . . .'

'Bankers?'

'Take your hand off my mouth.' He doesn't, not even when my phone rings. I have to elbow him in the Adam's apple. 'Take over research duties.'

The coach's bathroom is a dark and claustrophobic cupboard big enough for a couple of Henry Hoovers. Before sitting, I put the plastic lid down; her voice makes me feel ever so safe.

'Hello, love!' Vee shouts. 'I've missed you.'

Suddenly, I miss her, too. 'We'll be back soon. You got my text?'

'I'm on the edge of my seat. Tell me everything.'

I sigh. 'OK, where to start? My father has an on-off girl-friend. The church-mouse type – ineffectual, unattractive, nothing whatsoever to say for herself. Just totally *blah*.'

'I'm yawning just imagining her,' says Vee.

'Unfortunately, she comes with a daughter, who has an awful lot to say. The daughter's called Annie and last night Michael broke into her house.'

'You're shitting me?'

'He was looking for evidence that she's not a nice person – the fat-breasted bitch bullies him, Vee. It's calculated, too. Yesterday, the woman did a big-tongue face at him.'

Vee gasps.

'She's *middle-aged*.'

'She's damaged.'

'Michael's not a criminal, Vee. He just wants society to take him seriously.'

'I know, love.'

'Especially, by my dad – but he's too blinded by the mono-syllabic church mouse.'

Vee sighs. 'Ruled by the womb broom.'

There's a knock on the door. 'You all right?' Noah speaks through the hinge.

'Go away, I'm sitting on.' Then I continue, more quietly, 'Turns out Kathy Bates has a weird hobby.'

She laughs. 'Kathy Bates?'

'Seriously, she's her doppelgänger – when she was in *Misery*. Annie collects jars with *bits* in them. Each has a date on it. Michael will tell you they're the ashes of her murder victims.' I explain why they can't be. 'That'd make her the most prolific female serial killer of all time.'

'How many jars?'

'Not far off two hundred, in a cabinet in her study. If you knew her, you'd be intrigued, too.'

'Darling, I'm contemplating breaking in and having a look myself. We need samples.'

'Got.'

'Give me Michael's number. I'll call him now.'

'You're a legend.' I make it clear. 'I am *not* taking the piss. I'll pay whatever you think a fair rate.'

The offer, however, is rewarded with silence.

'Hello?' I look at the phone, put it back to my ear. 'Vee, can you hear me?'

'I'm actually having a sulk,' she states.

'What about?'

'About you being a bell-end. We're friends – by proxy, your family matters to me.'

That's how friendship rolls, I remind myself.

'Vee, I apologise. We are friends with brilliant benefits.'

'Babe, you burnt that bridge. Have you seen Tommaso?'

When I say 'Yes,' she yelps. The smug type best friends make when simultaneously shocked and delighted. That noise usually makes me irritated. How I wish I had something to yelp back about. Instead, sadness sits in my stomach, heavy as a goldfish bowl.

'It's such a long story.'

'*C'è qualcuno lì dentro?*', an Italian woman calls, rapping on the toilet door.

'Almost finito,' I tell her.

Vee is asking me, 'You're going to see him again, right?'

'Never. I promised.' I sigh. 'I'm a woman of my word.'

'To a fault.'

'I know.' Another knock on the door. 'Listen, I've got to go. I'm on the bus to Venice. Don't ask. I'll forward Michael's number now.'

'God, I want your life.' She doesn't, but I feel a fleeting

exoneration for everything I've ever done wrong. 'Now go,' she states. 'I've got his back.'

I trust her implicitly. When she's hung up, I blow a kiss at the phone.

The bridge that connects the islands of Venice to the mainland, Ponte della Libertà, is four kilometres long and far too narrow, with no emergency lane, making it unfit for purpose. When a Maserati undertakes us, I tell its bonnet, 'There's not the space for two – especially when one of you is a *coach*.'

'Don't look,' Noah tells me.

I study the lagoon.

According to the map, it's the shape of a battle shield. I can confirm it's not an overly friendly waterbody. The winter sun tries its damnedest to penetrate the water – to reveal depth, shade and tone – but this bit of the Adriatic refuses to sparkle its trademark navy blue. If I were to colour-match the Laguna di Venezia, it would be the shade known as Algae Green with a hint of Putrefied Poo.

'It's like the Great Grass Sea.' I shiver, turn to Noah and explain, 'I'm a Thronie.'

He frowns. 'Not a very good one. The Dothraki Sea is a vast inland region of *grass*, hence its name.'

'I was referring to its ambience.' The Dothraki are barbarians. Pressing my nose against the window, I monitor changes in marine infrastructure.

Emerging from the water either side of us, ramshackle fishermen's huts teeter, like sniper nests; visible as far as the eye can see, their bowlegs swathed in black slime. As are the gangrenous oak trunks that protrude in packs of two and three. Some have black sacks attached to their tops – the charred remains of hanged men.

'Where you at?' asks Noah. '*GOT*-wise.'

'Halfway through the third series.'

'You are in for a *treat*. It gets better and better.'

'Do not' – I swing to face him – 'tell me a thing. I'm very invested.' Then I point at the lagoon. 'What's with the tree trunks?'

'*Bricole*.' Noah speaks Italian. 'It's the limit of the navigable channel.'

'Listen to you,' I say, impressed.

'And the slim wooden poles with the nets are called *mussel farms*.'

I stop talking to him, until we arrive at Tronchero bus station. The pit stop is a grim fusion of medieval architecture, 1970s industrial units and tag graffiti. There, I tell Noah I'm going to walk, because he's patronising, and I don't trust him spoiler-wise. Noah doesn't give a shit. Gives me his blessing and heads towards a floating platform.

I mutter, disappointed, 'That's not very knight-like.'

The man has the auditory sensitivity of a moth. 'Then I suggest you get this *vaporetto* to *Guglie* on the *Fondamenta di Cannaregio*. It's just above the *Ponte delle Guglie* bridge.'

'When did you get so bilingual?' I complain, following him on board the No. 5.1.

'You were ages in the shitter,' he explains.

The word 'lagoon' suggests a tranquil body of water. This one is absolutely irate. Its currents are choppy and baffling. Vicious wave crests head-butt one another to death. Beneath the surface, there's nothing discernible; other than Weil's Disease, Cryptosporidium, E. coli and Swimmer's Ear. Ahead, the water slaps at buildings' sides and steps, leaving behind it a fringe of vegetation. Even the seaweed wants out.

'Ninety per cent of Venice's bowel movements are in there,' I say, hanging to the boat's side as we swing a violent right into the area's main thoroughfare.

Noah tells me, 'The *Canal Grando*.'

'*Tutti frutti*,' I say back, because Venice certainly unveils herself with a thumping *ta-da!* She's like a film set. Not a real one, a CGI one. The Lost Land of Atlantis (post-glory days). Its faded magnificence slackens the jaw.

If the Grand Canal has lanes, it's not apparent. Gondolas, sixteen-storey cruise ships, floating cranes and speed boats compete fearlessly for the straightest route to their destination, leaving the water positively crazed at the lack of nautical nonce.

Unlike the olden days. Before tourism, these buildings were palaces, their owners seafaring merchants – the oligarchs of their time. Their terraced castles sprung, magically, from the seabed, the architecture a surprising fusion of Christian, Byzantine and Islamic influences. Venetians were the doyens of high culture, back in the day.

Its majesty now jaded, most of these properties are un-occupied on the lower floors. The cost of keeping them from sinking into the lagoon would pinch Putin's purse.

Now people just come to stare. Like me.

The waterbus bounces on angry waves, because Venice does nothing to help herself – refuses to stop unfolding. Limestone bridges. A never-ending wall of the most striking windows, often with no concern for its neighbours. St Mark's Basilica and its golden dome that twinkles so fiercely it could be illuminated by a billion Swarovski crystals.

I say to Noah, 'We are going in the wrong direction.'

The plan is to get off the boat and jump on the No. 5.1 going the opposite way. Yet St Mark's sucks us inland. With solid ground such a precious commodity, you feel obliged to use it. Especially when the low sun sets the basilica's golden mosaics ablaze.

I'm surprised when Noah asks if I'd like to look inside.

'Jeez, *no.*' I won't draw God's attention to my presence. The wise guy already squats too smugly in the conscience. Showing Noah Google Maps, I say firmly, 'I've decided to walk.'

Noah takes my phone. 'OK, but I'm in charge of getting us there.'

'Please be more successful than last time,' I state. 'My job will be taking the whole place in.'

'Just do it silently,' he replies.

At first, foot traffic is moderate. We weave through tourists and narrow walkways, sneaking peeks at shops cluttered with Murano glass and Venetian masks. Deeper into the backstreets, the visitors peter out, as do the authenticity of the souvenirs. Good-humoured chatter is replaced by the odd boat's engine.

Important rules when browsing Venice's backstreets.

1. Don't say *Buongiorno* to anybody. It's not appreciated.

2. Neither is eye contact.

3. Or walking on the left-hand side. Which is often a problem.

The cobbled lanes range from five metres in width to just fifty centimetres. They are tangled as spaghetti and as hard to tell apart. Those who live here leave little evidence of their existence. Doors and lower windows are guarded by ironwork, ornate and hefty. Upper windows are neat squares, hidden behind shutters split and rotten, like an old boat.

This medieval labyrinth is the most antisocial place I've ever been. Sixty-nine minutes after we set off from St Mark's Square, Noah and I arrive at our destination.

Campo del Ghetto Nuovo.

Saturday is a day of worship and rest, if you're Semitic. We are alone in the district's central plaza, surrounded on three sides by the loftiest buildings we've seen so far. Their frontage is more spur of the moment and higgledy-piggledy.

Jews were prohibited from building outside their district; the only way was up – making single-storey structures rare. There's one here, though. The townhouses huddle around it, giving this courtyard the feel of an amphitheatre. Centre stage, a squat building with seven bronze panels on its wall – a memorial to the Holocaust. In the stalls, little shops with Hebrew signage; their wares, religious objects and books.

Where are you, Ruth? I look up at rooftops, originally servants' quarters, entrance via a hatch; their light source arrow-slit windows that lie on their sides. If I was my mum, I'd get myself one of those pads. Away from the blown bricks, fossilised struts and prying eyes of the Grand Canal – anonymous but safe, if a little cramped.

'Everybody keeps themselves to themselves.' I nod at Campo del Ghetto Nuovo and the whole Lost Land of Atlantis. My verdict, Tommaso did good.

Usually, I would recommend you stay outside of a surveillance zone, entering it only in disguise. Noah and I don't have the time.

Kosher House Leonardo is, as the crow flies, ninety-eight metres from the Campo de Ghetto Nuovo. A slender stone B&B built in the Middle Ages, its interior is clean and modern. Our room is at the top of four flights of stairs. Sparsely furnished – we have just a double bed, side table and wardrobe, all made of bright oak, as is the little square window and floor. The en suite is an avant-garde box of Murano-inspired tiles.

The reason I plumped for this guesthouse is because the website said, '. . . even Venetians couldn't tell you where it is'. It took us a few circuits before we discovered it burrowed inside a thin *calle*.

'I'll sleep on the floor,' Noah says, poking his head into the bathroom.

'We'll top and tail,' I insist.

'I don't trust you. Especially not that way up.'

'In your dreams. Now let's go eat. The best way to fathom a place is via its cuisine.'

'Can't,' he tells the toilet. 'I'm waiting for a Skype.'

I squint at the back of his head. 'You've never Skyped in your life.'

'Yeah, well. It's my sister.'

'*Hannah?*'

'We have to be very specific. She's in Perth, time difference and all that.'

This I ask, gently: 'Are you going to ask her what she knows?'

He doesn't say no. He takes his head out of the bathroom, leans against the architrave and talks to his feet. 'I don't know what I'm pulling up for her. We never spoke about it. We weren't allowed, then it became normal. She'd emigrated by the time she was nineteen. She's a sheep farmer now.' He crinkles his nose at how bizarre that is.

'When did you last speak to her?'

'Sometime in 2003.'

'Christ. We'll stay in and wait – as long as it takes.'

'No. I want privacy.'

'You don't.'

'Give me some sodding space, woman.'

Reluctantly, I hand him my laptop. 'Password is Khal Drogo. Two words. The o's are zeros.'

'You really *are* invested,' he mumbles.

'I will be changing it, soon as I'm back – to something non-*GoT*-related. And checking that you've not snooped.' I nod at the computer. 'You'll be able to see her head better. Bigger screen. How long do you want?'

His jaw re-clenches.

I perform a hand flap. 'Phone in when you're finished.' Then, grabbing my bag, I do as I'm told.

Antonio Banderas

I sit on a canal's concrete edge, my feet dangling half a metre above the water below. The channel looks stagnant in the dark – the walls either side of it are too tall; the moon can't shine on its surface. There's only one place where the water gets to shimmer – twenty metres along the bank from me a restaurant's lights flicker and tickle the water into life.

I wonder if she dines there. Her current identity honed, she works on procuring Husband No. 3. Some rich jeweller, I imagine. That gets me thinking about her new name. I choose one for her.

Bathsheba Abelson.

It suits her. Assuming she's brushed up on the Tanakh; which won't have gone down well, what with Bambi adoring God: specifically, the Catholic one.

My tongue dehydrates as I approach the restaurant. Like there's a chance she'll be there. Yet she's so close, I can practically smell her, and being that close makes anything possible.

The osteria's door is incongruously squat. Three steps lead to a wooden room and a litter of tables too close to their neighbours. I could be below deck. My guess: this was once a store for goods delivered by boat. The waiter spots me. I point at a table by the window. He nods, no nonsense.

My initial finding: the other patrons are not my mother. Just four German tourists.

Settling in at my table, I create space – push the condiments, cutlery and table adornment away. Put my phone on the place mat, my elbows either side of it.

As per usual, it's my job to save Michael's life. Though when I call, his line is busy. Just as well the waiter arrives to speak fast. He has no time for truck.

'You wanna know the best dish on the menu?' Sixties, eyebrows standing on full alert, a hand on his hip. Antonio Banderas, a five-foot-three Venetian one.

I speak fast, too. 'I do wanna know.'

'Liver and onions.'

'Not a liver lover. What else is there?'

'Onions.' We maintain eye contact. 'Saturdays. Not a busy night.'

'Understood. A bottle of house red and a basket of bread. Or have you run out of those?'

'No.' He turns with a little flourish.

I redial. If it rings, I don't hear it.

'Yes?' Michael snaps.

'Sup homeslice?'

'Who is this?'

'Your sister. Florence Love.'

Exasperated, he says, 'Seb just called, but I told him the truth. Yes, our hearts are too entwined, but I've got to consider the ethnics.'

'Ethics,' I tell the waiter, who plonks bread at my table, expertly uncorks my bottle, then tips it at the air. I grab my glass, place it under the bottle's neck. 'You told him to swivel, I hope?'

'Why would I ask him to do that?'

Not in the mood to explain metaphors, I look at the wine in my glass – an inky ruby. Take a sip – black cherry, black-berry and blackcurrant *avec* a hint of vanilla – I bob my approval. 'Do not meet him, Michael.'

'We're going out for a drink.'

I put the glass down, too heavily. 'You are not.'

'I am. Ask Dad. I want to put old ghosts to rest. You do it all the time.'

'It's my inability to put old ghosts to rest that's the problem.'

'Seb did it with a *girl*,' he reminds me. '*Maybe* he was just an egg donor. *Maybe* he was doing her a favour, but the damage is done . . .'

'Doing her a favour? He was sixteen years old.'

'But let me tell you something about *maybes*, Flo. They will cost you dear.'

I demand, 'Are you going to get back with him or not?'

'Not.'

'Swear on Dad's life.'

'This I do vow.'

An unfortunate fact of Michael's life: he yearns routine above all else, yet is unswervingly fickle. I take a sharp bite of bread and deal with more pressing issues. 'Have you spoken to Vee?'

'Vee who?'

'Vee *Na*.'

'Yes.'

'And you're going to give her the samples?'

'We're meeting at the drive-through at 20:00 hours.'

'Good. Trust her completely. In my absence, she's your responsible adult.'

Michael tells me, 'You do know that's discrimination and slavery.'

'I'm looking out for you.'

'Well, you're ruining my human rights. I'm a grown man.' He demands, 'What is *wrong* with you?'

Stumped, I say, 'I'll give that some thought.'

And I do.

Michael had a bit part in *Coronation Street*. He's a poster boy for healthy living and eating. My wingman during entrapments, he made me certain of my safety. Sometimes he'd barge in early, because the target's behaviour had been 'too wrong'.

I tell him a truth: 'You have saved both my bacon and my sanity a thousand times over.'

'And that is not my fault,' he says.

'No.' I smile. 'But it is the way we roll.'

How to find a missing person in a labyrinth with no name.

1. Have a spatial strategy

Tonight I will be employing land-use mapping. This involves dividing a map into smaller squares using an overlay grid. In the absence of tracing paper, draw straight on to the map, like me.

My search area is, thankfully, small. Just two hundred square metres, divided into four squares. Less fortunately, it's jam-packed full.

Surveillance circuit one: scour each square on foot. Look at everybody you encounter. Woman, man and child. Currently, I'm unsure if Bambi is alone. Maybe the pannacotta lover is with her. My sister and niece, too. Do this while familiarising yourself with the terrain. Ideally, by the end of this surveillance circuit, you'll know the patch like a local.

Surveillance circuit two: the aim this time is to make an actual map. If anyone asks, pretend you're a geography student; they *love* a colourful diagram. This one should include land function, every bit of it. Hotels, apartments, offices, churches, parks; jot down everything you see. Your target could be behind any of their walls. When back in the room, do a neater version of the map. A colour-coded one. In fairness to geographers, colouring in provides a welcome hiatus from empirical-data collection.

Surveillance circuit three: statistically, you are most likely to bump into a lost person during a third circuit of the field. A study of the lost at festivals discovered that those who kept moving in a consistent circuit were reunited with their friends fifty per cent more quickly than those who stayed still.

If you don't bump into your target, rinse and repeat the following day – this time peeking behind those walls.

2. Do not make any enquiries, discreet or otherwise
Not when you don't know the target's name. (Certainly, I can't use her last two. Or Bathsheba Abelson). Aside: women also make the best missing people – they're more careful, methodical and private. That makes me finish my wine in two gulps. Last time I saw her, she stuck out like a dead dog in the bath – elusiveness is no longer in her nature.

I signal for the bill. The waiter gives me the slip and waits, hand on hip, while I count out my euros.

'You wanna receipt?' I shake my head; nonetheless, he passes me a piece of paper. 'Tomorrow we have other dishes.'

'Glad to hear it.' I look at his note. He's written a telephone number and name. '*Angelo?*'

He does a coy nod, then tells me to leave. 'We need your table.'

I weave a route out through the empty seats. Then do not waste a minute. Time is money. And, in my profession, the night is your friend.

Surveillance circuit one complete, I return to the guest-house at midnight, to find Noah seated on the edge of the bed, as I left him. Only I don't recognise his face. It's ashen. My laptop sits open beside him.

'What's happened?' I ask warily. 'What did Hannah say?'

'Enough.' He turns the screen to face me.

I don't know what to expect – a close-up still of his sister? Instead, I see a black-and-white photograph. Two little girls in Holy Communion dresses. I don't move closer. I remain standing and shake my head.

He nods.

I gawp at the snap for a while. 'You've *found* her?'

'Hannah overheard something. A conversation between my parents.'

'When?'

'She was fifteen.'

My eyes are glued to the photograph. 'About Bambi?'

Noah ignores me. 'When Hannah asked about what she'd heard, Mum hit the roof. Then frightened the shite out of her. Things you don't threaten a lass with.' He's confused; it doesn't tally with his own memories of Elaine. 'Unless, of course, they're true.' He remembers I'm in the room. Tells me, unblinkingly, 'If Han repeated it, any of it, especially to me, we'd be swimming with the fishes. That explains her leaving so young for the other side of the world, eh?'

I gasp. Repeat my question less enthusiastically than before. 'Were your parents talking about Bambi?'

Pushing himself into a standing position, Noah walks robotically towards me, stopping two feet short of my face.

'I'm so sorry,' he says, planting a hand on my shoulder. Only he misses. A dead palm lands on my breast.

'Florence,' he tells me gently. 'I found them both.'

The Nun or the Bunny Girl?

The online article is called 'Twisted Twins' and was written in March 2002 by a Kiwi called Abi Hogan. New Zealanders have too chirpy a disposition; this one certainly treats her subjects with too much delight.

> *Who could be better as your partner in crime than your exact copy? Nothing confuses the cops more than a set of trouble-making twins. Here's some of the most notorious of all time . . .*

The title of her list is 'Double Trouble'.

Scrolling down it, I apprise myself of the company my mother kept.

The Krays – the 'greatest' mob bosses of all time. The Foxes – one a public drunk, the other a born entertainer, they eluded justice by pretending to be one another. The Spahalski twins – each independently ruthless and unaware they shared a personality disorder. Stephen Spahalski was gutted: 'I thought I was the only murderer in the family.'

The O. Brothers; the Han Sisters; the silent Gibbons twins.

At Twisted Twins No. 7, I falter. My heart punches, relentlessly, at my ribs. It takes a few reads because I struggle to absorb the context. Like an infant, I sound out words and sentences.

'The Galini Girls. They have a criminal nickname.'

Noah doesn't respond. Sitting on his side of the bed, staring at his socks, shaking his head, then nodding, engrossed in an internal conversation with himself.

Mine is more external. 'Ruth and Rina. Ruth *and* Rina. I

am a twat, a total twat. Of course that was what Tommaso
was saying.'

*Ruth and Rina were born on New Year's Day, 1951. Their
mother, Maria, died during childbirth. Their father never recov-
ered from her loss. The girls learned quickly not to rely on him.
Not that they needed anybody, not when they had each other.*

*Pictured Below: Ruth (left) and Rina (right) at their First
Holy Communion in Sasso Marconi, Italy.*

The photo is the only childhood snap I've ever seen of
my mum. I zoom in, try to decide which one she is.

Identical pudding-bowl haircuts, identical child wedding
dresses, identical smiles. Both hold rosary beads – this detail,
the only thing that tells them apart. Ruth cradles hers like a
wedding bouquet. Rina's dangles at her side, its little crucifix
on the floor, Jesus face down.

They could have been in The Shining, I don't say out loud.

Then my heart issues a corker of a jab – I think I remember
this story, vaguely; or maybe just its type. Over the years,
I've digested many articles like this, eager to understand the
intentions and truths behind those who kill. Like it's a lovely
diversion from my own shit.

*The Galini Girls did well at school and, at 16, both left home.
Ruth moved into the Convento di Santa Brigida and entered the
pre-novitiate phase of becoming a nun. Whereas Rina worked
as a florist by day and a bunny girl by night at a casino in
Bologna. It was there that she bagged the most eligible divorcee
in town – mafia racketeer Marco Ferrari.*

*On 24th June 1973, Rina returned home from a few days
visiting her twin to find her stepson, Matteo, in her bed. Dead.
Carbon-monoxide poisoning from a boiler that had been tampered
with.*

I look at Noah, beside me, wide-eyed. 'She has a fucking MO?'

Noah blindly sips a bottle of water.

That evening, Ruth Galini left her convent for the police station, suitcase in hand. There, the nun confessed to killing Matteo. When Rina discovered her twin's confession, she, too, visited a police station, claiming sole responsibility for her stepson's death.

The twins were dogged, sticking to their individual versions, neither of which married. Though they agreed on one thing – their intended victim, Marco Ferrari, was a wife-beater.

On 21st December 1973 – less than six months after Matteo's death – the Galini Girls were acquitted. A lack of evidence made it impossible to indict either of them. The sting in the tail – Matteo Ferrari had been a local hero, a footballing revelation. Just nineteen, he'd been signed as a sweeper for Bologna FC. The trial over, Ruth and Rina disappeared. The consensus, they'd played the Italian constitution like a fiddle.

Fury swept the nation. The Italians love only one thing more than their sons: football. The mafia's retribution was swift. On 2nd January 1974, Rina Galini was hit by a train.

Ruth's location remains unknown to this day.

Manipulative masterminds or misguided loyalty?

An instant and violent grief arrives. Because I know my mother's name. And her twin was called Rina.

'No. No. No,' I half wail for the woman I never knew. 'We called her Aunty Carina.'

Noah sits up, alarmed, pushes a tissue into my hand. 'You knew she had a twin?'

I shake my head. 'Just a sister. Mum pretended she sent us Christmas presents.' I hold my breath, try to stop crying.

Noah takes the tissue from me, puts it over my nose. I

protest. 'Dinosaur blow,' he demands, then mops up my face and takes the laptop from me.

'My mum was baptised Ruth Galini, Noah.' That starts me blubbing again. 'And she wanted to be a nun.'

'There are other articles,' he warns me. 'All in a similar vein.'

'Misguidedly loyal,' I declare. 'That's what Ruth and Rina were. Monozygotic twins are known for it. It's not their fault – they're a biological mishap. Imagine it – sharing too much empathy, experiencing one another's physical pain, speaking in synch . . .'

Noah interrupts. 'There are more detailed articles. There was DNA. One of theirs, but the genetics were too similar. The courts couldn't indict one or the other. There's also a suggestion that Rina and Matteo were at it.'

'Aunty Carina was sleeping with her stepson?'

'Maybe things were getting tricky. Rina wanted Matteo gone, in case Marco found out.'

'No,' I tell him.

'There weren't many years between them.'

'She was being abused by the husband – they said that in court.'

He manoeuvres my chin, makes me look at him. 'They said a lot of things in court. Most of which were quite weak.'

Depleted of energy, I whisper, 'Have I got her horribly wrong?'

Noah shrugs. 'When I knew her, she was lovely.' Then leans over to click on a different tab.

The webpage is a memorial page to Matteo Ferrari. The site's purpose: to raise funds for the Federation's Disability Football programme.

'The guy's virtually a household name,' I complain. 'There's a memorial park named after him, and an annual football tournament, and a statue in Bologna.'

'Hen, when did your mum have her first kid, Maria?'

I stare at him for a moment. 'Five years before me. *Ish.*'

'Bambi was tried for murder, gave birth, lost her sister, then fled her homeland inside of a year.'

'Who on earth was the father? She was a nun.'

'A nun with a bun on the run.'

'That's not funny.'

Noah agrees. 'We need to leave Italy now.'

My laugh is frenetic. 'I've only just found her.'

'The mafia have long memories. But *thanks to you*, Flo, she's safe. The best man is looking after her. What daughter can boast of having achieved that for her mother?'

'None in the whole history of civilisation.'

'Then there's her family. Maria and her wee girl, who are *your* flesh and blood. As connected to you as Michael is. Your *sister*, Flo, who has a *child* – think of their safety.'

'Paola.' I tell him my niece's name, like we're tight, when, in reality, she's five and doesn't have an inkling who I am. She's an angel, though. I saw her – tight Mediterranean curls, a terrible singing voice, the emancipation with which she used her little child body. Her wise eyes – they gripped me. Paola was so like me at that age, existing with an utter conviction that life had been designed for her.

A loyalty ignites within me. 'I have a sister,' I tell Noah. 'Another actual female relative. We frequented a womb. My confirmation name is her forename. Both named after Nonna, a woman I loved desperately, despite her being a figment of Mum's imagination.'

'Big shit,' he agrees. 'You can't put them in danger.'

'I won't,' I promise.

'The truth. That's what this case was about.'

I squint. 'Was?'

Noah is staunch. 'I won't help you.'

Tears threaten again, because what the hell is he talking about?

'I can't help you, hen. I've got a kid – I won't put the bairn at risk. This is the *best* way this can end – for Bambi, your family and mine. I don't want to be implicated in this.'

'Nobody cares about you,' I say.

'It's best I keep it that way.'

'Yellow-belly.'

'Come on.' He makes me turn around so we face one another. 'You know who she is now.'

'I haven't a clue who she is!' I shriek. Take a moment to pull myself together. Though my smile is still sad. 'There's no denying, it's less clunky on the tongue, eh? *Ruth Galini*.' I can't look him in the eye, so hold his hand instead. 'I'm not finished, Noah.'

'I won't help you.'

'But I have such an overwhelming dilemma.'

'You don't.'

'I do.' I tell him the humiliating truth: 'I need to know if she loves me.'

Our Father

I am now a one-woman band. Which is just as I like it.

That's a lie. It's also bad PI practice.

Never be alone in the heart of the Venetian mafia – the most ruthless of them all – when they unwittingly harbour one of Italy's most hated women. You definitely need bodies on the ground. Counter-surveillance. Noah would have been a good start.

I am Florence Love and do not need a single person.

I tut at my own blarney, slump over the canal's wall and daydream at the water. Noah's absence gives Venice a new light. A menacing milieu. The sunshine has a dirty tinge. The cold air smells of coffee-infused decomposition.

Instead, I imagine Tommaso watches over me. That gives me a buzz. Tommaso Bellini is indisputably a man of his word; unlike my wingman. I look up at a window on the opposite bank. Pretend Tommaso spies on me through its shutters; he'll be cursing my sass and bravery, but dangerously hooked, nonetheless. He said that to me once: *I'm dangerously hooked.*

I recall a fact: Italian men are saddled with a perilous passion. And we *never* made love. Of course, Tommaso has followed me here.

I rub my face and beg answers of a pigeon, 'Why didn't we just *make love*?' But the bird's too dead; just bobs. 'Our last kiss wasn't supposed to be the *last*. I kissed him on the knuckle and forgot to cherish it.'

Just as I forget to note land use, and the pedestrians who pass by behind my back. I look into the canal and stare at the past.

An hour ago, to be precise – when Noah abandoned me. 'I *will* get killed,' I tried to emotionally blackmail him.

'Which proves every point I am making.' He was folding dirty T-shirts and jamming them, thoughtlessly, into his rucksack.

'I don't believe you've seen an episode of *Game of Thrones* in your life.'

That softened his jaw. 'Give over.'

'You swore you'd be my wingman, fucker. What happened to being loyal to your clan?'

'I am. I'm choosing my son.'

'What am I going to do now?'

Noah stopped packing. He was sorry for saying it, 'You need to feel loved by her. I don't. My son doesn't.' Reading the stories of Ruth and Rina had given Noah clarity – a different one to my own.

'Anybody would think *I'd* murdered someone. You're being so cold.'

That stopped him packing. He came over and cradled my shoulders with his hands. 'You don't need to search for love, hen.'

'Ruth Galini is my clan,' I said flatly.

'You have it in spades.'

'Love?' I snorted.

'Me, for one.'

'I knew it.'

He didn't argue. Moved back to his rucksack. Reinstated folding and jamming.

'So, you going back to the wife?' I asked.

'Slovenia, actually. I'm meeting a friend.'

'No, you're not.'

'The lass I spoke to at the caves.'

'The over-enthusiastic kraut? When did you get her number? Do you even know her name?'

'Lilli. We chatted. You were in the lav.'

'That's not very German.'

He squinted. 'Her surname is *Busch*. Is that German enough for you?'

'Lilli Busch?!'

He ignored my pretend delight. 'We've messaged a bit.'

My disappointment was entirely unanticipated. 'You are an *actual* stalker. I'd stop telling random women you love them in spades, if I were you. That's not putting your son first. I thought you were rushing back to your clan – to be a proper and present father.'

I deserved a shove, at least. Instead Noah arrived, this time to place his hands on my face, cupping my cheeks like they were small glass balloons.

We looked at one another for quite some time.

Then Noah admitted, quietly. 'I would. You know . . . But *only* in another life. And assuming you underwent a personality transplant.'

'That's the worst compliment, ever.'

'It's all I got.' He kissed my forehead.

'But you'll be here, secretly, won't you? Keeping an eye on me, like Batman.'

'Hen . . .'

'Tell me you will, even if you won't.'

He said too sadly, 'I will. Aye,' then dropped my face, just like that. 'Train leaves in an hour.'

The reasons I know he's definitely gone: I listened to his footsteps in the corridor. Rule of thumb: the slower the walk, the more internal dialogue. Noah's footfall was brisk and loud, brimful with intent, fading away too cursorily.

I push the canal wall away from me. Administer myself with a sharp flick to the temporal lobe and remind myself why I'm here.

Mapping the Jewish quarter is not an easy feat.

One front door services who knows how many apartments above. Overcrowding meant that rooms were cut in two, horizontally, to create extra floors. Some of them aren't even apartments. Office space, dentist's, synagogues had to be built on the ghetto's rooftops. Thankfully, outside of the Campo and its immediate streets, the chaos recedes. The housing, the bakeries, the kosher restaurants, the Jewish bookshop are drab and utilitarian, compared to the rest of the islands, but stunning by the rest of the world's standards.

It's barely 4 p.m., yet the light fades. I stop in a little square to frown at a break-dancer – he performs for a café's clientele. No PPE whatsoever, hare-brained moves on cobbles. Literally screwing grit into his head, which injects a good deal of jeopardy, heightened when I receive four texts in quick succession.

Let it be Noah. I fumble for my phone, but the gut never lies.

It's the Antichrist, and she is fuming.
Where are they, bitch?
I want them back.
Now.
NOW.
Lips furled, I type back: *I sense venom in your full stops.*
Annie's next message is a lot of full stops. Followed by: *You've been in my house.*

There's a small, rounded turret squirrelled away in the rooftops – the glass dome is the only immediate clue as to the synagogue's existence. I use it as a spiritual channel. 'Dear God. I'm really, *really* busy just now. A quick solution would be more appreciated than you know. Amen.'

Quick as a flash, He's here, utterly tolerant of all religions; He'd be nowhere without them. *My child, you do the only thing you can at this point. The thing you always do. Take the blame.*

I waver, before acquiescing. Type:
Do you know you snore like a drunk donkey?
Kathy Bates top-trumps me. *I'm calling the police.*

Darkness sets in fast. I get out of the surveillance area and make my way to Piazza San Marco. There I sit cross-legged, my back against a pillar belonging to the Museo Archeologico Nazionale and look at St Mark's Basilica.

I don't want to go home. Not yet. But this phone call could mark the end of this particular attempt to find her. Which isn't fair, because I've come so far.

After a while, I pull free my phone. I don't even know if he'll answer. Goodness knows what he's heard via Darcie.

However, Dad picks up quickly. Then speaks too fast.

'Florrie. Thank God you've called. I'm at an absolute loss. No idea whatsoever how to deal with this . . .'

'What is it?' I demand.

Dad takes a lungful of breath. 'Michael's set up a *lair* in the Yellow House.'

I explain, 'It's his incident room. And he promised not to do private investigation without me.'

'It's very insidious.'

I ask this with one eye shut. 'What's he investigating now?'

'Annie.'

'Ah.'

'Did you know?'

It's difficult to judge how best to respond to this. 'About what?'

'There are blown-up photographs of her on the walls. He's been *inside* her house. Stolen old photos. Taken new ones of her – when she's at the bus stop, mostly. He's put handwritten notes up. I'm worried he's going to *harm* her.'

'What do the notes say?' I ask.

He whispers, '"Annie called me a spack. Annie told me

off for chewing. Sucking food sucks. Annie wants to have a baby with anyone – she asked me.'"

'You what?' I shriek. 'I knew it. I knew she wanted his sperm. Dad, it was me who broke into her house. I wiped the CCTV footage from her computer, took photos, followed her. The shots of her at the bus stop – I took those from a barn opposite. It's the ideal observation point.'

'You didn't. I can see Michael's glove in one of the photos.'

'I also obscured the lens of her security camera – for when I kill her for real.'

'We have to deal with your anger-management issues.'

'Enough.' It is time for my Dad to man-up. 'Cersei Lannister, Daenerys Targaryen, Brienne of Tarth – in fact, *all* the women out of *Game of Thrones* would have high-fived me, had they seen footage of my unmanaged anger. Not just them – all the women in the world, too. And most of the blokes. Dad, get with the game – nowadays, women are fully entitled to have a scrap. Especially when it's in the name of love.'

My dad remains silent, but it's a good silence, so I continue.

'Yes, I punched her in the mouth and, know what? It was a corker. I also tried to strangle her a bit, but she was too unwieldy. The gun in my hand was a packet of Marlboro Lights. Because, yes, I pretended to shoot her. Annie was blackmailing me with that footage – I was to ensure that you and Darcie never reunite.'

'Dear God. I didn't know.'

'You did. But you chose the attention of her mother over sticking up for your kids. I'm sorry for the C-word, by the way. Now, Dad, I'd love to chat, but there's a more prevalent issue. The police are going to turn up at the cottage any second. Annie knows Michael's been in her house. Only he hasn't. I have. Which is irrelevant, because you don't know a thing.'

'Michael!' he shouts.

My brother arrives in the background. I hear him saying, 'Press the woofer button. The *woofer*.'

'Dad has no idea what a woofer is,' I say, waiting for the speakerphone to kick in.

'Ask her what to do with the samples,' Michael is saying.

'I can hear you. Doesn't Vee have them?'

'She didn't want them all,' he complains.

'Why, how many did you take?'

'One hundred and sixty-seven.'

I freeze. 'The actual jars?'

'What jars?' Dad demands.

'*She* told me to. *She* said, take the samples.'

'I said *take samples*! Christ on a bike, Michael, where are they now?'

'In your bedroom.' He argues with Dad. 'She's not using it.'

'What's in the bloody jars, son?'

'Ashes.'

'Dad! Dad!' I try to get his attention. 'They are not dead people. I have Vee looking into it.'

'Her victims?' I hear Dad say.

'Yes,' Michael tells him. 'I think she's on a spectrum.'

'Stop it!' I shout. Then, quietly, 'Annie's calling the police. Whatever is in those jars is very important to her. Michael, hide the samples. But first, get the treehouse empty of incriminating evidence. Dad, you know nothing.'

'I won't have you take the blame,' he states.

'I don't intend to. A crime can't have taken place if I'm in a different country.'

'Where are you?' shouts Michael.

'I can't tell you. I need to confound the prosecution, what with my guilt not adding up. It's a flair I've inherited from our maternal side.' I'm shocked by my own audacity.

Not that Michael's listening. 'You're not allowed to not be in the country. Not without me. I get panicky, the lemonade fizzes over, I could die. Where are you?'

I remain as silent as Dad.

'Where the hell are you?' repeats Michael.

'Your sister will be back really soon.' Dad's voice is unexpectedly conspiratorial. 'You are coming home, that's right, isn't it, Florrie?'

'That is definitely my plan. Michael, go plug in the shredder. The police could be here any moment.'

'She better come home,' I hear Michael say, before doing as he's told.

Dad and I wait thirty seconds. The time is spent listening to Venice, which is an acoustic phenomenon. The absence of cars allows for an unrivalled clarity of sound. It's akin to sitting in a recording studio, the most delicate sounds amplified – a cough, a footstep, the slap of a mallard's wing.

Then six o'clock arrives, like now, and every campanile in the Lost Land of Atlantis chimes. More than a hundred bell-towers compete, each with their own tone and story. The result is an epic symphony.

It can be quite alarming, if you're not braced for it. I have to put a finger in my ear.

Dad's voice is quiet and urgent. 'Where are you?'

I look up at St Mark's, at its yawning arches and minarets. 'I'm so close, Dad.'

When he replies, something is different – his voice has been swapped for another; a replica of the one he'd used when demanding I stop looking for Mum. It involves an unswerving throat polyp growl.

'OK, Brienne of Tarth, know this – everything I did was for you and Michael.'

I stop him there. 'Daenerys Targaryen.'

I imagine he performs a head bob when he says, 'Mother

of Dragons.' There's certainly a smidge of reverence in his voice. 'Your conclusions may not match mine and you'll likely disagree with my methods, but we can't worry about that now. I need you to be battle ready.' He pauses. Decides what my weapon should be. 'I have a little psychological intelligence.'

My father doesn't do psychology; not using his normal voice, anyway. And I'm glad, because it unnerves me . . .

'When a partner dies, or you lose a child, it's unimaginably tragic. Yet, those left behind had an identity before. But *twins* – they have a plural identity. The death of one leaves the other permanently broken. Please be gentle with her.'

I reassure him, 'She's my Achilles heel,' then, wait for other useful information. When none arrives, I ask, 'Is that it?'

'You're also grounded.'

My smile is thin. 'That's never sounded so appealing. Assuming your companion and her pet Antichrist are off the scene. What are you going to say to Darcie?'

He doesn't hesitate. '*You come with too much baggage. Fourteen stone of it.*'

That is the funniest thing he's ever said. 'You can ground me for a year, but *only* if you say exactly that.'

'We have visitors – that was ruddy quick.' Dad swiftly wraps it up. 'I'll hide the jars, play dumb. You will make your father an oath.'

'Anything,' I swear.

His gravitas is spine-tingling. 'Come home to me, Florrie.'

A Crock of Joy

For a while, I was her missing piece.

I remember.

Or maybe Bambi's loss gave my memories a rose-gold hue. That her dependence on me was endearing. That, when I got her to stop thinking, it proffered in me a sense of accomplishment. Especially when I made her giggle. Living in an emotional vacuum is unhealthy, Dad had explained; and, according to my memories, I was emotionally mature so accepted her foibles in the definite knowledge I could fix them. The reason – she loved me most.

When we watched *Columbo* and dissected his methods, she'd confide: 'We are quite the peas in the pod.'

It transpires I wasn't the right pea, though. Simply a squatter; a pale imitation of its previous occupant. Not that I blame her. Losing a twin has to be the ugliest blow. The implosion certainly toppled Bambi backwards and over an edge.

I imagine her as a mannequin, being carried naked on to a boat under the arm of a witness protection officer; soon to be given a new name and the opportunity to become whoever she wanted to be.

Pushed on by my father's complicity, I spend the rest of the day searching – and ignoring Annie's increasingly frantic texts, an example of which is this:

I want my fucking jars back NOW!

I've never heard her swear before. Her tone is also indicative of someone who is failing to call the police. Dad confirms it. Sends me a message.

False alarm. Was the ASDA man.

That gives me purpose. Woolly hat pulled low, I study everybody I pass. Peek through the slivers of light between shutters; they expose little, just a hint of net curtain. The shops are fluorescent with yawning windows, in comparison, making staff and customers easy to clock. The restaurants are the easiest – I loiter outside, pretending to scrutinise wall-hung menus.

At the osteria in which I ate yesterday evening, I come face to face with Angelo. He uses the window as a mirror, smooths his black hair behind his ears, doesn't smile or wave when he sees me staring back. Just collects a bread basket, placing it on the table at which I sat last night. When I don't come inside, he adds an empty wineglass.

I'm pleased for the wood and occasional lighting, but especially the warmth. I take off my coat, rearrange the table's accoutrements and Facetime Vee.

'Darling,' she says. 'I was just about to call. Michael brought me *all* the jars – can you believe it? My first conclusion is – the cat's out of the bag.'

'I spoke to Dad earlier,' I nod, pushing in earbud headphones.

'Where are you?' she squints at her screen.

'A restaurant. Have you managed to look at the contents?'

'Indeed. I've been in the lab. When I say "I've been in the lab", I asked someone to check for me while I waited impatiently.'

I hurry her along. 'And what are they?'

'Detritus, mostly.'

Angelo fills my glass. I reposition the phone so he can't see its screen. There's no need; he bickers with another waiter.

'Can you narrow it down?' I ask Vee.

And so she props up her tablet in front of her, enabling her to fold her hands and look like a newsreader.

'Jar one. Dated 12 March '87. A pinch of sub-base – that's crushed aggregate. They use it underneath driveways or patios. Jar two. Sixth August 2004. Soil. Alisol in type. Very acidic with clay-enriched subsoils and a high nutrient-holding capacity. Indigenous to hot areas, Africa-hot.'

I interrupt. 'Less information.'

Vee does a face that says, *Oooooh*, before continuing. 'Jar three – bird seed. Jar four – wood chippings. Jar five – a mixture of sawdust and fragments of glass. Jar six – grass. You're very bossy.'

'It's something I'm working on,' I apologise. 'How many did you test?'

'Ten.'

This I say quietly: 'Any bones, human or otherwise?'

She shakes her head. 'They could be trophies.'

'Do not tell Michael that.' My face is no-nonsense. 'What we do know is she has something to hide – she's not called the police.'

'Want me to key her car?'

I smile. Then stop; a text has arrived. 'Did you hear that? I've got another message.'

'Who from?' demands Vee.

I grin. 'Annie. It's just one word. Blimey, Vee – she really wants them back.'

'What word?'

My imitation of Annie is a guess, because I've never heard her beg before: *Please*.

'Shut. Up.' Vee leans forward and frowns. 'Is it right that I hate her so much?'

I tell her a truth. 'If you didn't, I'd be offended.'

We say our goodbyes and, soon after, Angelo saunters to my table.

'Wanna know the best thing to eat?'

I nod, because mental lethargy arrives, heavy as a crashmat.

'Sarde in saòr,' he states.

'Is it offal?'

'No, it's very good.'

I grin. He does, too, which is quite alarming. 'You have Hollywood teeth,' I tell him.

'I'm lucky,' he agrees.

Then I point, silently, at his choppers. Because I am at the beginning of an epiphany.

Everybody goes to the dentist. That narrows down a search. Though her appointments would be few and far between. I don't have a year. Neither can I be at every surgery at once on the off chance she has a check-up.

I drop my finger. Study Angelo for other clues. His tresses are long enough to scrape into an undersized ponytail. 'What about your hair?'

'It's my own.' He bends towards me. 'Pull it.'

And I do, because my mother has fat brown curls and not a single grey. In fact, on the day we met (the most fraught of my life), Bambi's hair refused to flake.

'I need a hairdresser,' I decide. 'How many hairdressers are there in Cannaregio? Exactly. Give or take.'

Angelo confides, 'The best is Leopardi's, next to Chiesa Evangelica Luterana.'

My Italian is pitiable, so I feel positively bilingual when I tell him. '*Chiesa* means church.'

At last, sighs God. *Your epiphanies are very protracted.*

He's right – I half laugh at my own stupidity.

'Angelo, I would like to go to *chiesa*. A Catholic one.' His look suggests I am infuriatingly sexy. 'I wanna know the best one.'

You don't wanna know the best one! snaps God. *Catholics err towards the shortest route.*

I add, 'By which I mean, which is closest to Campo del Ghetto Nuovo?'

Angelo nods. 'Madonna dell'Orto. Cannaregio, 3512.'

Jubilant, I stand up, offer Angelo my hand and say, 'May the Lord be with you.' Why, I'm not sure. In return, he takes my hand, kisses its knuckle roughly; lets it drop. The fury in his eyes tells me I'm magnificent. And, for one glorious moment, I agree.

I exit the restaurant with purpose. Then return, because Angelo shouts after me, 'You wanna pay the bill?'

The church is shut when I arrive in its courtyard. Yet candlelight from within makes the rose windows' glass dance. For a good minute, I pretend my mum is having a cup of tea on the other side of that window. In utopia, she'd be living in the cloisters, back among her own kind, because that was the dream. But I get too urgent a bowel-flutter, so need to jog back to the en suite.

Before I leave, I take a photo of the opening times.

9 a.m.

A noble building of orange bricks and white marble detailing, Madonna dell'Orto's bell tower and onion dome dominate the skyline – a massive middle finger to its surroundings. Its façade is decorated with small arches, bas reliefs with linear motifs, and twelve niches, each home to an Apostle.

I come in peace, I nod at each of them, then venture inside for morning Mass.

Colossal pieces of artwork; vertiginous ceilings; Gothic arches and Grecian pillars; the thundering organ jangles both air and nerve – it makes for compelling evidence that there is an Almighty.

Genuflecting at a back pew, I rest on the kneeler and assume the praying-hands gesture. Enjoy the energy, which is hypnotic. Catholicism makes puppets of the lapsed. The prayers and congregational responses are designed to hoodwink you into being a better person. I find the whole thing very confusing. Because, yes, its history is blemished and it might be a cult; but it's my cult, which, as a scientist, makes no sense at all.

The entrance procession begins.

Please don't be High Mass, I pray, because they are both lengthy and in Latin.

The priest holds two graceful fingers aloft, moves them as though they're a conductor's baton in time with his greeting.

'*In nòmine Patris . . . et Filii . . . et Spiritus Sancti.*'

'Amen,' we say.

The service lasts for an hour twenty. It's time enough to scour the small congregation thirty times over; and the servers, coveting their candles, incense and processional cross; and the balcony behind me, where sisters and nuns fondle their chaplets.

I consider interrogation techniques.

Bambi Love is not your average perp. Rule of thumb: the fragile require a less hard-sell approach, cross-examination-wise. Crushing them mentally is banned. The preferred approach being, the Co-ordinated Behavioural Response – its philosophy, to adapt your technique according to the subject's foibles.

I'm an old hand at that. Yet the complexities of this case mean I'm saddled with an encyclopaedic list of questions. Here're some of them:

- Is it ever nice to run away from a daughter with abandonment issues?

- Did you know Fergus was a paedophile?

- Carbon monoxide. Discuss?

- Were you and Eric Steensen doing it?

• Pannacotta Man. That's three people I know you've slept with. *Three*. Is that too many for a mother?

• Your first daughter, Maria – did you love her more than me? More than Michael, who has special requirements, a nuclear family being one of them?

But my tone is unconducive to forging a bond. I turn down the volume on my own issues, aim for detachment.

• I'm not here to upset you. Just to understand how one might go about premeditated murder.

• Dad said you were his soulmate, which is really nice. Do you have similar feelings or is he a bit deluded?

• Your twin was Rina. I remember you called her Carina. It was her death, wasn't it, that left you banjaxed in the head?

• Is empathy a tricky concept – not that I'm judging?

Things must slide. The likelihood: our time together will be rushed. At long last, the congregation files from the church and I decide on my final questions. The Four Prongs, I call them. They are necessarily pithy.

1. Did you and/or Rina kill Matteo Ferrari?

2. Why abandon us for a country that hated you?

3. How did you kill Fergus?

4. Why don't you love me any more?

A day spent hanging around the church has left me deplete of conviction. The six-thirty service was a High Mass too far. I have seen no one relevant to the case. Even God played hooky.

Now I sit in La Cantina del Vino, a cicchetti bar situated a short walk from Madonna dell'Orto on the Rio della Madonna dell'Orto. It's busy. Communion wine kick-starts a thirst; the congregation certainly enjoy their nightcap. Me, too. I sit on a high stool at the window.

Outside, the Murano glass streetlights make the canal flicker pink. The cobbles and courtyards boast an equally romantic hue, as do the pedestrians. On the downside, amethyst is a terrible light for successful target recognition.

I rub my eyes. Surveillance is intense at the most dispassionate of times. Today, I've definitely overused my eyeballs. I have to squint when my phone vibrates. The text's a blur.

I'm happy to come and collect them. Annie.

That's the nicest thing she's ever said to me. Gagging for a row, I call her straight back.

'So what's the deal with the glass urns?'

Her tone is clipped. 'As I said, I'm happy to collect.'

'This isn't an eBay transaction.'

'For heaven's sake, what do the contents matter? It's extremely personal.'

'It's not. Not when I hold all the cards. Or jars, in this case.'

She does an irritated yelp. 'They're of sentimental value, Florence. I don't expect you to understand that.'

The dignified thing would be to undermine her with a Cruella De Vil laugh. But I'm too defensive. 'Yes, I do, which is why I have a family and friends. What have you got, apart from the monosyllabic mother you terrorise? You don't do sentimental things. You're a witch. An actual witch.'

Her own Cruella De Vil laugh suggests I'm right. 'George

warned Mum and me that you were disturbed. I googled your symptoms and there's a name for your condition. Hold on, I'm just getting it up.' She pauses.

If she were here, I'd give her a Glasgow kiss.

'Here it is. Passive-aggressive megalomania.'

'You've so made that up.'

'Afraid not, lovey.'

She's messing with the wrong person. 'Give me the *Merriam-Webster's Medical Dictionary* definition.'

Annie remains silent.

'Come on, Kathy Bates. I want the universally accepted definition of a passive-aggressive megalomaniac. Apparently, it's right in front of you.'

'I want my jars,' she hisses.

'Because, far as I recall, I've never ever been passive-aggressive. I'm incapable of it. Non-verbal aggression, avoiding confrontation – not on my radar.'

She has nothing.

'Pretending to pull something up on your computer – I'm cringing for you. Just admit it, the spice jars are trophies. That's why you haven't called the police.'

'Yes,' she sighs. 'Let's call them that.'

The woman's a bugger to penetrate. 'What star sign are you?'

That disarms her. 'Aries.'

My laugh is sardonic. 'I fucking hate Aries. Their egocentrism is always the death of them – thank God. What's in the jars?'

'Florence,' she states, 'I'll make this very easy for you. I will collect my jars at a place of your choosing. I will delete the security footage and you'll not see or hear from me or my mother ever again.'

'Until the next time . . .'

'Our parents have parted company. It's over.'

I grin. 'What did he say to her? His *exact* words.'

'Do we have a deal?'

'Not until I know if you're a serial killer or not.'

This, Annie growls: 'They're my jars of *joy*, Florence. Mementos.'

'Of what?'

'The times I've felt unbridled contentment.' I can hear that her jaw is clenched.

A collector myself, I understand the attraction. I collect information – the garage is stuffed full of books, medical journals, OS maps and leaflets. This, I consider a healthy extension of my identity. Annie's reasons for being a collector are definitely more menacing. She comes across as the unloved-child-seeking-comfort-by-accumulation type.

'Did you pulverise your mementos in a pagan ceremony?' I ask.

She refuses to open her teeth. 'They are whatever we stood on at the time.'

'Who's *we*?' I take a greedy gulp of wine.

Annie says this as though it's perfectly normal: 'They're all the times I fell in love.'

I cough it back up. 'A hundred and sixty-seven times?'

She says, strictly, 'I'm very in tune with my emotions. People like me feel a lot of love.'

I shake my head, sadly. 'No, *lovey*, they don't; they crave it. They also spume bile when they see it going on between others. There's a name for your condition, but I'm not going to give you an excuse. Stay away from my family. I'll return the jars myself.'

'When?' she asks quickly.

'When I'm back from my hols.' I hang up and finish my drink in one.

The spice jars contain the ashes of Annie's happiness – that would be heartrendingly poetic if she wasn't so odious.

And so I find myself with a sudden luxury. Time.

Annie won't call the police, meaning Michael's out of the woods and I don't have to return home *tout de suite*. It's only nine o'clock, yet my eye muscles throb, all six of them. Lack of sleep exacerbates eye strain. Leaves you at risk from glaucoma, eye spasms and ischemic optic neuropathy.

Which is the reason I don't recognise her at first.

The Hips Don't Lie

I stroll back towards Kosher House Leonardo. The raindrops, infrequent but fat, foreshadow a downpour. When the couple wander past, I'm too busy massaging my nasal bridge and rummaging for an umbrella. Mechanically, I glance after them. Though it's a few seconds before I drop my head to the side; check out the woman from a different angle.

My initial thought: she walks like the Harmony hairspray girl from the seventies.

Activating the spring facility on my umbrella, I follow them along Fondamenta Madonna dell'Orto, the canal slopping to our left-hand side. Remaining a good ten metres behind, I examine the woman's back: this is a person of interest.

Height: 5.8. *Check.*

Build: slim. *Check.*

Style: sophisticated. Tight black trousers tucked into fur-trimmed ski boots. Her dark wool coat is knee length and belted. Her headscarf, a vibrant duck *à l'orange*, is worn Audrey Hepburn style, its loose material swung back around her neck. *Check.*

Walk: appears to be one of my own repertoire of walks. Though this woman glides with a more natural panache. *Check.*

Be warned. Only rooky PIs dare to believe. Cynicism is key – the evidence should stand up in court – and there are boxes this POI doesn't tick:

Her demeanour: she appears not to have a worry in the world. Bambi Love would be brittle and adrift, not making new friends. The companion is squat with theatrical arms, half her age and walks like he straddles a bucket. The real Bambi Love wouldn't be walking outside, let alone throwing her head back and laughing out loud.

That laugh. Time stops dead. My neck muscles wane.

I've not heard it in twenty-five years.

Positive identification *cannot* occur until you see a POI's face. The umbrella's ribs tight to my head, I speed up. Pull back, because I'm being reckless. Swap my beanie for a scarf – its colour is a muted version of hers.

Whoa there, I remind myself. *Nothing is ever that serendipitous.*

But just in case, I take a picture of her back. Apart from her Holy Communion photo, it's the only one I have. I zoom in on her headscarf, look for clues as to her hair colour.

The bridge that cuts across Rio della Madonna dell'Orto is constructed of dog-eared wooden planks. I tail them across it and along Calle Loredan, left into Fondamenta della Sensa, and over another bridge where, suddenly, they wave one another goodbye. It's reassuringly perfunctory, the man continuing onwards, the woman turning right into a side street.

A criss-cross of alleys, grey and identical in the dark, I trail her for less than two minutes. We're a spit from Campo del Ghetto Nuovo – I lodge a similar distance from it, just in the opposite direction.

Her destination is Calletta Stretta – a walkway wide enough to accommodate two people, at a push. By the time I peek around its corner, a front door has already banged shut. The cobbled avenue comprises twenty-one doors. Ten on either side and one on the far wall. Knocking on any of them is foolhardy, particularly given I don't know her name.

I scan the immediate vicinity. There's an alley between two buildings – boarded up for years, the wooden slats have split and dropped.

It's a job to squeeze inside. Once I manage it, however, the view is ideal – directly into Calletta Stretta. The hiding space is tight, mind you – I have to remain standing, my spy scope resting in the horizontal gap between boards, lean my temple against the wall, then wait for eight and a half gruelling hours.

Akin to a Chinese water torture cell, rain drips from the guttering four floors up. Agitation and sleep deprivation are relentless foes – the throb in my eyes intensifies and escapes, spreading into my temples, cheeks and jaw. For an hour or two I contemplate going mad.

5.38 a.m.

A bright blob. It bobs deep inside Calletta Stretta. My yap is beleaguered – it definitely gets bigger. Then there are arms, legs and a body. A woman. A whole one, she emerges from the darkness. A street lamp throws light at her face – her features sharpen. Glancing left and right, she shows me both profiles.

Bambi Love. *Check, check, check!*

My mother appears uptight. My guess, she wants her bed as much as I do. She was big on sleep, if my memories aren't fake.

Anxious not to lose sight of her, I tumble from my hiding place, gouging my palm on a spike of wood. I squash my mouth into my bicep and scream. It's excruciating. I don't look at the damage, just wrap it tightly in my scarf, dig the hand into my pocket; walk fast, try to swallow the pain.

The tangle of walkways is familiar to me, yet I don't take enough notice of their names. I lag behind her, holding my arm. Like Donald Sutherland in Daphne du Maurier's *Don't Look Now*, prior to being murdered by a female dwarf. Though I don't call out – no way am I making that mistake again. This time, I intend to corner her, physically. And then mentally, using a Co-ordinated Behavioural Response. If only

I could remember the Four Prongs; Christ, my hand hurts like hell.

I know she's about to arrive at her destination, because she slows down, digs in her bag. Pulling free keys, she pauses at a shop door. Employing a tomboyish saunter, I continue straight past her.

This is her scent: bloomy, citrus and soap.

Chanel No. 5 fact: Coco wanted a fragrance as complex as a woman, while emphasising the whole, not the sum, of its parts. The resultant perfume should be banned. It's too full of intrigue.

The shop door clatters shut.

I about-turn. Stop at the window. It's dark inside, except for a door-shaped corona at the rear. My eyesight adjusts. I can make out flowers, black as cardboard cut-outs, buckets of them. Tommaso has given everything so much thought. How am I to get over him now? A flower shop – it's too perfect.

The real Bambi *loved* flowers. Our garden was a rural idyll, bursting with blousey blooms and climbers. It remains as she designed it, though Dad's less detail obsessed than she. Then there's her home in Calabria Bagnara – its walls were drenched in flowers, her front patio invisible for terracotta pots.

Mum has locked the door behind her. In the absence of a bump gun, I use a pick. I first made one of these for a GCSE project. This version is a few on, but the principle remains the same.

Bend a wire hanger into an inverted L – this is your pressure pin. Repeat with a second piece of wire but, on the inside of the L's short line, add grooves. Think: a rake for a Borrower. Grooves facing down, insert into the keyhole and wiggle. This pushes the pins down. Now insert the pressure pin and wiggle.

My right hand pulses. I can only use its fingertips. It takes longer than usual to align the lock's pins.

I close the door silently behind me.

She's in the back room. I hear her singing.

Singing.

That makes me mad. And relieved. And endeared, because her supra soprano is shocking, but mostly sad at the song she chooses to wail. It used to be 'The Flower Duet' from Delibes' opera *Lakmé*. Now it's the tune from the British Airways advert. I circumnavigate flower buckets to lean against the door's architrave and look through the gap.

My mother stands at a workbench, snipping at stems, occasionally stopping to concentrate on an impassioned high note.

I am *utterly* unaware that I've joined in.

She turns too sharply, our flower duet petering out before it gets started.

Like a naughty child, I step into the room and hold out a placatory hand, because my mum is catatonic with shock.

Usually, when Michael hasn't breathed in a while, I hold his nose. I don't know Mum well enough, so I try to touch her arm. As expertly as Michael, she dodges my hand, because the scarf has dropped free.

Tissue destruction extends through the epidermis to the subcutaneous tissue – my palmar anatomy gapes. In layman's terms: it looks like a small bomb has gone off in my hand. There is blood all over me.

'Oh, shit!' I shout.

Mum won't look at it. Just stares into my eyes. Her apology is heartfelt: 'I am going to faint.'

'Jesus Christ, is that my bone?' I demand.

But black walls close in on me.

When I come round, I'm on the floor. My mother is passed out beside me.

*

Mum sits holding her cheek. 'You hit me?'

I promise her, 'I was checking you weren't dead.'

'Well, I'm not.' She's genuinely sorry about the fact.

The protectiveness I feel towards her is murderous. 'That's very defeatist. Do you have any idea what I've been through to find you?'

'Don't,' she warns. 'I'll weep.'

'For who, exactly?'

'For all of us.'

'No,' I tell her tear ducts, because her bottom lip wobbles. 'We haven't time. I can't be here for long. We need to talk.'

She mouths back, 'I'm too emotional.'

So I tell her something about me . . .

'False Memory Syndrome is a condition that centres on a trauma. Reinvented memories become ingrained. Everything you are is defined by it. My memory? A woman called Bambi Love who *adored* me.' I lean towards her. 'Did I make it up?'

Her fingers lift and hover in the space between us. I shuffle closer, to help her out – but she doesn't touch me – she says the most beautiful thing I have ever heard.

'They put you in my arms, and I said to your daddy, "She has the eyes of a woman who's a thousand years old. Life will be bearable now," I said.'

'Was it?' I smile.

'You became my sun in the sky.'

My head floods with Disney birdsong.

'But now, I'm just scared.' She points to her chest. 'Of feeling anything in my heart.'

I look at her décolletage. At a fine gold chain. With what could be one misshapen rosary bead. It's not, it's a cornicello – an Italian amulet that wards off evil.

'Your horn of hope,' I whisper. Of all her sins, this was the one that stung the most – the fact she forgot to leave it to me. She's letting me touch it now, though. 'It looks like a baby dragon's tooth. Their newborns are called wyrmlings or whelps.' I look up and ask, 'Who gave you this?'

'My sister,' she says quietly. 'You are very like her.'

The birdsong is accompanied by the actual animations from *Sleeping Beauty*.

'Surely that means I'm very like you, too. You were identical.' I let go of the necklace, cup her cheek and say, 'I know, Mum. About everything.'

'No?' Her eyes plead with mine.

'Yes. Now, I need medical attention. The unofficial sort. I'm not ready to die, not before we've spoken. Half an hour, it's all I ask.'

'*Santo cielo!*' She remembers my hand, looks for her bag, drags her bottom towards it, pulls free a phone, makes a call. 'Hold on, if you can, piccolina,' she says.

'It's just, I could have septicaemia and my tetanus is out of date.'

Her Italian is different to her English – fast, strict, intelligent-sounding. Her words are alien as Dothraki, except her last two – '*Sta morendo,*' she says, before hanging up – which has something to do with death.

Pulling herself to her knees, she writes on a Post-it note and hands it over. 'Go here now.'

I shake my head. 'You'll do a runner.'

Keys jangle in the shop's front door. 'The blood,' she mutters, pushing me out of a back entrance. 'I have to clean it. You know where it is?'

I look at the note. *Madonna dell'Orto.*

A further fact about serendipity: when coincidences arrive like flying ants, it's usually a friendly warning of imminent doom.

At the church, I sit on a step and panic – my arm's on fire up to the elbow. Lockjaw, gangrene, a necrotising subcutaneous infection. Using my good hand and the wall, I get up and make my way to the portal doors, not expecting them to be open: it's barely 7 a.m. Yet one is. Slipping inside, I slouch on a pew and say to God, *This is not how I planned it*.

A baritone voice replies, '*Andiamo*.'

The man is not God, but he is the size of a rhinoceros. Obediently, I follow him through the nave, a side door, a corridor and into a kitchen. Waiting on a plastic chair is a young woman and her medical box. Dressed in civvies, apart from the rosary beads, she gently picks up both my hands, comparing one with the other.

'*Merda*,' she states.

My smile is slim. 'That's what I said.'

Nineteen or twenty years old, I would guess she's in the pre-novitiate phase of becoming a nun – just like my mum was when her life imploded. I wonder if this girl knows who I am. Whether she considers me foolhardy or loyal for not letting my mother go. My gut tells me – she doesn't know or care. I am simply in need.

While I bite on a towel, she removes every splinter from my palm. Tenderly, she cleans it, as though it's stigmata, then anoints it. The sutures are neat and the bandage is massive. Co-codamol is administered orally, while she holds the glass to my lips. Finally, she cradles my swaddled hand in both of hers, and prays.

'*Ave, o Maria, piena di grazia, il Signore è con te. Tu sei benedetta fra le donne e benedetto è il frutto del tuo seno . . .*'

If she's reading my Last Rites, I don't care. Her innocence is as palliative as a pre-med. When she indicates that I'm to remain seated, I say, '*Grazie*,' put a cheek on the table, close my eyes and wait for the painkillers to kick in. I'm not sure how long I sleep for, but when the Rhinoceros prods me awake, I find a small pillow under my cheek and a rug over my knees.

I look up at the clerestory window – the sky has a noon hue. '*Andiamo*,' states the Rhinoceros.

More corridors, then a large oak door. Its iron hinges squeal when he yanks it open. In front of us, a haphazard stone staircase leads downwards. His chin jut tells me we're going in. I don't expect him to close the door behind me.

The darkness is alarming at first. The only thing I can see: water glistening back up at me at the bottom of the stairs. I take the steps, timidly. Wonder how many other bodies bob dead below.

Eight, it turns out.

The basement is a catacomb. A foot deep in lagoon, the water acts as a mirror; its pillars appearing twice as long. I must walk a sturdy plank to get to Bambi Love, who perches, vision-like, on a sarcophagus ahead. Faint downlights twinkle in the water around her like spirit orbs. The stone coffin on which she sits appears to hover ethereally. I enjoy the sensation of walking on water.

'Well, this tops all my graveyard tours,' I smile, thinly, on arrival, then sit opposite her.

She just stares at me. Allows herself, finally, to see me. I don't know how or where she's got her courage from, but she doesn't even blink. Simply sucks in every last detail of my face.

It makes me shy. Especially when she stretches a hand across the stone lid. I watch my own hand slide towards hers. Our fingers tangle.

'My little girl,' she says.

Twittering bluebirds clap their wings excitedly, because an orchestra is playing, and a male voice warbles a magical tune. *I have but one song, one song, only for you, one heart . . .*

Then she warns me. 'The dead are the only people we can trust now, piccolina.'

The Four Prongs

When I ask my mother about my aunt, her eyes wander to another life.

The whimsical expression is one I've seen before. Instinctively, I relax.

'You know who hit some nails in the head?' she muses. 'Shakespeare.'

Bambi becomes Helena from *A Midsummer Night's Dream*, an Italian one, who hasn't learned her lines properly. 'We grew in a womb together, like the double cherry. Seemingly parted, but there's such union, you know; when two berries are moulded from one stem.'

I frown, because I don't remember her being particularly well read.

She nods, understanding my conundrum. 'It's hard for others, sometimes, to understand the relationship between twins.'

'I understand,' I reassure her. 'They're a biological mishap – there's no room for anyone else.'

I'm wrong. 'Rina Galini had the room. All high hopes and no idea how to make them real. *Her* mistakes were too full of implications. Never mind, twins are there before everybody and all else.' Pausing to reminisce, her eyes dart between sorrow, joy and confusion. 'Then you had the Galini Girls. They had no mama, just a papa who missed her too much . . .'

Bambi Love fact: her storytelling is still mesmeric. Her expressions stretch from crown to collarbone, unconsciously conveying every sentiment, her emotions morphing in a trice.

Such uninhibitedness – it's like I spy on her through a hole in the wall.

Especially as she addresses the occupant of the coffin beneath her elbows: 'I'll tell you, shall I, all about Ruth and Rina?'

The key with my mum was this – remain as quiet as possible. The longer she forgets you're there, the longer she'll keep her tale going.

I make my whisper sound like it's from another dimension: 'Yes, please.'

And so she continues.

'They were like two stereo speakers – giving the same answers, singing the same songs; they fooled the teachers by pretending to be the other. And their father; usually, he was too drunk to notice. They even dreamed the same dreams – but only at night. When school finished the Galini Girls took different paths.

'Rina met a man. He promised her the moons of Jupiter. Young, a little lost, stupid – she married him within a month.' She blames herself. 'Then again, Ruth had become too much about God, you know?'

I do. Growing up, she'd been His biggest fan. And her own worst enemy – I recognise her facial expression; I've seen it often enough. Though, at the time, I was too young to put it into context – at seven, you assume there's nothing of much consequence beyond your nuclear family.

Today, that facial expression falls into place. Regret – and how it haunts her. She bobs, as though unhinged.

'And all the while, Rina's husband was breaking her will and her bones. Yes, we wished him dead, but it was always fantasy. One day, we planned to bash him on the head with a brick; the next, poison his frittata with moonseed. None of it involved breaking a boiler.' She remembers I'm here. Looks up. 'Neither of us knew anything about boilers.'

'Matteo's death was an accident.' I nod.

Her shrug is weary. 'Maybe not. Marco was a monster. He had more enemies than friends. Matteo was all he cared about – he paraded the boy like a trophy.'

I frown. 'Why on *earth* did you both admit to it?'

She frowns, too. 'I did because she did. For one crazy second, I thought, she's gone and really done it. Tried to bump Marco off, but got the wrong Ferrari. But she hadn't thought of the prison cell, piccolina. We're claustrophobic – she would have gone mad in the head.'

In the other dimension, I'm slapping her with a pool noodle. 'You pretended you murdered a man so she didn't get claustrophobic, irrespective of the fact that neither of you did anything?'

'We were a biological misfit,' she mutters defensively.

Defensive is not good. I emphasise her attributes. 'Loyalty is a precious quality, though.' I clarify. 'Assuming its use is appropriate and in proportion.'

'You always understood.' She leans across the tomb, conspiratorially, like I'm visiting her in prison. 'The trial was quite the spectacle. She made things up about herself. She was doing a course in gas pipes. I'm not a plumber, piccolina, but there's no course in *gas pipes*. She said God told her to do it. He didn't.'

'She was pretending to be crazy.'

'But *why*? I didn't do anything.'

'Surely you told her that.'

This was apparently the problem. 'I never got to speak to her again.'

'Ever?'

She speaks as though she's hearing it for the first time, too. 'We were kept apart until the start of the trial. We couldn't confer, you see. The only times I saw her were in the dock. She wouldn't look at me.'

'Did you tell the court your sister had lost her mind; that neither of you had done it; about Marco being a maniac?'

She nods, a little absurdly. 'At the police station – I couldn't keep my story up for two hours. I told them about Marco and his cruelty. I said, "I know nothing other than my sister is not capable of such an act." It made us look worse. I had given the prosecution a motive. They wanted to be quick, because Matteo Ferrari was a big hero, and now he was a household name, too – the nation was gripped. All the eyes were on the Bologna *polizia*, you know. Italy wanted a good story.'

She gives the media its due. 'The papers gave it to them. School friends sold lies about us. But the Ferraris – they were as quiet as snakes. A court decision was of no matter to them – they had their own plans.'

'The courts proved you both innocent,' I say weakly.

'In Italy, insufficient evidence means only one thing – the police messed up. They wanted two heads on a pole.'

'I'm sorry,' I say. 'Bringing this all up – it must be unbearable.'

Her eyes become fond. 'You thought of me first, always.'

I hold my throbbing hand – the one she's forgotten to ask me about – and do a stagey sigh, 'I seem to remember that's my job, right?'

'I suppose it was.' She can't talk about me in the present tense. I'm grateful for her second wind. 'When we were acquitted, I was rushed from the courthouse into the back of a van. The police took me to a safe house, I don't know where. It was on an industrial estate of some sort. A warehouse – bomb- and bulletproof, they told me, so I had nothing to fear. A door led from a workshop to the upper floor, which was like a make-believe hotel. One that had armed guards to keep its visitors alive. The rules were strict – you had to be anonymous. It was forbidden to leave your room; you might identify the others being held here. And vice versa. Only two people came in and out. A protection officer in blue jeans and a T-shirt with David Bowie on it. And a counsellor, because I was now one of the two most hated women in the country and had to become a different person, pronto.'

'One who was not a twin?'

'For our own protection, we were kept apart. The public outcry was huge. They, like the mafia, wanted retribution. We wouldn't last a week, they said – unless we went our separate ways. Do you know, when you become a protected person, they give you two weeks to learn by heart everything about the new you. Then they show you a video of your new home. I could choose the country and my Christian name.'

'*Bambi?*' I frown. 'It's not exactly run-of-the-mill in Dorset.'

With no humour whatsoever, she replies, 'I was, a little bit, taking the piss.'

'Oh,' I say.

'With no shadow of the doubts, I was reuniting with my sister. The authorities could burn in hell. I knew she'd be thinking the same; counting the hours until we were together again.'

I squeeze her fingers, but she pulls them gently free, squashing her hands between her crossed legs, whispering new secrets at the dead doge.

'I got a message to her,' she tells him, ashamed. 'The councillor agreed – because of my distress levels – though I couldn't see her. It could be just one sentence.' Bambi dusts the tomb's lid with her fingertips. 'It was a mistake. But you see, as children, we felt each other's pain – a broken toe or a bee sting. Once, in the playground, I knocked myself out. My sister was in the chapel, but fainted, too.' Confusion narrows her eyes. 'When did I stop *knowing* her?'

'What was the message, Mum; the one that would help your distress levels?'

'I told her that I was pregnant. Six months gone, I hid it under a girdle. She will know that I am scared witless, I thought; that I need her because she is wiser than me.'

My mother stops talking. Looks at me blindly.

I make excuses. 'It sounds like she was having a break-down.'

'So, why wasn't I having one, too?'

We look at one another silently. I'm not sure how to respond.

'It was like God unplugged us from one another,' she complains.

'I do understand,' I reassure her. 'I refused to accept you were dead. There was no lightning bolt. I'd have *felt* it.' I ask this less enthusiastically. 'Did you feel *anything* in the moment that Rina passed?'

Her expression is the one you'd wear having been shot in the head. Except Mum talks. '*Oh, mio Dio.* No!' Half stands up. Horrified, looks for an escape.

I half stand, too, ready to tackle her into the swamp if she flees. I reassure her I'm an idiot. 'I don't know what I'm saying . . .'

'I thought . . . I thought . . . I don't know what you know and what you don't . . .'

I try to explain: 'My curiosity – it's like Tourette's.'

'Piccolina, it was *Ruth* who died. She wore my clothes. She had my identification documents. She jumped on the train tracks so that I could live. With Rina gone, nobody was having Marco's baby.'

My mouth gapes for a while.

Like a child, she asks, 'Is that disappointing?'

'No, no.' I sit back down. 'My head's just, you know, recali-brating a new route.'

She defends her poor choices. 'I was so young and got dazzled by the glitz.'

While I re-examine her face. Bambi Love was a gangster's moll. I can think of no world less suited to her. A new compassion evolves in me; a fiercer one. I tell her off, 'You're not the dead one.'

'I am. On paper. And in my soul.'

'Not in mine.'

Bambi's grief, however, is too terminal. 'Ruth was supposed to wait for us.'

'She gave her life so you and your child could have one.'

'I didn't want a life, not without her.'

'You should honour her gift.' I talk shite.

'She took her life – God doesn't forgive us for that.'

I do, says God.

'He definitely does,' I say.

Eyes wide, she asks, 'How do you know?'

This is what God says to me:

white noise

'I'll tell you why,' I squint. 'Since when has it been a sin to sacrifice yourself to save others? Far as I'm aware, that's what Jesus did for us – died for *all* our sins, even the crappy ones.' I scour my memories of GCSE history. Point. 'What about the Catholic priest who took the place of a Jewish prisoner in a starvation cell? He deliberately died and definitely got into heaven.' A quote arrives – for a split second I attribute it to *Game of Thrones*. '"Greater love hath no man than this, that a man lay down his life for his friends."'

That does it. Bambi crumples into herself. Though she refuses to cry. Instead, enlisting muscle and sinew, she shows me what interminable grief looks like. It is horrendous viewing. Makes me hold my breath, because Anne Hathaway is a fraud; it's my mother who dreamed a dream in times gone by.

The silent anguish, her contorting face; tears are dripping from my own chin before I even realise I weep. When Mum notices, she becomes firm. 'It's best not to think about it.'

Halfway from all the answers I need, halfway from never seeing her again – there's no time to pussyfoot. I scrub my face.

'Mum, does Maria know who her father is?'

She nods, strictly. 'Joey Nucci. A cousin. He and his wife, Donatella, brought her up as their own. Their village was one thousand kilometres south of Bologna. They already had six children – who would notice another? Maria was safe and cherished. And I got better.' She points, fascinated, 'Do you know what happened when they discharged me from the hospital for my emotions?' I shake my head. 'They took me straight back to the safe house. *Orientation* – that's what they called it. Their job was made easy, now the world thought I was dead.'

Christ, I'm keen for Pannacotta Man to be her redeemer. 'But you found love in the end, didn't you?'

Playing with her naked wedding finger, she gives this some thought. 'No.'

'Your companion at the airport?'

That produces quite the nose-crinkle. 'That's Joey. I'm no pervert, piccolina – he's a blood relative. You know, I didn't know that Donatella had died until I returned to Italy. Joey gave me a safe place again. Such generosity, given the stakes. I had no protection.' This she says, excited, 'But I had a family once more.'

It's my turn to look down at the tomb. Somehow, Bambi wangled herself a new safe haven, and it was the most perfect alternative to the Loves.

No, no, no, I tell it.

Yes, yes, yes, says God. *You lobbed a grenade at her last chance of happiness.*

268

I blame Father Benedict. I'd met him in Tuscany while searching for her and, if he'd kept shtum, Mum wouldn't have known I was in the country. Which means cousin Joey would not have slipped me her address, while she hid in a confessional box down the road. The mafia were already watching me – the psychopathic priest put them in ridiculous danger.

'How do you know Benedict?' I ask.

Tutting, she confides, 'Alcohol is not his friend.'

'Last time I saw him, he put a gun in my mouth,' I state.

Her response is too philosophical. 'The stakes are high. It's Joey and Benedict who were once close. They grew up in an orphanage in Siena. Though they hadn't seen one another in many years.' She leans forward and makes this sound a lovely thing: 'Until you turned up.'

Shame makes me wince.

'Joey confided in Benedict many years before, when he was adopting Maria. It's OK,' she reassures me, 'in those days, he was sane. Trustworthy. Too true to his word. Especially with the mafia. Father Benedict's problem with them was that he lacked a vital survival tool – hypocrisy. There was a price on his head.'

I suddenly remember. 'Joey, Maria, Paola – where are they?'

'Same place. It was just me who moved on. Benedict saw to it.'

He did not.

Things I won't tell her about Benedict: he now lives in a converted church on a mountain road in Sistiana with Massimo Sattori. Another ex-priest who is an actual legend. Known internationally as The Eradicator, I'd marry him, were he seventy years younger. Their safe house is an unhappy one. Diametrically opposed, intellectually and moral-compass-wise, Benedict and Massimo share only one thing – a hatred of organised crime. I don't know what Benedict did or why, but The Eradicator certainly gave the mafia a boda-cious tooth-flick.

The irony: Massimo is also Tommaso's godfather. My informed guess: it's them who collude to protect Bambi Love.

Yet I can never repay their altruism. What I can do is make the universe promises. Like, for my entire life, I will mourn Tommaso Bellini and live in the past. While so doing, I will send Massimo such heartfelt vibes – the poor man is doomed to incarceration with a soul-sapping nemesis.

That's better than having nobody, says God.

Limp, I look across a coffin at my mother – she is beautiful, broken and very much alone.

What the hell have I done?

God deals in bald-faced truths: *You didn't listen to your father.*

My forced grin is as much for me as for her. 'And then you came to Lymington? I *love* Lymington. Michael and I went to the Yacht Haven not long ago.'

'Michael.' She does a slightly hysterical cry. 'My boy.'

'He's so well.' I tell her quickly. 'He was on *Coronation Street*.'

'*Davvero! Coronation Street!*'

'He's a credit to you.' My need to make amends is all-consuming. 'The baby Jesus – you'd say Michael was a dead ringer.'

'And you were my little Virgin Mary. Exactly the correct hue. When you started school and weren't chosen for the role, I wrote a letter of complaint.'

'That is mortifying.'

'You got the lead the next year.' Her smile's impish. 'And the year after that.'

She's back in the storytelling zone. For now, my guilt eases.

'I like boats – they don't remind me of a single place or

person. Like here, I suppose.' We look around the mausoleum. Then she remembers my hand – holds it in both hands, like it's a dinosaur egg.

'She went a bit overkill with the strapping,' I say.

Mum reassures me, 'She didn't.'

An aside about me and death: I never want to meet it. Its eventuality tormented me as a child; it still does. A fear of death is called thanatophobia, and I have it. For the first time in my life, however, I actually don't care. It'll be my punishment.

It doesn't help that she's being quite maternal.

'Poor Florence. I'm so hopeless with blood and gore, do you remember? If I cut my finger you'd say, "You're turning into a zombie again, Mummy."'

'I got the zombie idea from *Sapphire and Steel*,' I tell her. 'You couldn't watch it on your own.'

'You weren't supposed to look.'

'I peeked.'

Her smile breaks my heart. She likes me, despite all I've done. 'It made me resolved. I thought, if a five-year-old can watch it, I can too. Now, how did you hurt yourself?'

'I tripped on to a spike of wood. It could have been my throat.'

She gasps. 'But for the grace of God.'

'I could have died.'

'You still might,' she says.

'Of what?'

She's not entirely sure. Reassures me, 'We all die in the end.'

I squint. 'You're a laugh a minute, do you know that?'

She does mischievous eyes. 'And you were the clumsiest child, always falling over a pocket of air.' *There* she is. The real Bambi Love. 'My little fairy elephant.'

See how she now tickles my bandage with her nails. I try

to summon the sensation of her doing that on my actual skin. But the ache in my palm is relentless; our time together unforgivably short.

'Lymington,' I remind her.

In so many ways, she's like Michael. Different, but the same. 'When they told me I was coming to England, I said, "As long as I can see Europe."' Her entire face smiles. 'And with industrial binoculars, you could. What a life we had, huh?'

Between jail, the trial, a high-security psychiatric hospital, losing a twin and a daughter, 'orientation', she hadn't been outside. Just arrived in a foreign country and pretended to be someone else. That's an appalling turn of events.

Yet Bambi's face says otherwise. It was the best thing ever to happen to her.

She confirms it: 'I guess happiness just fell plop on my plate.'

'Really?' I squeak.

'It was love at first sight.' She is telling me, inhaling, as though the stagnant water is meadow-fresh. 'He looked like Ryan O'Neill.'

'Eric Steensen?'

She looks appalled. 'Your daddy.'

'He did not,' I snigger.

'We were free and in lust, like Oliver and Jenny in *Love Story*. The night we married, he carried me into the cottage and got my dress stuck on a nail. The skirt ripped up to my hip.'

'You told me.' My memory pumps a triumphant fist. 'Also, on my sixth birthday, you picked flowers from our garden and made me a beautiful posy. You said, and I quote, "It's just the same as my wedding bouquet, piccolina."'

'African daisies.' She points a long finger, lengthened further by a shiny nude almond. 'If you tap the flower's head, the seeds fall out. We planted one each year on the anniversary of our marriage. Romantic, huh?'

My mother and father grew African daisies from the seeds of her bouquet. My bottom lip starts to tremble. 'Dad still does it,' I say; remember the letter Annie stole from the post office.

She'd wanted Dad out of her and Darcie's life from day one. That precious airmail envelope was a bribe; in return, I was to help the Antichrist in that quest. As a result, I discovered Dad was writing to a PO Box in Calabria. Although addressed to Maria's daughter, Paola, it was meant for Mum. This is what he'd written:

To let you know, after much thought, I've decided to replant the African daisy. The badgers have returned, happy and well. God bless x

I thought it perfunctory. A code, more than likely. Michael and I were the badgers. But the African daisy? Now it's clear. George Love was telling his wife that his feelings remained unchanged; at least for another year.

'You were so in love. Happiness was plopped on your plate. Why leave him? Us? And of all places, Italy?'

'Ah,' she says regretfully. 'Piccolina, there was a situation.'

An interesting fact: there are no hard-and-fast rules about refreshment consumption in a burial chamber.

I have my wish. Mum and I are ladies who lunch. Though we refrain from putting our cups on the tomb and cradle our biscuits in napkins on our laps.

The pre-novitiate nun had brought them in – along with two co-codamols, an *antibiotico* pill for the *infezione* and a doggy-bag of sutures and dressings. She and Bambi had then spoken soft and fast Italian. I noted that, throughout, they held each other's hands fondly. Jealousy made me want to tell the girl, *I'm the blood relative, the daughter, the one who made her feel safe.* But she doesn't know who I am. Curiosity's not in her repertoire. She just carries out the will of God.

Alone again, Mum dips an amaretto in her coffee, and continues.

'Two men knocked on the door, out of the blue. Daddy knew as soon as he saw them it was trouble. You see, they were from the Servizio per le Informazioni e la Sicurezza Democratica.'

I shake my head.

'The Ministry of the Interior. They wanted to puff out the Ferraris, along with some other key players. "A mafia purge", they called it.' Her head does a confounded rattle. 'They should know, of all people. Mafioso never go out with a puff. "A hundred times, no," I said. Because I didn't want to be a star witness – what person would? However, my co-operation was too important to them. They needed Rina Ferrari to come back from the dead.'

'Oh, Mum.' I don't know what else to say.

'They put the bloody willies up me. Perhaps this, perhaps that. Perhaps they couldn't promise to protect us any more, you children. Perhaps we could all go wherever we liked, after my testimony. Australia, Iceland. I didn't want another new life.' She takes a sip of espresso. 'I liked our one.'

'But it was the British government who protected you. What the hell has it to do with the Ities?'

I'm wet behind the ears. 'International politics is decided by powerful people. I'll tell you a thing about the intelligence services in Bologna: they're not always good men. Not like Eric – he fought, with teeth and nails. Told his big boss it was too dangerous, that I had human rights. But the National Crime Agency has its own agenda.' She shrugs. 'The trial was likely to last a year, maybe more. Eric, your daddy, Elaine – we all knew, I'd probably get thwacked.' She shakes her head, disappointed. 'I didn't.'

Good God. I finish my coffee in one.

'The Italian intelligence people did as they promised, looked after me well, then offered us a new start. Daddy, Michael, you and me. Together. I was very strict about that.'

'All of us?'

'"No way, Jose," I told them. "I come as a pack of four."'

I check again, 'All of us?'

She nods. 'Belgium. I would be a florist, and your daddy a tennis coach, once he'd learnt Flemish. I had it all planned out.'

'*Really?*'

She says this dramatically. 'We didn't go. I know, I know.' Her eyes beg me not to judge. 'Guilt, my girl, is a wicked affliction.'

'I'm not grasping this.'

Hand on her heart, she swears, 'Daddy never forgave himself.'

'Dad said *no?*'

'I understand.' She tells her knuckles a terrible truth. 'I'm a dangerous woman to have around. Michael would have been first – a son for a son . . .' Her voice peters out.

'Sweet Jesus,' I mouth.

'I was back on the Ferraris' radar. Old ghosts are so dogged.' She puts a palm in the air. 'Don't try to fix me.'

My heart nosedives – some things are too broken. 'Did you go to Belgium?'

'For twenty-two years. What a lot of life that is! The funny thing is, my moments of happiness couldn't fill a day.' She explains. 'I made gloves. And lampshades – for the gift shops. *Urgh!* One day, I snapped. You see, all that time, I had a piece of secret information – it played on my mind for too many years.' She suddenly whispers, 'Twenty-two years before, during the Ferraris' trial, I'd been granted a visit – Joey. He gave me his address. I'd been planning my journey there for ever.'

Now she teaches me to suck eggs.

'You must take a lot of windy routes. My journey to Bagnara Calabria included twelve trains, four buses and a hundred kilometres of walking. Naturally, I was in disguise; the simplest changes – this hat or that scarf – it makes people quite useless at recognition.'

She is totally unaware that I have a Diploma in Private Investigation and a business that specialises in it. Neither is she interested.

'My plan, to glimpse Maria – that's all. Then I would go back to the gloves and lampshades. Piccolina, I'd never even seen her.' She half laughs. 'I couldn't leave.'

For a split second, I'm resentful. 'But you were awful at being invisible at the airport. How are you still alive?'

Her shrug belies a cunning that comes with having been a wanted person for most of your life. 'I don't go out much.'

I stare, then say, 'Let us pray.' I need to think. Close my eyes.

Because a while back – when the past was falling into place for me and I refused, point blank, to stop looking for Mum – my dad had been crystal clear.

You're dabbling in events that are extremely dangerous . . . Do not look for your mum . . . I cannot help you or talk to you about this again . . .

I thought him a coward.

And her.

Too many amends to make – I've no clue how I can make things better.

My eyes spring open. Mum pretends to have hers shut. 'Amen,' I say. Then walk around the tomb, sit by her side, cup her chin.

'You do know, Mum, that you were *it*. The one – for Dad, I mean. He never moved on – just stayed behind, right where he was. Putting his children's safety ahead of all else, especially

276

above the love of his life. That shows great sacrifice and . . . *nobility.*'

Memories of Dad make her eyelids lazy. 'He was like my knight.'

'He's mine now.'

She smiles, relieved. 'I wouldn't have it any other way.'

I stroke her hair. Tell her, softly, 'I am so sorry – I wouldn't stop turning up. It's a mistake I'll never repeat – you'll never see me again. But, for both our sanities, I have to believe I'm here for a reason.'

'What is it?' she asks, like I have all the answers.

I don't, but I go with this one. 'To inform you that your husband still loves you wholly and blindly – you were and will always remain his soulmate.'

I love the face she pulls – her smile is wonderful.

She taps a temple. 'I talk to him all of the time, in here. I'm not sure he always listens – he has very selective hearing – but some days I *know* he hears me, because he talks right back. I have to be in the mood, though. Some days, I ban myself from thinking about anything at all.'

Tomorrow, she can have a day off.

'And then there's Uncle Fergus,' I say. 'Whatever happened to him?'

Mum hadn't expected me to mention him. I'm not sure why. Lips ajar, she waits for elucidation. I use the opportunity to inhale her breath. Coffee, with a hint of apple-scented lip gloss – it gives me a love shiver. As does the scent of her pheromones, as familiar as my own.

'I wasn't in England when that all happened,' she says at last.

'When Eric was killing Fergus?'

She doesn't flinch. 'Eric was convinced Elaine was having a love affair with him. She wasn't – Fergus was a creep, and

I told Eric so, but still he hated him. I think there's some history, you know.'

'Probably.' I'm grateful for her ignorance.

Then Bambi remembers something. 'We were going to be private investigators. I taught you.'

I smile. 'You were preparing me for all the eventualities.'

'I was Jaclyn Smith. And you were Kate Jackson.'

'Was I?' Right there – a lost memory.

Yet, instinctively, I do a sexy gun pose. She swishes her hair to one side and places her hands together like she prays. In the actual shot, Kelly Garrett wears a white halter-neck bikini. Whereas Sabrina dons an androgynous lumberjack shirt.

'You were always the sexiest one,' I complain. 'And I'm sure I was Cheryl Ladd.'

'Wrong hair colour,' she states.

I frown. 'There's a few things I don't get. Like, why Eric needed to disappear.'

Her smile is replaced with mild irritation. 'Because of another case.' She flaps a hand, dismissively. 'A dangerous one. Do you remember, we went on stake-outs?'

'In the Yellow House.' I nod. 'How dangerous?'

'Ireland – we were sure he was hunting the terrorists. Your daddy built that treehouse and I painted it. I like yellow.'

'Mum, no offence. I have to ask. Were you a bit in love with Eric?'

'His eyebrows flaked.' The thought of seborrheic dermatitis makes her swallow a retch. 'Have you seen your father?'

'Ryan O'Neil.' My smile is sad. 'Eric framed you – you realise that?'

'No, my girl.'

'Kind of, he did.'

'If he did, it was for our mutual benefit. Eric protected me every day for twelve years. Daddy and he were close like thieves.'

'Did Eric or Dad say that? That it was for your mutual benefit?'

'They said nothing. I know nothing. Your father just said that Fergus would not be a problem any more.'

'You wrote suicide notes.'

'That's all I did. I was gone when it happened.' She assures me, 'Fergus was a bitter and spiteful man. He resented my relationship with his brother. With you children, too. Most of all, he hated that George and Eric were so close.'

Two things strike me here:

1. She knows nothing about Fergus's perversions.

2. George had a bestie.

That's big; men don't have many of those. Especially dads. Unlike girls, they lack the evolutionary need to talk – when they do, it's a subliminal alliance.

'Your uncle listened to private conversations. He knew about me – not everything, but enough to use as a big stick.' Without blinking, she says, 'Taunting his own brother. And me – it was mostly me. That was hard for us to live with. It made Eric's blood boil – his job was to keep me under the radar. Fergus liked us on the tenterhooks.'

Before asking this, I hone in on her face. A micro-momentary expression lasts one-fifteenth of a second, give or take. And my next question is a biggie.

'Have you any idea how they killed him?'

'No!'

'For example, you know they used your car, right? Eric, Dad and Elaine.'

There it is: a mini-explosion of facial data.

I'll slow it down for you . . .

Eyebrows – smash down towards the glabella. Upper

279

eyelids – rise. Lower lids – flatten. Mouth's lateral commissure – stretched earward, pulling the lips slim.

When these four actions occur simultaneously, it's the universal micro-expression for fear – the type one enlists when unable to face the truth.

'I have not one single clue about any of that business. Apart from the letters we wrote, I wasn't part of it.' She issues me a grave warning. 'And if you tell me the details, it will be a dagger too many.'

I am acutely aware that, given my sins, it's the least I can do – I act as clueless as she. It's water under the bridge, anyway. Bambi Love is innocent of first-degree murder. *Check*.

That leaves just one thing to ask.

I'll be honest: I hope the following question is met with vehement denial and a shedload of assurances. Especially as I struggle to say it out loud.

The ball in my throat is called a globus hystericus, and there's nothing funny about it at all. It insists I burst into tears – we're having quite the grapple.

'Why don't you love me any more, Mum?'

'Ah.' She shuffles her knees around to face me.

I stop her there. 'That is the cruellest thing anyone's ever said to me.'

'May I touch your chin?'

Please! my eyes shout.

'I'm not sure I have the right any more.'

'Well, you do.'

Bambi tips my jaw up. I'm to look into her pupils, infinite and black as deep space. I think I see life in there, but it's far, far away; teeny as a molecule.

She knows I've seen it. 'I'm playing with fire, my girl. I've learned not to get sentimental about you. That won't change, ever.'

That hurts.

Yet I'm not to take it personally. 'I'm in denial and a little too dead to do anything about it. You understand?'

'No,' I mouth.

She releases my chin, puts a hand on her hip. Does that thing she does – uses a fascinated tone, as though she's not the topic of her own gossip.

'Over the years, I have had therapies – CBT, IPT, MBCT; I can't remember half the names. I remember the tablets, though – Xanax, Tramadol, Temazepam, Zopiclone; I could go on for five minutes. I have eaten mood-boosting foods, had acupuncture, art therapy, reiki; drowned my sorrows and smoked cigarettes.' She whispers the last two: 'I've also read books on Buddhism and had my colon irrigated.'

I don't know what to say. That's a lot of information.

'Nothing worked.' She nods.

I mutter things. 'If you can't love me, who can?'

Like I'm five, she tells me off. 'I knew you better than anybody, even myself – such unconditional love, you were concerned by nothing but us. You rescued me. Don't you remember my favourite word?'

I should know it, stockpiling memories like Annie does joy jars. I spout a guess. A ridiculous fucking guess.

'Denouement?' Ashamed, I explain: 'It means the resolution of a narrative . . . It's in my top ten.'

Using a thumb, she decides to neaten my eyebrows. 'There's a word I love more.'

I'm too emotionally banjaxed to play, so stop using my neck muscles. Mum's having none of it – again holds my chin aloft and gives me a clue. 'I loved it the most when you said it.'

Late to the party and out of breath, the answer arrives in my head. Parked too deep, and for good reason. Immediately, my globus hystericus becomes as big as a pear. There's no way back – I submit to my parasympathetic system; twenty-five years in the making, my sobs are desolate and cathartic.

And all the while, she watches each and every tear, communing with them telepathically, or so it feels. The odd one, she swipes away; maybe their *raison d'être* doesn't stand up. It takes ten minutes before I'm depleted of emotion and able to talk once more.

'Your favourite word' – I do a double intake of breath – 'was *Mummy*.'

Her shoulders drop, relieved. 'Children forget so fast.'

'I didn't. I was a prodigy. I won competitions for remembering.'

'Did you?' She examines my hairline, like she'd forgotten I had one.

No. But I passed exams, with knobs on. When is she going to ask me about those? Never. Because she said, "I've learned not to get sentimental about you. That won't change. Ever."

I watch her smack her knees once, then just come out with it. 'I put you in a box.'

'Wow,' I tell her.

'It's a very beautiful box. It took nearly three decades to build.'

'What fucking box?'

Of course, she doesn't flinch. She was married to the mob. 'A very thought-out one,' she promises. 'Like Noah and his ark. Only, I've designed a box, not a boat. And it's not so much a box. More like a block of marble, you know, with no insides.'

'How big is it?' I demand.

She puts her finger and thumb together – there is no discernible gap. 'It's got to be small to fit in my head. I've decorated it,' she reassures me. 'Because now and then I visit its walls. But not inside – because here's the miracle. In the core of the marble is a teeny bubble of air. You can't even see it with a telescope. But if you could, you'll find that, inside, it's bigger than a universe.' She tells me straight, 'I don't go there.'

'Because it's filled with me?'

Her head jiggle is uncertain. 'The real you is in there somewhere. Lost among all the other lives you may be leading. There are too many. Possibilities bouncing off other possibilities, spinning away in too many directions. That bubble is a horrible place to live. The chances you are happy are a billion to one.'

Physics fact: they're not. 'You've switched your feelings off.'

'No. I chose just one reality for you and stuck with it. I've painted that reality on the surfaces of the marble block. I know I sound mad, but it's horses for the courses.'

Her dictionary of choice is still *The George Love Vernacular*. Why hasn't her husband been boxed and banished to a parallel universe? She gets sentimental over him. And Michael. This doesn't seem fair.

Closing her eyes, Mum gives me a snapshot of her artwork.

'There's a mosaic of you in a mortar-board hat. I had to use a sander – one you wear as a belt – to scratch the marble; otherwise, my little tiles wouldn't stick. A hundred thousand of them, I picked each one myself. The oil painting of your wedding – my, *that* was a labour of love. It could cover Basilica Sancti Petri. You know the funny thing? Your children are in it, too. Because you were wiser than me, piccolina. At twenty, you knew things: mostly, that you didn't know your own mind. Your children: two joyful mistakes. Both tanned and boys. One will be a doctor, the other a vagabond. The type who gets right up the nose, unless you're his mother. I'm proud of how you keep him in line. And your husband! Dangerously handsome, like a young Richard Gere. But not a scallywag – an ex-priest, who left his religion because he loved you more than even God himself.'

My smile is sad. 'And because he got a member of his congregation pregnant. Twice.'

'Out of wedlock.' She nods. 'There was a bit of a scandal.'

I feel sharp pity. She's made up a pretend me.

She flaps a hand. 'And my girl, you're strong – everything I longed for, it happened to you.'

I stare at her, until she gently elbows me. 'I'm a fool.'

'No. That's a really good survival tool.'

'It was.' She reminds me of something else I've loused up. She's sorry to admit it. 'You're melting my marble.'

'I shouldn't be. You got every detail right. Do not tell me my future, though. You'll spoil the ending.'

She shakes her head, as though she's the Snowman, slowly dissolving, feet up. 'I'm starting to love you again.'

I never stopped, I don't say. I remind her of those walls. 'Can me and Richard Gere have a hall pass?'

'A pass for which hall?'

'Khal Drogo from *Game of Thrones*. I know it's greedy.' She doesn't have a clue. 'Alternatively, we could make a pact.'

Her eyes tell me to make it good – and quick – too fast, she's remembering what it is to love. But how can we make a pact that will satisfy our losses for ever more? Two people with different pasts and future needs.

'Freedom,' I state.

'I'll never have that,' she sighs.

'From guilt.'

Now, she listens. 'How?'

'By snatching every moment of joy we can, knowing the other is doing the same. If we do it together, we'll feel condoned.' She doesn't look against it. 'No pressure, but we need to fuse our priorities for ever. *Now*. We won't get another chance. Then everything will go back to how it was yesterday. But not until you swear this: you will put me right back in that box.'

'It's too late.'

'I like it in there,' I growl, then point at the dead doge. 'On his grave, you'll go and get a life. And when you laugh, or forget, or feel inexorably contented – it won't matter. In fact, it'll be brilliant, because we'll be working as a team.'

I remind her, 'Swear on the dead guy.'

She turns to place her forehead on the stone coffin. 'On the life of Marcantonio Mocenigo, I do swear to collect happy moments.'

I explain, 'There'll be an element of competition, too. Who can collect the most moments – there's extra points if you can draw one out.'

She smiles. 'Still so competitive.'

'I get it from Dad.' I am unapologetic. 'From when he played tennis. We'll compare notes when we're in heaven. Agreed?'

That distresses and pleases her in equal measure.

God reminds me about me: *My child, the jury's still out.*

Ditto. I remind Him that it's a two-way street.

When the oak door squeals open, my mum shuffles to the left.

Our time is over. Just like that.

'There's a bar mitzvah,' she tells her knees. 'I have to finish the flower arrangements.'

'Oh,' I say.

'It has a theme. *Frozen.*'

'Back in my box already.'

'Girls have them, too. Only it's called a bat mitzvah.'

For a while, I regard her knees, back. Pat one of them goodbye. She grabs it before I get up. Her hug is more of a faint. Repeatedly, she apologises into my breast. '*Scusa, piccolina. Scusa. Ti prego, perdonami. Scusa . . .*'

Before she lets me go, she kisses my cheek. Wet, fat, Italian kisses.

The one I give her back is protracted – I hold her head and forget to breathe. Then I leave, walking the plank towards the stone steps, not looking back.

'Florence.' My foot falters on the first step. The accent, its inflections and musicality – she says my name exactly as it was designed.

It occurs to me, quite suddenly – I don't yet know hers.

When I turn, she is holding my bag of bandages aloft, just like she did in our kitchen in Dorset. Only, back then she'd dangle a lunch bag, PE kit, hairbrush; and she always said the same thing.

'One day you'll forget your own head.' Today, I see past her fake exasperation. Look a millimetre beneath the façade. A new emotion effervesces. Absolution – not the full monty, not yet, but a start, nonetheless.

I point. 'You're one up already.' Snatching the bag, I smile. 'Let the games begin.'

'One all,' Bambi Love shouts after me.

Ik heb een dokter nodig

Tuesday, 9 December, 2014. Arrivals –
Bournemouth Airport

I spot Dad before he does me and my heart does a bunny-hop.
He looks unbelievably sweet and a tiny bit mad. The lolloping
gait, deerstalker hat and Barbour; the sign in his hands.

Florence Love, my daughter, it says.

The voice I use is four octaves higher than my usual resting
pitch. 'You are so embarrassing!'

'Michael made it,' he says. 'He said you'd probably forgotten
what we look like.'

I grin. 'I've been away for a blink in space-time.'

Our cuddle is long and gentle – his clothes smell of boiled
vegetables. He tells my hair, 'You've been gone for much
longer than that.' Then, holding me at arms' length, he asks,
'Have you grown?'

'Maybe a bit.'

Then he notices my hand. Whips it aloft. 'What in sweet
Jesus have you done?'

'The strapping's a bit over-enthusiastic,' I say.

'You could use it as a pugil stick.'

'I could not – it hurts like the Dickens.'

Note: on the plane, I decided to respect my father more,
so have banned myself from swearing ever again (in his
presence).

'I got impaled on rotten wood.'

'When did you last have a tetanus?'

'Back end of 1984.'

His eyes widen. 'I'm a terrible parent.'

'I had to make my own dentist appointments, too. We'll see how it looks when we get home.'

Home.

We walk to the car park, me bouncing on the melody of that word, Dad slightly further ahead, my rucksack bending him double.

'Hindus say, "Home is where the om is",' I say loudly.

'Do they?' he calls back.

'No. But it's good, eh?'

'I have no idea what you're talking about.' Still, he smiles – one side of his face is flooded with crow's feet. I wonder if I should tell him anything; instantly dismiss the thought. If I've learned anything, it's that George Love will broach a subject when he's ready.

In the meantime, I make sure he knows where we're at.

'Belgium, though. Seriously? Can you imagine Michael attempting Flemish?'

His footsteps peter out. At his side, I stop to look up at him. 'I'm going to teach him some, though, just for the crack.'

He gazes down at me.

'*Ik heb een dokter nodig*,' I say. 'That means "I need a doctor."'

Dad opens his mouth and shuts it a few times. Then makes a pledge. 'I will try and be . . . *better.*'

'You will never change.' I command it of him. Then bend the knee, which is quite the gesture in Westeros. Flowery words embarrass Dad, so instead I inject my voice with a passion that verges on wrath. 'For everything, I thank you.'

He looks either side of us. Then tips his chin at me, once.

We leave it like that.

Inside the car, while Dad fine-tunes his cockpit, I take a packet of ibuprofen from his glove compartment; dry-swallow four.

'So, where's the brother who couldn't live without me?'

'He's having a ceremony in the paddock.'

'Sounds about right.'

'Vee is his yogi. Cleansing his karma, apparently.'

That perks me up. 'She is *seriously* hysterical.'

'She's certainly the other one of you.'

Hand on my heart, I've never felt prouder.

He even ruffles my hair. 'I've a feeling you girls are going to be trouble.'

'Tell me about it.' I am joyously complete. 'I could do with a karmic boost myself.'

The paddock is a short walk from the cottage. Twenty metres uphill. Owned by a farmer who's forgotten it's his, we've tended to use it as our own. As children, we would camp in it, because Dad could see us from the kitchen window. Not that our expeditions ever lasted long – Michael's too petrified of the paranormal. I designated it an Area of Outstanding Natural Beauty for a geography project. Michael even had a birthday party there – the bouncy castle faced downhill. It was carnage.

Dad no longer cuts it in summer; it's too florid a canvas of wildflowers. In late autumn, however, he'll give it a trim.

Today, Vee stands out particularly. Sitting crossed-legged on the grass. Her headscarf, an astonishing cacophony of aquamarine, Mauritian turquoise and Caribbean blue – the sun's obsessed with its sequins, over-examines their dimples. Her head shimmers like a mermaid's tail.

Underneath, she wears a full-length navy puffa coat and wellies. Elbows on knees, palms up and cupped, she talks to Michael, three metres to her left. Wearing a onesie, Uggs and the guest duvet, his eyes are squeezed tightly shut.

Dad whispers, 'She's dissolving negative thought patterns before they take control of his life.' We move a few steps closer. His David Attenborough impression is better than

Michael's. 'And now we witness the cleansing rituals of the Greater Spotted Love . . .'

'Shush. I want to listen.'

Vee is saying, '. . . an emergency meditation for when the pressure becomes like lemonade and threatens to pop out of you.'

Michael's outbreath is beleaguered. 'Because it does.'

'And why is that?'

'I'm too nice.'

'It's a beautiful thing,' she says. 'But the ancient Punjabis were clear – if you lose yourself, you're of no use to anybody.'

'I'm too selfless,' he tells the ether.

'They also understood the importance of not dwelling on old problems.'

'How old?'

'Anything that happened prior to breakfast.'

'Hallelujah.' He can get with that.

While Dad hovers on the sidelines, I join them, sit down opposite Vee. She makes happy O's of her mouth and eyes.

'Love the scarf,' I whisper. 'Is it solar-powered?'

'Julien Macdonald,' she whispers back. 'Seventy squid in the sale. Morden's.'

Michael jerks his head at the sky, like he's genuinely blind. 'Is that you, Flo?'

'Noooo . . . I am a figment of your imagination . . .'

'Vee, can you hear her, too?'

Smiling widely, she states, 'And this, Michael, is the power of karmic cleansing. Open your eyes.'

On seeing me, he scrambles backwards. 'Woah.'

'It's powerful shit,' I say.

He asks Vee, 'What's it done to her hand?'

'I just fell over,' I reassure them.

'A cliff?' He puts his hands on his hips.

'No. If I had, I'd be dead.'

Vee puts a stern finger in the air. We are to be silent and close-eyed. Her cadence is instantaneously hypnotic. 'Using the hourglass method of breathing, we will now achieve peace and classy dignity. Tell yourself: *I rock*.'

'I rock,' we say.

'Now stand up.'

We do as we're told. Though Michael's no stranger to the ceremony – he's waiting for her cue.

Vee delivers it with a touch of the pantomime. 'Time to cleanse, my karmic friends!'

I frown. They shout words into a wind not strong enough to macerate them. Vee has the mouth of a sailor. Dad's discomfiture, however, has less to do with that; everything to do with Michael's long list of grievances.

'Annie is a swamp monkey . . . Seb did coitus with a girl . . . Florence abandoned me to go abroad on her own. I would never do that to her . . . My own father didn't believe me . . .'

When Dad wanders back to the cottage, I follow.

The kitchen table showcases a cake stand. Three tiers, each piled with glazed petits fours. There's also one yellow balloon and a card – from Michael, I assume – welcoming me home.

'I only called this morning to say I was coming back.'

Dad nods, 'He was beside himself. And he will be again soon.'

'Just not today,' I smile.

So does Dad. 'He's such a conundrum. Do you know he saw Sebastien?'

'God, yes, I forgot. How did it go?'

'Your brother took a date.' Dad signals outside. 'I don't imagine Sebastien got a word in edgeways.'

'Vee?' I laugh. 'That is genius.'

He laughs too. On and off, for a good five minutes. We're

infected by the type of amusement that squats in your belly then resurfaces of its own accord.

My eyesight – unlike Dad's – is twenty-twenty. When I clock Michael standing poised with what looks like a priest's thurible, I swiftly redirect Dad's attention.

'Can you look at my hand? It feels like a rat's gnawing through my metacarpus.' Sitting at the kitchen table, I ensure his back's to the window.

Dad unwinds the bandage like it's a toilet roll. 'Is there anything under all this?' The excessive swaddling is a godsend. Behind him, Michael swings the censer from a long chain, apparently anointing the paddock.

Oblivious to what materialises behind his back, Dad gasps; and I wince – the cool air is as abrasive as fibreglass.

'Florrie, I think we need to pop to A&E.'

At first, I haven't the courage to look. When I do, I say one word: *Hoerezoon*, which is Flemish for the son of a whore.

'Wrap it back up,' I beg. 'Quickly. I can't look at it.'

Bewildered, he picks up the used bandage. Gazes at its ever-increasing spot of blood, culminating, at its end, in a soggy claret-and-brown palm print.

'There are new ones in my bag.' I bob my chin at the kitchen top. 'I'll need co-codamol too. And diazepam.' He falters. I'm not in the mood. 'Dad, I can see my flexor digitorum superficialis. You keep them in there, above your head. Behind the soup you're never going to eat.'

If my palm had a paint colour, it would be chartreuse yellow.

I concentrate hard on Michael and Vee performing bows, specifically the Añjali Mudrā. *Namaste*s over, they hug like AA support buddies. Then, finally, they high-five – a gesture suggestive of them having nailed a boxercise class.

When my bag clatters on to the flagstone floor, my head shoots left. Its contents scatter and smash. Yet Dad fails to lean down and pick them up. Instead, he grips the worktop, his knuckles grey.

Panic seeps up and into my face.

'Dad,' I say quietly. But he's too busy having a terrible medical emergency. 'Dad!'

His turn is sluggish. I gasp when I see his face. He weeps. Though it takes a while for me to see why. He holds something aloft – like a warrior might show off a severed head. Only it's not body parts but a thin golden chain.

'Hers?' he whispers.

Eyes on stalks, utterly cured of pain, I wiggle my bad arm; remind him I can't put the thing on by myself.

He's all fingers and thumbs.

'Oh. My. God,' I tell him, feeling its little horn of hope.

He stands back. Shakes his head, dazed.

'I feel more hopeful already,' I say girlishly. 'Don't you think it looks like a dragon's tooth?'

He can't deny it. 'It's very House Targaryen.'

Michael bursts into the kitchen. 'That was so spiritual.' Then he points at my hand; 'That is disgusting.' And to Dad; 'Why are you crying?'

'We need to get your sister to the hospital,' he says.

Michael nods, instantly proactive. 'I'll shave and blow-dry my hair.'

Even Vee, who is a medical coroner, winces when she sees the wound. 'You might need a bit of reconstructive work done on that, love. George, she *definitely* needs the diazepam.'

I agree. 'I'll be all right as soon as I've had some drugs. Then I really want to go to Casualty.'

Dad flaps, looks for his keys, change for the car park, argues with Michael, who's desperate to ablute. While Vee re-bandages my hand.

'I have *so* much to tell you,' I confide.

'I feel sick with anticipation,' she whispers back, then sneers at Dad's bottle of pills. 'Two milligrams? It's hardly worth the bother. You'd get more of a lull from a simple carbohydrate.'

She hands me five. Pops a couple in her mouth, too. 'Just to take the edge off.'

For a few minutes, she and I sit in easy silence. Now and then, I shake my neck, so I can feel the cold tickle of metal.

'That ceremony,' I ask. 'How many denominations do you reckon you offended?'

'None. You can misuse religion as long as it's for good.' She waves the issue away. 'We'll burn in hell together.'

Trouble is, I've other plans for the afterlife. But I'm always on for a fall-back. 'Just as long as we're in a different fire pit to Annie. She's been texting me about the bloody jars. I'll give them back another day.'

Dad is shouting, 'Let's go!'

When Vee guides me to the car, I acquire a limp. I'm not sure why, it just feels respectful, given everybody's efforts.

'Text me when you've seen someone,' she demands. 'And *The Theory of Everything*, as soon as you're up to it.'

'I'm there,' I say, then, as an afterthought: 'Glastonbury. Next year?'

Her look is hateful. 'I'd rather tongue-kiss a shark. How about wine-tasting in Provence?'

'That works. I definitely haven't been banned from there.'

Once in the car, I buckle up and glower at Michael. 'Why am I in the back?'

'It's my turn.'

'I'm dying of an unspecified infection and you're pulling rank.'

He turns and points. 'And do *not* be popping up like that again, not every time I do karmic cleansing.'

'Deal. Dad, slow down.'

Our father panics. Having forgotten to fiddle with a single knob or mirror, he drives too erratically. I use my functioning arm to clutch the door handle. Double-check with Michael, 'What if we have a case and I have vital information?'

'Only then,' Michael agrees. 'And only if I can be boss?'

'Just as well I'm promoting you then.'

The melodrama with which he turns to face me – he actually utilises slow-mo. It's hard not to smile. Especially when he speaks. Gravelly and resolute – he could be Maximus Decimus Meridius, if he wasn't saying: 'Go on.'

'You, partner, are now the assistant boss.'

'Which involves doing what?'

'Working in the shadows, acting like an assistant, but actually being assistant boss.'

Michael's own voice returns. 'Really?' He puts his fingers on his cheeks.

'Really.'

'I *have* to text James.'

'You do not,' I state, then wince out loud. 'Dad! What is wrong with you? You've been driving for a hundred years and still can't navigate a speedbump.'

Michael is rubbing his skull. 'They should ban you when you get to fifty. Why are we driving like Starsky and Hutch?'

'It's an emergency, son.'

'You've given me a haemorrhoid.'

'Haemorrhage.'

'I do know.' He turns the radio on.

For a mile or two, we listen to Smooth Dorset FM, Dad glancing at me in his mirror, his look one of bewildered fascination – not with me or my face but with the yellow cornicello that once belonged to his wife.

It still does, I tell him with my eyes, *and always will, for ever more, and then some*, because the benzos are kicking in.

Michael pulls free a Tupperware container. 'Tartlet?' We've

not had the chance to answer before he's slapping the lid back on. 'I forgot napkins.'

I'm in a drug-induced charitable mood, so undo my seat-belt, get on to my knees and lift the parcel shelf. There's a kitchen roll in the boot. Beside it, I spot Annie's spice jars. Wrapped tight in a roll's worth of cling film, they're like a mega-pack of giant batteries. Michael hates the woman – but not as much as glass rattling unconstrained in an open space.

'Nice job!' I shout back at Michael. 'The cellophane.'

'I put them in date order, too.'

Holding on to the headrest with my chin, I shout, 'Dad! I am not wearing a seatbelt!'

'Put one on then. *Now.*'

'And they've been through the dishwasher,' says Michael.

I whizz my head around too fast – it takes a moment for my ear liquid to settle. 'You did what?'

My brother has no loyalty. 'It was Vee's idea.'

'Annie's joy?' I whisper-shout, falling back on to my bottom. 'What did you do with it, Michael?'

'I let it free.'

I cover my mouth. Examine his hair; look up his nose and at his shoulders – he's covered in bits. The incense censer's finial pokes from his bag.

Spitting something from his tongue, he admits, 'It was more of a sacrifice.'

'*No way!*'

Dad is trying to parallel park when I start giggling. When Michael joins in, too, we're thrown out of the car. The frozen air hits me like a shot of sambuca. Dad has to shuffle me into A&E, because I'm too busy pointing at Michael and laughing like a lunatic. 'You are in *so* much shit.'

Putting Old Ghosts to Rest 101 – Tip #4:
The Big Crunch

Nothing in life lasts for ever, not even the multiverse, assuming you err towards a cyclic cosmological model and its inevitable Big Crunch. For the sake of your sanity, buffer yourself from the surety of cruel endings and small deaths . . .

• Embrace impermanence. Eras wind up and new beginnings present themselves. This can be a bane; it can also be an adventure.

• Put your faith in DABDA. This model is not science, it's unsubstantiated hypothesis. Indeed, Professor Robert Kastenbaum, a leading authority on death, says the model lacks proper research. My suggestion to him: stop being so defeatist and do some then – it has legs.

• The last A in DABDA stands for Acceptance. Fresh status quos require fresh mantras. Use mine if you like:

Alice found Wonderland via a deep fucking hole and many a plot twist.

Warning: Don't say this out loud. It will get lost in translation. The best epiphanies are kept close to the chest.

Case closed

ACKNOWLEDGEMENTS

Aside from the usual culprits – Jo Unwin, Lucia Campanella, Daun Rosam – I would like to heap praise upon my editor and partner in crime, Frankie Edwards. Your personal investment and positivity has been unflinching and integral in both my journey and Florence Love's. I know what this has meant to you too. Flo and I will be *forever* grateful.

So how did it all begin?

a Girl CALLED LOVE

Scott 'Scat' Delaney is a world-famous jazz singer. He has ample opportunity to stray and his girlfriend, Alice, needs to know she can trust him.

Step up Florence Love, Private Investigator.

Florence has just ten days to entrap an A-Lister. Whilst sticking to her cardinal rule: One kiss, with tongues, five seconds – case closed.

A master of body language, evolutionary science and nifty disguises, her approach is unconventional, her success rate excellent. But targets are rarely as beautiful as Scat. Never fall for the target.

That is very bad form indeed.

Once you've met Florence Love, you'll see the world in glorious technicolour at last.

And then she did WHAT?

In the
NAME of
LOVE

Retired, technically, Florence Love is a long way from her London Private Investigator glory days. But her latest target is achingly personal.

A ration of Montepulciano in her water pouch, Flo finds herself racing around Italy on a borrowed Vespa in the name of love. Bambi Love, specifically. Her mum – missing for twenty-five years. The one case that's still unsolved.

To find Bambi, maintaining focus will be critical. Florence must not be distracted.

Not even by a beautiful, goosebump-inducing Italian stranger with mafiosi friends and a habit of suddenly disappearing himself, who knows far more than he's letting on . . .

The Florence Love series is available now in paperback and ebook

© Jonathan Ring

Louise Lee was once a Geography teacher. When oxbow lakes no longer floated her boat, she took the next, natural step in her career progression and became a Private Investigator. Memorable cases include a high-functioning bigamist with three wives and six children, who was set to marry a fourth; and losing a target because George Clooney started chatting her up in a bar.

Louise undertook an MA in Creative Writing at Birkbeck, and has had work commissioned by BBC Radio Four. The Florence Love series follows the life of an irreverent, thoroughly 'modern' PI who specialises in entrapment, and Louise would love to hear from fellow Florences – drop her a line on Twitter @louise_lee1.

If Louise's mum is reading this, the books are in no way based on her true experiences. Honest.

Get to know Flo a bit better
here as she divulges her
thoughts on some
Very Important Matters . . .

How to set up an operational PI company in less than a day

Pick a name for your firm

Though avoid names that publicise what you do. Super Sleuths or Cheaters R Us are big no-nos. Choose something that will evaporate on a client's bank statement.

Get a website

Phone up India and ask a freelance web designer to put a five-page spread together pronto. For twenty-five quid a page, they'll come up with logos, photos and hyperlinks. You simply email them the content.

The content

Steal it from someone else's website. Thoroughly rejig it otherwise that's plagiarism. Inject the requisite amount of empathy (it's often missing in a world dominated by alpha males). Insert some philosophical memes (they justify the client's need to overstep a mark). Here's a quote you can use to validate the need to spy on a loved-one:

'To acquire knowledge, one must study; but to acquire wisdom, one must observe.'

Marilyn vos Savant said this – officially the most intelligent person in the world between 1986 and 1989. The punter will take her seriously. Never underestimate their need to be condoned.

Another quote you're welcome to:

'In our struggle for freedom, truth is the only weapon we possess.'

The author: His Holiness the 14th Dalai Lama. Enough said.

Ensure your website has a feminine touch

Whilst avoiding the spa-break look. You want to ooze classy yet corporate – it insinuates surveillance teams, spy gadgets and forensic facilities. In this industry misrepresentation works a treat. Don't feel too bad. None of your clients will be able to afford more than two operatives at a time, let alone the use of the inflatable weapons analyst in your pretend forensic laboratory.

The truth about your business: it's just you and a rucksack now. One that contains hats, glasses, hairpieces, a Dictaphone disguised as a pen and a wireless camera poking through the strap. Yes, it gets more exciting as you make a bit of cash and can invest in the GPS tracker, spyware and a second-hand van but, in truth, you don't need much to start.

You have a name and functional website set up. What now?

Pay Google to advertise it. 100 quid should get you to the top of the search results for a minute or two. Give it a day and you'll have your first job.

You no doubt wonder: hold on, I've not had a bean of training?

Whilst waiting for job No. 1 to roll in, download a 'How to Become a PI' book. In the absence of a government-approved NVQ, this will teach you the basics in a very basic way. PIs are not scholars. A lot are ex-military who require quick, shouty answers. This is good. You can read it in one hit, and then re-read when waiting for job No. 2 to roll in.

Don't be surprised at the tasks that fall into your remit – traffic accident reporting, repossessions, debt collecting. Though, be warned: PIs who head in such directions tend to be without the imagination to make it in the field, proper.

NB. Concentrate especially on a chapter that covers the Data Protection Act. Once you know it like the back of your hand, search in between the lines. Getting around that bit of legislation will become your *raison d'être*.

Finally, you have read and re-read your how-to book – what next?

Throw it into the chiminea and go learn the proper way – via the soles of your feet. The truth is, you work it out as you go along. If a case feels compulsive, you'll become obsessively resourceful in your need to unearth the truth.

If not, you're in the wrong job.

Charlie's Angels, the TV show – a power discussion

Yes, it was 'jiggle TV'. Yes, when the Angels went undercover it was exclusively as sexy people (sexy waitresses, sexy construction workers, sexy clown skaters). And yes, the scripts were sometimes rubbish. Yet it remains in my top five most influential TV shows ever.

The reason: *Charlie's Angels* is a lovely example of socio-anthropology working at its most productive. The threesome is so admired because, contrarily, the Angels weren't actually very sexual. Breathtakingly beautiful with excellent fashion sense, maybe, but if they had a libido, biological clock or, indeed, a clitoris, they never threw it in our faces. That was good. I was only five.

In short, *Charlie's Angels* was a show about professionalism and mutual respect, whilst looking hot, which is exactly what girls wanted in the late seventies/early eighties. That desire, for me, still stands today. Most especially, the chance to dress up whilst going deep undercover.

Disclaimer . . . Feminism is a big subject. I'm not always entirely clear what it is. But the Barrymore Angels are a travesty. I wouldn't trust one of them with my boyfriend, which was the entire essence of the original TV show's charm.